DON RICH

COASTAL PAYBACKS

A 'Shaker' Denton Novel

Coastal Adventure Series
Volume 3

FLORIDA REFUGEE PRESS, LLC
2019

Library of Congress PCN Data
Rich, Don
Coastal Paybacks/Don Rich
A 'Shaker' Denton Novel
Florida Refugee Press LLC

Edit/Proofreading by: Tim Sauter
Cover Photo by: MJ0007

Published by FLORIDA REFUGEE PRESS, LLC, 2019
Crozet, VA
Copyright © 2019 by Don Rich

Dedication

To my friend, David Thatcher Wilson, whose stories and pictures of his childhood summers on the Eastern Shore of Virginia have been so inspiring.

And to the past, present, and future boardmembers of the West Palm Beach Fishing Club, and the Palm Beach County Fishing Foundation. For their creation and continuation of the rich history of that great organization. And for their dedication to the education of the next generation about that area's great fishery, and the need to protect it for those that will come along after them.

Preface

The thing about old friends that haven't seen each other in a while is they like to reminisce and catch up. Which is exactly what was happening with Murph Murphy and an old pal of his. They just happened to run into each other at a marina restaurant in Riviera Beach, Florida. Or so Murph thought.

Another thing about old friends that are catching up is that it can really be boring to others. Especially people who had worked as hard earlier in the day and were now as tired as Murph's girlfriend and partner, Lindsay Davis, was. But, not wanting to spoil his fun, she excused herself and headed back to their boat to crash, leaving the two men alone to swap stories. It was a decision that may very well have saved her life. What the two men didn't know was that they were about to be joined by a third man, one with a gun and a plan. It was a dangerous combination, and the evening was about to take a very dark turn.

Chapter 1

It was Friday about 7a.m., on a bitterly cold winter morning on the Eastern Shore of Virginia, or, as we locals like to call it, ESVA. My name is Marlin Denton and I was getting an early start to my day. I pulled up to Albury's Boat Works in Magotha, a tiny town on Magothy Bay, on the ocean side of the peninsula. This is just a few miles north of Mallard Cove Marina, down on the tip of ESVA, a place where my fiancée, Kari Albury, and I call home. This boatyard is owned by Kari's cousin Carlton; he's repairing one of our boats and building us another one. I was here to check on the weekly progress of both, half an hour before most of the yard crew was due to arrive. The one that Carlton is repairing is my vintage wooden Chris Craft forty-two-foot aft cabin called *Why Knot*. Picture tons of varnish, chrome, and higher maintenance than one of those women from any of the "real" housewife reality shows. She's here getting fixed after being damaged in an explosion. How that happened is another story, for another day.

Because of the explosion, and as a part of the repair process, we are swapping out the old gas engines for brand-new diesel ones. It's worth the added expense to me because it's a heck of a lot tougher to make diesel fuel go "boom" than gasoline. Having personally been on the receiving end of the "boom", I don't have any desire to go through *that* again. See the mention above about that other story... Anyway, we are also making a few subtle changes that will make *Why Knot* more comfortable for both Kari and me to live aboard together. She should be ready to "splash" in about three weeks, well ahead of schedule. I'm really happy about this part, because in the meantime Kari and I are living on our friends' houseboat, *On Coastal Time*. We'll move aboard *Why Knot* once those friends, Murph and

Lindsay, return from their winter fishing trip down south.

Michael "Murph" Murphy and his girlfriend Lindsay Davis are busy chartering their forty-seven-foot Rybovich sportfisherman, *Irish Luck*, for a string of Florida winter billfish tournaments. It's a nice way to stay warm all winter and get paid for it. And they get paid very well. In addition to their "elite charter" fee, they are also one of the top crews around in winnings. They took first or second in the top two richest tournaments in the mid-Atlantic last summer, bringing home seven figures in prize money. Yes, some fishing tournament purses have now broken through the million–dollar mark. Shattered it, in fact. And Murph and Lindsay just added to their string with another win in the Islamorada Winter Invitational Billfish Tournament, pocketing a large Calcutta. That's the usually huge side bet pool of tiered cash winnings. On their boat, the charter clients know upfront that the crew keeps a portion of all Calcutta proceeds, and the anglers split any purse winnings with them as well.

Oh, and the bit about it being an "elite charter?" That's because *Irish Luck* is kept to the highest maintenance standards; she looks as good or better than the day she was launched. Because of this, they only charter to people who respect their boat as the piece of floating fishing art it truly is. You'll need a recommendation from another client of theirs before they'll put you on the schedule. You can get away with doing that when you are as hot on the fish as they are right now.

Anyway, sometime this spring we'll move over to our own houseboat, which Carlton's crew is currently building next to *Why Knot*. It's going to be called the *Tied Knot* and will be slightly larger than our friends'. She will also have a few amenities that theirs doesn't, including a private sundeck and built-in hot tub. While she'll be similar to *On Coastal Time*, she'll be a little bit longer, wider, and higher at over seventy feet long, twenty feet wide, and including the sundeck, she's three decks high.

Both *Tied Knot* and *OCT* (my shortened nickname for *On Coastal Time*) are more properly called "house barges"; meaning they have no propulsion system. Most houseboats have inboard/outboard setups, the absolute worst idea, ever. It means that the outdrive unit, the part with the propeller, will always stay in the water. This makes it susceptible to barnacles, marine grasses, electrolysis and a host of other trip ending issues that you usually discover only when you need to move the boat. As in, right before a hurricane hits, or when you have a hull breach. By not having an engine, it also means that we don't have any holes through the hull for shafts, exhausts, or water intakes. Invariably, these are the things that become trouble points, can cause leaks and in the worst-case scenario, they can make you sink. By not needing any of those, we avoid that risk. We also avoid having to put a ton of money into a propulsion system, as well as its maintenance. Much better to rely on a tow from a boat that gets used often. Reliability is never overrated when it comes to boats.

I walked through a small door into a huge heated workshop that can accommodate up to three boats, side by side. Going from the cold, dry outside air, my senses are suddenly assaulted with the smells of epoxy, paint, paint thinner, bedding compound, varnish, and sawdust. Everything that makes a boatyard smell...right. You know how some people love the scents of perfume in a department store? This combination of boatyard smells has the same effect on me. In the summer these scents would be wafting all through the yard, spilling out through the huge open access doors of this and the other half dozen buildings just like it. Plus, a couple dozen more boats are usually over in the rail yard and even more on the concrete slab of the "do it yourself" area, each contributing to this aromatic mixture.

The rail yard is the open-air section of the boatyard where some boats are moved after being pulled out of the water by a ways. Over the summer a lot of bottom paint and less critical finish work is accomplished here, especially things below the waterline. The DIY slab gets similar work accomplished, but boats are hauled over there by a mobile strap hoist and it only has half the weight capacity of the ways.

Carlton has the largest ways on ESVA. This is the equivalent of a giant, steep concrete boat ramp equipped with railroad rails. A huge angled platform with a mobile cradle moves down those rails until it submerges under the water. Boats then load onto it like they would a trailer, and once hauled out of the water they are moved around the yard on those wheeled cradles via the rail shuttle. It's a very old system, but it's capable of safely hauling anything from an outboard to huge shrimpers and work boats. Oh, and big house barges.

I love this place, the work that gets accomplished here, and watching the craftsmen ply their trades. Most of them are ESVA natives, and many are practicing those same crafts that their forefathers did before them. In this world where so much is now done with robots and soulless machines, boatyards are one of the few places remaining where those that work with skilled hands are still revered. It's reassuring to see there are places where this is still the case.

I climbed up the staircase of the scaffold that surrounded the hull and stepped onto the aft deck of *Why Knot*. Those aforementioned craftsmen have now fitted her with a new salon door; the old one was a casualty of the explosion. Looking beyond it, I saw that the salon's new deck had now been covered in vintage style cork flooring, which had already been coated with several layers of polyurethane varnish. The galley's new cabinets and lockers have also taken shape; some are now larger than their original counterparts. These are a few of those changes I talked about earlier. However, the new cabinet and locker doors still have the same vintage style anchor-shaped vents that she originally came with. Again, these were all cut by a human craftsman, not by some computerized C&C machine. And there were some upgrades to the galley that we've tried to camouflage; a microwave and a convection oven hidden behind a wooden cabinet front, a larger built-in refrigerator and freezer, and more storage for cookware. But it was all designed to look as original and just as vintage as her hull. Another upgrade is the large flat screen TV which raises up out of the counter that divides the galley and the salon. A salon is the nautical equivalent of a living room. If the TV rig sounds cool, trust me, it is. If you ever want to see real creativity at work, visit a boatyard.

My cell phone rang, breaking the silent spell that all this held over me. I saw that it was my friend who was also one of Kari's bosses, Dawn McAlister. Her calling this early in the morning wasn't usually a good sign.

"Hey, Dawn, what's going on?"

Her answer chilled me. "Lindsay called us for help. Murph apparently disappeared last night down in Riviera Beach. Casey's flying down, and he needs you to go with him." Dawn is all business in serious situations, short on talk, and long on action.

"How soon do we leave?" No time for hesitation on my part. If Lindsay called for help, things were bad. Over the past several months she's become like a sister to me, and Murph like a brother, so there was no question that I was going.

"Wheels up two minutes after you get to the plane."

"Thirty-five minutes. I have to pick up some clothes."

She replied, "Kari is packing for you right now. Don't slow down in the parking lot. Linds is freaked,

Marlin. He's apparently been missing for ten hours, but she just discovered it."

I was already out of the shed and running to my truck. "I'm on my way."

Chapter 2

Dawn was right, I didn't even park my old Ford Sport Trac at the marina. Kari was already standing out in the parking lot waiting for me, my bag in her hand. She was on her phone. "Hold on, Linds, I have to load him." She threw my bag in the back seat, kissed me goodbye through the window, and said, "Love you. Be safe."

"I will. Tell Lindsay to call me when she gets off the phone with you. Love you too." With that, I sped across the parking lot and headed north on US-13. Two minutes later, Lindsay called. I've heard her mad, happy, sad, and even drunk, but never rattled before. This wasn't good.

"Mar, I'm so glad you guys are coming, I didn't know what else to do, or who to call. The police say I can't even file a missing person's report for another day and a half. They think he's off drinking with that guy, and that he'll show up. But he left his phone under the table, and he never goes anywhere without it. He was sending me a message that he didn't go on his own."

"Slow down, Linds. What guy? What happened? Walk me back through it."

"We're staying here in Riviera Beach at the same marina where Casey used to live back when Murph worked for him." Casey Shaw was Kari's other boss, and Dawn's fiancée. "We were having dinner here at the tiki hut place last night when this guy walked in and spotted Murph. He came over to our table and sat down. Murph called him 'TW'. They apparently knew each other from 'back in the day', and Murph used to work for him. When TW sold his boat, he introduced Murph to Casey.

Anyway, I was tired, and went back to the boat and fell asleep. When I woke up this morning, I realized Murph never came home last night. I walked up and down the docks looking for him, but he was nowhere to be found. I went up to the restaurant, and they had his cell phone; he had dropped it under the table. I talked the manager into calling and waking up the bartender that had worked last night, and he remembered Murph and two guys leaving together. One sounded like that TW guy and some other guy in his early twenties. He remembered all of them because the young guy paid the tab, even though he never sat down or even had a drink, but he paid in cash and left a big tip. He thought they went down the center dock together, which is where we're tied up."

"Linds, is it possible he came back to the boat and then left again?"

"No! I wake up anytime anyone so much as steps on the boat. So, there's no way that he came home then took off again. And it's so frustrating that the police won't even help. I guess they see so many people that are just partying down here, and they usually turn up a day or two later. But that wasn't what happened now. Something's happened to Murph, I can feel it."

"Hang in there, we're on our way. We'll be at your boat in about three hours. Don't worry, we'll find him. It's gonna be okay."

"Hurry, Marlin. I'll meet you at the airport. Please hurry. Something bad has happened to him, I know it." She hung up.

I called Kari, "Hey. Call Linds back and keep her busy on the phone for as long as possible. Keep her mind off this as much as you can, she's really scared."

"I know, she sounds really bad. I'll do the best I can, but I feel kind of helpless up here. At least you guys will be on the ground in just a couple of hours."

"I'll call you as soon as we know something. Hopefully, there's a reasonable explanation for this, and he just got caught up with some friends. But I don't know. This doesn't feel right to me either." I said.

I met my friend Casey Shaw at the Accomack County Airport where he keeps his Cessna CJ–3 jet. Casey is an investor and developer who has large real estate holdings in both Virginia and Florida and uses the plane to go back and forth. He also owns Shaw Air; a charter aircraft company and this plane is part of that fleet. Shaw Air's chief pilot, Sam Knight, would be flying us today. Dawn wasn't kidding; we were airborne two minutes later.

Sitting beside Casey back in the cabin I asked him, "Do you have any idea who this guy TW is that Lindsay was talking about?"

He nodded his head. "His name is Tim Wilton. He was Murph's first boss. TW had an old Pacemaker sportfisherman over on Singer Island, back seventeen or eighteen years ago. Murph was just a kid then, working the docks in the afternoons and weekends trying to pick up freelance jobs as a mate and boat washer. TW hired him to babysit his boat over in West End, Grand Bahama for that summer while he flew back and forth on the weekends. He saw that Murph was responsible and had a lot of drive, so he took him on. Murph was also honest and trustworthy, two things that TW desperately needed in a boat sitter for a rig that was left over in the Bahamas. Plus, being just a kid, it also meant that he was cheap labor. Murph was anxious to break into the boat business, and figured that if nothing else, this would be a great reference for him in the future.

But the people that TW hung out with though were nothing like Murph, who guarded the boat like his own when TW was back in the states. If Murph hadn't been there, I guarantee that at the very least TW's liquor locker would've been emptied, and the boat quite possibly might have been gone as well. His crowd could be rough on occasion.

This was about the time that I first met Murph. I had an old 31 Bertram that my first wife and I used to run back and forth to the Bahamas that summer. I was in my early twenties and had already started a successful career in real estate investment. Murph was seventeen, and a good kid. Like I said, TW was impressed with Murph, and ended up hiring him straight out of high school the next year as his full-time mate. Murph worked for TW the next two years, until Wilton went off to be a 'guest of the state' for a few years. He supposedly was a developer and contractor but that was just his cover, and how he washed some of the money. The story I got was that he financed and organized loads of grass that were coming into South Florida."

"Murph would've never had anything to do with that, Casey!" I said.

"No, he wouldn't. And TW was smart enough not to have anything like that around his own boat. As far as Murph knew, his boss was just what he said, a real estate developer and contractor. He had a hard time coming to grips with the idea that TW might in fact really be guilty of what he had been accused of. I don't need to tell you how loyal Murph is to his friends."

I nodded. "And if he still has those doubts about TW being guilty, then he wouldn't hesitate to sit and have a drink with him."

"Exactly," Casey said.

"But why take off with him?"

Casey said, "There's no way that Murph would have voluntarily left Lindsay alone and by herself there."

"So, you think he's been kidnapped," I said. It was half a question and half a statement.

Casey said sadly, "My oldest best friend and mentor was murdered in the parking lot of that same marina right after I moved up to ESVA, and he was a friend of Murph's too. He knows all too well how bad the neighborhood is. There's no way that he would have left Lindsay alone there overnight. They have security and cameras, but it's the Palm Beach County waterfront. A

14

lot goes on down there at night. They're probably staying at that marina because there weren't any other slips available. It's high season in Palm Beach; next to impossible to find a transient slip anywhere, much less that close to the inlet. Speaking of security, you brought your pistol, right?"

I always carry it with me back in Virginia, and I knew my concealed permit was valid in Florida, too. "Yeah. And if I know Kari, there'll be extra mags and ammo in my bag as well."

"Good. That may be high-value real estate around the marina, but two blocks west of there are hookers, drug dealers, and gang bangers, all out in the open. You can't drop your guard around there, though I know better than to think that you would."

I nodded and settled back in my seat. This wasn't my first ride in Casey's plane. In fact, I'd been in about a dozen different types, makes, and models of private jets, mostly as an additional passenger, not the primary one. Though I'd recently come into enough money that I guess I could charter one now if I ever wanted or needed to. But all of that was also another story from another day. Right now, I'm just glad that it was a direct flight, and that we didn't have to mess with the TSA. Meaning we could carry our firearms loaded and onboard with us.

We were both nervous about what we would find when we got down there, so we lapsed into silence most of the rest of the flight. When we landed at North Palm Beach County Airport, Lindsay was already there waiting for us and hugged Casey and me as we got off the plane. The temperature was a shock; about thirty degrees warmer than when we left Virginia. I hoped Kari had taken that into account when she packed my bag.

"Still no word?" Casey said.

"Nothing, Casey. I'm so glad that you both are here; I feel like we'll get some answers and find him now." The relief showed on Lindsay's face.

Casey took her keys to the rental car, and we loaded in for the ten-minute ride to the marina. Casey was a West Palm Beach native and had lived here for all but the last year and a half of his life. Having someone who was so familiar with the area was going to be a huge plus. He had lived aboard in this particular marina for well over a decade, from the time of his first divorce until he and Murph left to build Bayside Resort on the Eastern Shore of Virginia. That was where he now lived aboard his yacht with Dawn.

Casey wasn't kidding about the neighborhood around the marina. It looked like something out of a made-for-TV movie. Drug deals were happening out in the open, and hookers were strutting up and down the sidewalks. There was a high-security fence with cameras and an electric gate back at the marina parking lot. Despite those precautions, Casey's friend had been murdered right at this gate while waiting for it to open. It had been an attempted carjacking that had gone terribly wrong. The whole thing had been caught by the security cameras which helped lead to the capture of the carjackers. I knew that Casey hadn't been back to the marina since the murder, and I couldn't even begin to think of what must be going through his mind right now. To have had a friend die here was bad enough, but now to find second friend missing from the same location must really be overwhelming. We parked the rental, then hurried down to *Irish Luck* where Casey and I were both in for a big surprise.

"Where the hell is the Rybo?" I exclaimed.

Lindsay said, "Oh, this was going to be a surprise when we got back up to ESVA. Murph made a side wager at the Islamorada tournament. One of the anglers was a huge Rybovich fan, and he fell in love with the old *Irish Luck*. He wanted to trade this for it and have us throw in a big chunk of cash. Instead, Murph turned it into a wager where if we won, it was an even swap. And that's what happened."

16

The boat sitting in the slip with *Irish Luck* written in gold leaf across the varnished teak transom was not a vintage forty–seven–foot Rybovich sportfish but was instead a sixty–foot Merritt. In addition to being two decades newer and more than a dozen feet longer, it was also several feet wider. Foot for foot, the Merritt was much lighter, and several knots faster. And worth about twice what the Rybovich was.

I wondered if somehow this wager figured into Murph disappearing. "Who was this lunatic that made that bet with you guys?"

Lindsay said, "He's a big country singer, I can't think of his name right now. But you'd know it. He had a hit song about some river up in North Florida, and he had another big hit about happy hour with that singer from Key West? Anyway, he's a really nice guy. He has a collection of Rybovichs, and he wanted ours badly."

I knew who she was talking about, and I couldn't see how he could be in any way connected with Murph disappearing, but at this point, I wasn't willing to rule anything or anyone out. We went aboard and walked into the salon, where Lindsay called Murph's name without hearing any response.

Casey and I dropped our bags on one of the salon's built-in sofas, then he turned and headed to the dock with both Lindsay and me in tow. We followed him up to the tiki bar Café, where he sought out the owner, a guy named Red.

"Casey! Haven't seen you in over a year, since you stole my chef. I hear he's even in magazines now. I just thought he was just a good fry cook."

"Yeah Red, that's why he left. But that's not why I'm here. Murph disappeared from here last night, and we're trying to find him. We need to take a look at your surveillance tapes."

Red folded his arms across his chest. "Yeah, well, you're not a cop with a warrant. Tell me why I should help you after you stole my cook."

I could see that Casey was running out of patience with this guy. It was easy to understand why this idiot would have lost Carlos Ramirez. He was no longer a fry cook, but a culinary powerhouse in charge of all of Casey's new ESVA restaurants.

"Because after what happened to Dave here, and now apparently to Murph, I can easily get Channel 5 to interview me about everything that's happened. And I can guarantee that would not be good for your business."

Red frowned and after a long pause said, "All right, let's go back into the office."

It turned out there were numerous high definition cameras that covered the open-air dining area, and one that had a long view of the center dock. Red ran it back to where Murph and Lindsay were finished with dinner and TW joined them. We sped up to the point where Lindsay left, and a few minutes later they were joined by a man in his early twenties who never sat down, he just stood. Right before Murph and TW got up to leave with him, the stranger reached a hand inside his windbreaker. The camera angle was good enough and the image clear enough to see that TW tensed. Then the three of them walked out of the image and were picked up again by the center dock camera.

Casey had Red zoom in on the image, and they could clearly see that the stranger now had a pistol stuck in Murph's back. They watched the trio walk to the second boat out on the right and go aboard. Red fast-forwarded through the rest of the night until almost dawn, when Murph and the stranger reappeared. Again, the stranger had his pistol stuck in Murph's back. They walked toward the camera and the base of the dock. Murph looked up at the camera and mouthed the words "Help me" right before they turned toward the floating dock. I heard Lindsay's sharp intake of breath. I reached over and squeezed her arm, but I knew that what we all just saw was tearing her apart.

18

Murph and the stranger climbed aboard what looked to be about a thirty–foot long center console boat with three outboards, or "trips" as they're called around the water. We could see the boat leave, and it looked like it was headed around Peanut Island, and for Lake Worth inlet.

Chapter 3

Without a word Casey left the office, making a beeline for the second boat on the right on the center dock. We had seen three people go into it, but only two had come out. Chances were good that TW was still aboard. The question was if he was still alive or not. When we got to the boat, which turned out to be a Hatteras sportfisherman somewhere in the mid–sixty-foot range, we saw there was a yacht broker's sign attached to the flying bridge railing. Meaning that there probably wasn't a crew living aboard nor expected around anytime soon. Owners usually liked to cut expenses on brokerage boats.

All three of us stepped down into the fishing cockpit, making our way to the salon door. The top drawer in the tackle center next to it was partially open, and we could see a door key lying inside. It was a very poorly kept secret around the docks that this was a common hiding place for boat keys. Casey tried the salon door handle and found it was already unlocked. He and I both pulled our pistols, and the three of us went in.

There was no sign of anyone in the salon, so Casey yelled, "TW! Are you here?"

At first, there was no answer. But then we heard a knocking sound coming from down somewhere along the companionway. We told Lindsay to stay in the salon and watch the dock through the windows, since she didn't have a weapon with her. Casey and I went down the companionway and into the first stateroom, where we found TW trussed up with zip ties and duct tape. He had been kicking the hanging locker at the end of the bunk where he had been left. We quickly freed him and removed the duct tape that was acting as a gag. Then we yelled for Lindsay to come down with us.

Casey asked, "TW, what the hell happened? And where's Murph?"

He replied, "My son has him. They're headed for Bootle Bay on Grand Bahama Island. He's after the money."

"What money? Why is Murph with him, and why are they going to Bootle Bay?" Casey wanted answers, and fast.

TW pointed at his ankle, which had a GPS tracker locked around it. "Because the Feds know where I am, twenty–four hours a day. They want the money too, but I've been telling them for fifteen years that there isn't any. If I left the country, an alarm would go off somewhere. I'm not even allowed to leave the county, much less the country, for the next year. I told Timmy that, so he decided to take Murph instead of me."

Lindsay asked angrily, "Why does he need Murph?"

"Because Murph delivered the money to my partner fifteen years ago. He knows Murph, but he doesn't know Timmy, so he wouldn't be likely to give him any money. I gave Murph the password that he needed to tell my partner so that he would know it was okay to give it to him."

"Not possible! There is no way that Murph would have moved money for you. Murph's a lot of things, but he's no crook. If he moved any money, he didn't know about it. And didn't know you were turning him into a criminal," Casey said angrily.

"You're right Casey, Murph is as straight as they come. Even back then as a kid, he'd never knowingly have taken piles of money out of the country for me. He just thought he was delivering furniture to my partner on the sly, ducking the huge Bahamian import duties. My partner had just built his house over at Bootle Bay, so he needed all kinds of furniture. I sent big overstuffed chairs, recliners, and mattresses. Only these were all stuffed with bundles of cash. The salon of my boat was piled high with that furniture. Murph never had a clue.

So, after Murph came back I put the boat up for sale, and that's when I got you two guys together and he started working for you. I made sure he was clear of me before all the indictments came down, and I was arrested. I didn't want any suspicion thrown on him just because he had worked for me; that could've wrecked his life."

Wilton made it sound like he was being so generous, having helped Murph find a new job, and making sure he wasn't around when the crap storm hit. I could see Casey was getting more and more angry.

"You son of a bitch! Don't try and make it sound like you were being so good to Murph. You were just making sure he was well clear of you so that the Feds wouldn't find him and figure out that he might know where the money went! This wasn't about him at all; this was about you!" Casey almost spat this last part out.

"Actually, it was about Timmy. I set it up with my partner to make quarterly transfers from a Bahamian shell company to a commercial bank account back here in the states. It was supposed to look like it was profits from an island resort being transferred back to the US company that owned it. We actually are partners in a restaurant and small marina over on the other side in the village at West End, and one down on Abaco. The money that was transferred stateside was treated as legal profits, and that company paid taxes on it like any other multinational based in the US. I just had him add in some extra cash with each transfer, laundering it. I gave Timmy's mother access to the bank account. She was only supposed to take out so much each year for them to live on until I could get back here and start providing for the both of them again. The remaining 'washed' money was supposed to fund a new, legitimate development company that I'd start when I got out. Meanwhile, my partner continued investing some of the rest of it over in the islands.

But it didn't work out that way. Once I got back here, I found that the commercial account had been almost zeroed out. Timmy's mother, my old girlfriend, had convinced herself that she and Timmy were entitled to all of it. Then I find Timmy out running around in a big center console with 'trips' on the back, and his mother living the high life in a condo in Palm Beach. Now the well has run dry, and Timmy decided to find the source of those deposits. He didn't know exactly where it was coming from, but his mother knew enough to send him looking for me after I recently got released.

I heard Murph was going to be in the tournament last week, and I hunted around until I found him. Timmy was following me and figured Murph was my partner with all the money until I convinced him last night that he wasn't."

Casey's eyes were ablaze. "And now your son has Murph, who he won't need any longer once they get to the money."

"He won't hurt him, Casey. He just wants to find the money and come back home. This is all his mother's doing; she didn't used to be this way but now she's a real bloodsucking leach. Timmy's not that kind of kid."

Lindsay threw it back at him. "No, he's only the type of kid that kidnaps people and holds them at gunpoint. And I didn't see his mother with him. Come on guys, we're wasting time."

Casey leaned into TW, "Just who is this partner, and where do we find him?"

Suddenly TW looked frightened. "First, you have to promise me that you won't hurt Timmy."

Lindsay leapt at TW, grabbing him by the shirt and throwing him up against the hanging locker. "You want a promise? I promise you that if Murph is hurt, Timmy is going to get that back tenfold. I'm telling you, the only chance you will have of ever seeing your son alive again is if you tell me exactly where he is, and we get to him before he hurts Murph. Otherwise, I'll shoot him myself. Do you understand me?" She slammed him against the locker again for emphasis. At five foot six, she was almost half a foot shorter than TW, but the muscles in her arms stood out as she pinned him back. A year of working the fishing cockpit had left her toned and strong.

TW looked over pleadingly at Casey, "I'll give you fifty grand to bring Timmy home safe."

"Blood money for blood, TW?" Casey was disgusted.

TW said, "There's no blood attached to that money. We only ran grass, no hard stuff. Nobody got hurt, ever. Hell, today there are people running those pot dispensaries that are looked at like they're really smart businesspeople. For selling the same stuff that I went to jail for more than a decade over. The only difference between me and them is they have to keep records and pay taxes. And that's why the Feds are still after me, only they don't want to tax it, they want to take it all. The funny part is that I've been paying taxes on it for fifteen years."

TW probably would have kept talking if it weren't for the fact that Lindsay hit him in the mouth right then. "I don't care. I don't care about you, how much time you spent in prison, or your kid. I only care about Murph. Now who's your damn partner, and where can we find him?"

TW's eyes got big and he reached up to check his jaw. He looked at Lindsay and then over at Casey. "At the back canal of Bootle Bay take a right, the last house on the right. It's Billy Thompson."

Now was Casey's turn to be surprised. He turned to the others, "Let's go."

As they were going across the salon TW called from the companionway, "Please don't let him get hurt, Casey. He's the only family I've got."

Casey kept going, out the salon door, down the dock and onto the Merritt. He turned to Lindsay, "What's our fuel like?"

She replied, "We just fueled up. Sixteen hundred gallons, enough to go about eight hundred miles at cruise. And she cruises at about twenty-six knots."

"Marlin, you start the generator, get the shore power, and the stern lines. Linds, you get the bow and spring lines. Let's go."

If there's one thing about Casey, it's that he's decisive. And in this instance, he knew all the players, and he also knew where we were going. Which made him the only one out of all three of us. I guess you noticed I hadn't been saying much. Yes, Murph and Lindsay are very good friends of mine, but for over fifteen years, Casey and Murph have been like brothers. What Lindsay and I didn't know was there was much more to this back story.

Casey cranked up the twin ten-cylinder MAN diesels, barely letting them warm up before signaling me to take in the stern lines. It's a good thing that he had lived in this marina for over a decade, he knew how fast the current ran through here, and he was used to dealing with it. While this boat was now slightly familiar to Lindsay, neither Casey nor I had any experience running big Merritts, though I guessed that it would be somewhat similar to his fifty–five–foot Jarrett Bay sportfisherman. Pulling straight out against the current was not an issue, but you had to be ready to buck it as soon as you cleared the slip and made your turn to head out of the marina, when it tried to shove you sideways. Casey made it look easy.

Lindsay and I joined him up on the flying bridge, as he merged into the channel on the west side of Peanut Island. At this time of year in manatee season, the fastest we were legally allowed to go was idle speed. The big mammals tended to hang out around here in winter because of the warm water outflow from the local power plant on the west side of the channel. We would have to totally clear the east side of the island and enter the inlet before we could get the hull up on a plane and run.

Casey had the helm seat in the middle of the bridge, while Lindsay and I sat on one of the bench seats on the starboard side.

"Who is this Billy Thompson?" Lindsay asked.

"Wild Billy Thompson was the guy that got me started in flying, and someone that Murph and I fished with quite a bit. He's an interesting character, always seemed to be more than flush but yet not quite rich. We were actually flying buddies for a while. He owns an Aerostar airplane, which is what got me interested in that model, and how I ended up buying one as my first plane. A few years ago, Billy dropped out of sight, and then I heard whispered rumors that he had been involved in the grass trade. But I had never seen any evidence of that. He was easy to get along with, and a lot of fun to fish with. I didn't have a clue that he was in with Tim Wilton; they hid that connection well. That's why it caught me so off guard back there."

I asked, "So, what and where is this Bootle Bay place? It sounded like you were familiar with it. Have you been there before?"

Casey nodded. "About sixty miles east of here on Grand Bahama island. Over fifty years ago some developer dug an inlet with two connected, but perpendicular canals. They were laid out in an 'H' pattern, parallel to the shoreline. They never had a lot of luck selling the lots as the bottom had dropped out of the island land rush. Last time I was in there was over a decade ago, and not even a quarter of them had houses then. And I seriously doubt there's been a building boom in there since.

It's about four miles southeast of West End. I looked at a couple of lots but decided against buying any. The average boat length was already getting longer by that point. It was tricky enough getting my old 31 Bertram back there, so you can imagine with this rig it's going to be like putting a cork in a bottle. The canals are narrow, the turns are tight, and the place is overgrown. And of course, the house that we have to get to now would have to be the one that's farthest in from the ocean. Probably why Billy built his place there; it would make a great hideout and he was unlikely to have a lot of nosy neighbors coming around. Heck, I may have even been the one that originally pointed the place out to him on a fishing trip. Now I know where he went when he disappeared."

We turned east, passing in front of the old Coast Guard station. We were still having to travel at idle speed as we passed it, but that changed right after we cleared the island and passed "Annie's Dock" at the north end of Palm Beach. This landmark was situated at the beginning of the inlet and the end of the idle speed zone.

Casey pushed the throttles forward, and the big Merritt responded like the racehorse that she was. She planed out inside of fifty yards, despite the five-and-a-half-ton weight of all the diesel in the tanks under her fishing cockpit's teak deck. Her standard cruise was twenty–six–knots or about thirty miles–per–hour, but Casey was pushing her well beyond that now. We passed the end of the inlet's riprap jetties and entered the Atlantic Ocean where Casey set our course at 105 degrees. This should bring us right in on Bootle Bay in about an hour and forty–five minutes. Technically, we should first clear Bahamian Customs at Old Bahama Bay at West End to be legal. But we were about three and a half hours behind Timmy Wilton, so no doubt Casey had decided to worry about that part later, if at all.

We had a light west wind with a following sea that was building the farther we got offshore. The Gulfstream current was in close today, and we hit it only about a mile out. We could tell because the sea changed direction slightly, getting more of a crosshatch wave effect to it. Like a living thing that moved back and forth both onshore and off depending on the day, this warm current runs north at between two and six mph. It varies in width, and again it depended upon the day, but it can be up to fifty miles wide as it makes its way up toward Virginia before swinging offshore and heading across the Atlantic to the United Kingdom. The sea changes from this current probably had more effect on Timmy's boat, since it looked like it was half the length of the Merritt and would be a lot lighter.

Fifteen minutes out, the swells were now about four feet, and the crosshatch had become more pronounced. Not that this mattered to the Merritt, as she cut through them like butter. But if Timmy had run into the same conditions, it was likely that he would've had to have had to throttle back a bit. The main thing we were worried about was that his lead did not increase as we pushed to catch up with him.

None of us said anything now, we knew we were racing against time. Chances are Timmy and Murph were already at Bootle Bay, and hopefully, Murph was still safe. Casey had a tunnel vision look on his face, focusing on the water ahead watching for any flotsam in our path that could damage the Merritt's hull or running gear. I knew he was probably trying hard not to think about what could be happening to Murph. I glanced to my right at Lindsay, who was staring down at the deck with pursed lips. She had to be going through absolute hell right now.

I'm not an overly touchy–feely kind of person, but I reached an arm across her shoulders and pulled her to me in a half hug. She reached up and grabbed my hand that was on her shoulder and squeezed it in appreciation without looking up. My heart was really going out to her now. She's normally a very strong person, but her Achilles' heel is Murph. They had been through so much together over the last year and a half; two people more meant for each other than any couple I know, except Kari and me. And Lindsay had been the one who had helped us get together, which had landed her uncomfortably in the middle a couple of times along the way. I owed her, big time.

I wish that Dawn, Kari, or both of them had been able to come with us, as they are both such good friends of Lindsay's. Not that I wasn't, but I knew she would feel more secure with her two best girlfriends around her. Those three were tight, and Dawn was kind of the mother hen of the trio. Then I had an idea.

"Hey, I haven't had a chance to tell Kari about what we found, and where we're going. Would you mind texting her? I promised I'd keep her updated. And Dawn needs to know, also."

Lindsay looked up and gave me a wry smile, "And it keeps me busy too, right?"

I nodded sheepishly. "Something like that, Linds." I looked at her as she gave me a sad but appreciative smile and squeezed my hand again before letting it go. Then she pulled out her phone and started to text. I pulled my arm away and leaned back on the bench seat.

Like Casey, I was trying hard not to let my imagination run away with me. TW swore that his son wouldn't hurt Murph, but he had also originally believed that his son and his son's mother wouldn't steal money from him, either. After almost fifteen years in prison, I seriously doubted that he knew his kid very well, and that's what really concerned me.

If everything goes as planned, we should now pull into Bootle Bay in an hour and a half. We were almost out of sight of the tallest condominium on Singer Island, a forty–three–story monstrosity that is the last thing you see going over to the islands, and the first thing you see coming back. I had made a similar trip over to Walker's Cay and back several years ago with my late uncle, and I remembered it from that. Back then the building was a concrete skeleton, having been ravaged by back to back hurricanes, and people had been almost giving the units away due to their association's repair liens. Now, new people were laying out up to seven figures for those same units. They have a thing down here called "Hurricane Amnesia" and it can be a really expensive and even deadly disease.

Ironically, on that trip, I had passed the very same marina we had left out of this morning, back when Casey lived there and Murph was working for him and I didn't know either of them. Who could have ever figured years later that this day would be in store for us?

Lindsay finished her texts and looked up at Casey then me. She hadn't even bothered to tie up her beyond shoulder–length blond hair, which was now blowing around her face a bit. Lindsay is very pretty and has wide shoulders which add to that look and feel of strength that I mentioned before, but it's a sexy kind of strength. Last summer I saw her "wire" tuna and marlin, wrapping the leader wire around her gloved hands in that epic tug of war in the cockpit. But now those strong shoulders were drooping, and she looked much older than her twenty–six years.

"I can't ever repay you guys for dropping everything and racing down here to help me save Murph. I don't know what I would have done without you two. I don't know what I would do without him."

I said, "And you're not about to find out anytime soon. We'll get him back, don't worry." I glanced over at Casey, who did look worried.

She said, "He makes me laugh more than any guy ever has before. We even laugh sometimes when we're..."

"Whoa, Linds! Too much information. Look, we'll find Murph, and get you two back to...laughing...in no time." I smiled as she looked over at me with a slight grin, the droop back out of her shoulders, just like I had hoped. Now to keep it this way.

Chapter 4

After what seemed like forever, but really was barely over an hour, the western end of Grand Bahama island came into view on the horizon. We were lined up straight on Bootle Bay inlet. Ten minutes later Casey was throttling back, dropping us below planning speed and down to idle, letting the stern rise and draw as little water as possible before we entered the shallow inlet. We hadn't seen any sign of Timmy's boat since coming within sight of Boodle Bay. Not that we would have known exactly what to do if we did. His rig was so much faster than ours in all but the worst seas, and we were now only in three-foot rollers.

Casey asked, "Locked and loaded?" We both answered in the affirmative. Casey and I both were carrying our pistols that we brought with us, and Lindsay had grabbed a Glock from the weapons cache that she and Murph always carried onboard. He continued, "Okay, the plan is to use our boat to block the narrow canal, and box him in. Shoot for the engines if he tries to get around us. Under no circumstances is he to get by us and make it to the ocean." We both nodded.

The tide had started coming in about half an hour before, but we were still stirring up silt as we entered the shallow inlet, splitting the difference between the rock jetties. I was glad that Casey was at the wheel instead of me; these were tight quarters.

"Looks like someone built a fish camp ahead; that wasn't here ten years ago when I came through. Lots of the trees are gone too, must have been that last hurricane. Now if the trees aren't all down in the canals, that'll be a bit of a help," Casey said.

There were a couple of outboards tied up at the fish camp, which actually looked more like a small hotel, but so far no sign of any boats with three engines. Up ahead was our first turn to the right into the entrance to the "H" shaped canal system. Casey kicked the starboard gear into reverse, spinning the bow until he almost lined up with the center of the channel of the western canal. He was right about the width, there would be no reversing course once we entered the canals. They had definitely been built when the average boat was much shorter. This canal was probably slightly less than seventy feet across, but with shallow sloping sides. With what *Irish Luck* draws, the running gear would definitely hit if we tried turning around.

I gave the fish camp another visual scan as Casey started us into the canal. Fortunately, I saw no one about. An unknown boat of our size going into this narrow canal system would certainly draw attention if anyone had been around. Then I focused my own attention back down the canal like Lindsay and Casey. He was right, there hadn't been any building boom since he had been here last. The canal was about two thousand feet long, and yet I could only see three houses. One of those yards looked cared for, probably the only full-time resident. But there were no other boats in sight.

None of us said anything since we were laser-focused on the canal. About a thousand feet ahead on the left was the intersecting connector. When we reached it, Casey kicked the port gear in reverse, pivoting again and pointing the bow down the middle. Still no sign of Timmy's boat, or any other boat. But we should see it when we make the turn into the last canal, about four hundred feet ahead.

"When I make this last turn, Lindsay, you check down the right-side canal, and Marlin, you cover the left. I don't want this son of a bitch sneaking up behind us."

"Got it," Lindsay replied.

"On it, Case." I was about as keyed up as I could get right now. As Casey made the turn, the only boats down the left side were all the way at the end, a couple of commercial scows tied up at a vacant lot. I spun to the right, expecting to see Timmy's boat at the end, but the canal was vacant. My heart sank, and I could see that Lindsay was now devastated. Again, I squeezed her shoulder as she stood there looking numb. I didn't know what else to do or say; this wasn't good.

Casey took both transmissions out of gear, then put both in reverse.

I asked, "We're leaving?"

He shook his head. "No, I'm going to turn around and back down to Billy's, so we'll be bow out in case we need to leave in a hurry. Or in case Timmy still comes in behind us, no sense in him seeing the name on the transom."

Casey is one sharp dude, always thinking a few steps ahead. He backed us past the connector canal, then stuck the bow back into it, making the water equivalent of a three–point–turn. Then he slowly backed us the thousand feet down to an old "A" frame house, the last one on the right, just as TW had said. There was a short and narrow dock with plenty of depth in front of it running parallel to the only seawall along the shoreline. We tied up alongside, using our port stern and spring cleats since there was only enough space for half our boat on the dock. We couldn't see any movement through the house's windows, but there was an older SUV parked on a crushed shell driveway next to it.

All three of us stepped onto the dock, still carefully watching for movement within the house, and again seeing none. Since Casey knew Billy, he was the first up the steps onto the back deck that overlooked the canal. He knocked on the door, which hadn't been latched, and it swung inward.

"Billy? You home? It's Casey Shaw." From somewhere upstairs came a muffled thumping sound. We went through the door into a big living room and kitchen combination. It was empty. At the far end down a hallway was the front door, and there were two doors off the hall that proved to be a bathroom and a guestroom. Both were empty. Again, there was thumping coming from above. Casey led the way up the living room stairs into an open sitting loft. There was one door at the back of it, and the three of us moved over to it. Casey opened it from the side and peeked inside before the three of us rushed through it. There was a man bound and gagged in the middle of the floor of the master bedroom. Casey went over to him as Lindsay and I checked the bathroom and the closet but found no one else.

Casey removed the duct tape gag and was greeted by a string of profanity for his efforts. Billy had obviously been "worked over" from the looks of his face; a split lip, black eye, and swelling around his cheekbones and jaw. "When I catch up to that son of a bitch partner of mine and that bastard son of his, there's gonna be hell to pay!"

I winced at the use of the term, "bastard," but that's another one of those stories from a different day.

Casey questioned him while he cut the zip ties that bound his hands and legs. "Was Murph with him?"

"Yeah, that was why I let the two of them in. I didn't see the gun in his back until it was too late. Hurry up with those ties, we still have a chance to catch them."

Lindsay jumped in, "Was Murph okay? Where are they?"

"Yeah, he's fine, and so am I, thanks for asking." He said sarcastically. "They're on the way to my bank in Freeport. And just who the hell are you two?"

Casey made hasty introductions as he helped Billy to his feet. He was a couple inches shy of six feet with shaggy salt and pepper hair and a build that had been thickened in the middle from years of island living. He said, "C'mon, we'll take my truck." As we hurried

35

over to the stairs, he spotted the Merritt outside. "Wow! Nice rig. Yours, Casey?"

Lindsay piped up, "Mine and Murph's."

"What, are you some kinda heiress or something?"

"Not hardly. How long ago did they leave?" She was staying focused, and best of all, hopeful sounding.

"Maybe half an hour. They should be getting to Freeport about now, and then they have to dock and get a taxi to the bank. It's twenty minutes straight down the Queen's Highway from here if I floor it. Like I said, we might be able to head 'em off before they leave there."

Freeport/Lucaya is the largest town on Grand Bahama island with about fifty thousand residents and most of the non–tourism-based businesses. We piled into the old, rusty SUV, and Billy took the turn onto the Queen's Highway on almost two wheels. I know that you are thinking; four lanes of smooth asphalt. Un uh. Barely two lanes of crumbling pavement down the middle of a narrow section of scrub-covered coral island. But Billy was taking it at the speed and with the skill of a NASCAR driver, passing in places I wouldn't have dared, and somehow only managing to run only one car off the road in the process. I looked at Casey up in the passenger's seat, and I could swear he was relaxed. Not me or Lindsay, partly because of the danger Murph was in, and partly because of Billy's driving. If we weren't so busy being scared and worried, we might have enjoyed the occasional water views across the flat lowlands.

"The kid went nuts when I said there was only fifty grand left of uninvested cash of his old man's. That's when he started tapdancing on my face, but I wouldn't tell him anything. He found TW's remaining cash in my desk drawer, but then he spotted my bank book with four hundred grand in that account. I told him it was mine, not his old man's, but as you can guess, he didn't care. He figured there had to be more and found ledger copies for the inn and boatyard that TW and I went in on together down in Marsh Harbour.

That, plus the little marina and restaurant here in the village is where the money comes from that I send stateside. We bought it all with the cash we had from the old days, and now we're legit. Kid didn't want to hear it. He's planning on running down there after he cleans out my account. Gonna take Murph with him, because he knows Harcourt Rhinehart, the guy who runs that operation for me. Figures that Murph might be able to talk him out of what we have in the bank down there, too."

A little over twenty hair–raising minutes later we were passing the commercial harbor as we arrived at the outskirts of Freeport. Two minutes after that, Billy pulled up in front of the bank. We all raced in where a quick look around the lobby confirmed that we were too late, again. Billy barged into the manager's office, with the three of us in tow.

"Stanley, please tell me that you didn't drain my account!"

"Billy, calm yourself, mon. Even wit' dat boy having your passbook, a note from you, an' your passport, it sounded too fishy for dat."

"Thank god."

"We don' keep that much in US money here anyway. So, I could only give him a hundred thousan'. Supposed to wire the rest."

"You gave him *how much*? Please tell me you didn't send that wire."

The Bahamian smiled, showing off a row of perfect, pearl white teeth. "Dat boy don't seem to understand de idea how to relax on island time. I tol' him dat I would send it in de mornin', dat our internet is down. I wanted to stall him until I could check wit' chew myself. I knew you could make de transfer on your own computer yousef if dat really be what you want."

I saw that Billy looked a bit more relieved, despite the apparent loss of a hundred grand. "Good thinking on that wire. I guess I owe you for not sending all of it."

Stanley grunted. "So, I'm guessin' dat note be a fake, an dat he copied your signature off de passport."

Bill nodded, still fuming over his six–figure loss.

Lindsay jumped in, "Did he happen to say where he was tied up?"

The manager shook his head. "No, but I followed him outside. Sumthin' jus' seemed not right."

"Gee, ya think?" Billy was still pissed.

Stanley ignored the jab and continued, "So, like I say, I followed him outside. He had a cab waitin'; it was my cousin's cab." He took out his cell phone and dialed a number. "Percy? Stanley. Where you take dat boy from de bank? Okay, good. Tank you, cousin." He looked up at us. "Lucaya marina. Dropped him off fifteen minutes ago."

We raced out of the bank, and Billy floored it over to the marina. Three things were bothering me. The first thing was that we were winging it; we had no plan, making it all up as we went along. The second was that we were all carrying pistols in a foreign country which we had entered illegally. I don't know for sure what Bahamian jails looked like, but I had a hunch and no desire to find out if I was right or not. Third, where was Murph? Stanley hadn't mentioned another man with Timmy, so I'm assuming he was alone. Billy said Timmy needs Murph once he gets to Marsh Harbour, so he should be alive and healthy, but where?

Five minutes later we arrived at the marina and started scanning the docks for the three–engine center console. I spotted it just exiting the marina and heading out the inlet. The exhaust bubble trail led back to the fuel dock where an attendant was counting cash. I raced over there with the others following me.

"Hey, that guy who just left here, did he have another guy on the boat?"

The attendant looked at me disinterestedly. "Why you wanna know dat, mon?"

I reached into my pocket and pulled out a twenty. He still looked bored. I pulled out another twenty, and he perked up a bit. "Now, what about the other guy?"

"I didn' see nobody else, but he tied up for tirty minutes an had me make sure nobody get near dat boat." He smiled, so I knew there had been more cash involved.

I asked, "He say anything else?"

"Yeah, wanted to know how long to Great Sale Cay tru de Lucayan Waterway. I tell him about two hours. He can make it dere easy before sunset."

"We can too if we step on it," Casey said.

Back in the car, I asked him what the Lucayan Waterway was.

"Almost ten miles of narrow canal, cut all the way across Grand Bahama Island, just south of Freeport. Wide enough for two boats to pass, but shallow as heck on the far side, maybe four feet deep, with two fixed span bridges, one we can't get under with our tower. But we'll have a closer, even more direct run to Great Sale from Bootle Bay, we just go past West End and cut over to the flats between Sandy Cay and Memory Rock."

I knew about the flats; a sandy shelf on the interior of the Grand Bahama Bank that mostly ran between eight and twelve feet deep. It sounded like Great Sale Cay was in the middle of it.

Lindsay looked shell shocked. "He didn't see Murph onboard, and neither did I from the dock."

I smiled at her, "He was there alright, that's why he didn't want anybody around the boat, in case Murph started making a racket. If he has a 'head' in that center console, I'd bet that's where he stashed Murph."

She looked at me and I smiled, then she brightened a bit.

"So, Casey, what's on Great Sale Cay?" I asked. In the Bahamas, *cay* is pronounced *key*.

He replied, "Two miles of scrub, beach, and more no–see–ums than you want to deal with. Those are like mosquitos, only give them a mouthful of tiger shark teeth, then shrink them down to the size of a pinhead. Damn things travel in packs, and they love the beach, just like tourists." Casey glanced at Lindsay, hoping to get a smile, but she was now back to being worried.

"I know, we ran into those things down in the Florida Keys. I hate them. Have you ever been to this Great Sale Cay before?" She asked.

Casey nodded. "Great Sale is a popular anchorage for boats headed down the Abacos. It's roughly midway between West End and Green Turtle Cay. The Abacos have their own version of the Intracoastal Waterway; a series of barrier islands a mile to two miles offshore of the two main islands which together stretch almost a hundred miles.

It makes sense Timmy would want to anchor off there overnight, there's shelter from sudden winds and enough privacy that would make it less likely for Murph to be discovered. And if you aren't familiar with the water along Abaco, you don't want to try to run it at night."

I had the beginnings of a plan starting to formulate in my head. Casey must've seen the wheels turning, as he cocked his head slightly while looking at me and said, "What?"

"This might really work to our advantage. First, we're pretty sure we know where he's headed tonight. Second, depending on how many boats are anchored there, we might have the privacy that we need in order to be able to overpower Timmy without attracting attention. We have to separate him from Murph and from his gun. And I've got an idea how to do both." I told them all what I had in mind, and I saw grins and nods. Now, we just needed there to be a minimum number of boats at that anchorage tonight, and a maximum of luck.

Billy drove us back to his house like he was in race with a hundred thousand dollars riding on the outcome. Because he was. We all boarded *Irish Luck*, and Casey idled us back out to the ocean where he took the Merritt up to cruising speed.

"Lindsay, do you have a Bahamian cruising flag aboard?" Casey asked.

She nodded. "Yes, it came with the boat along with the quarantine flag. So, I'm guessing were not going to be clearing customs?"

"No. We can't with Billy onboard, we couldn't explain how he got on the boat if we didn't already make landfall. And the kid has his passport. We should be okay though so long as we don't get stopped by the Bahamian Defense Force boats. With the Bahamian flag flying, it will look like we cleared Customs down in Freeport."

Casey looked at Lindsay, knowing the next two and a half hours until we reached Great Sale Cay were going to be an eternity for her. "Why don't you and Marlin go down and make us some sandwiches, since none of us have had any lunch."

I knew he was trying to keep her busy, but I figured that he might also want the bridge to just he and Billy, so that they could have a private talk. I followed Lindsay down the ladder and into the galley in the salon. She was just going through the motions as she made the sandwiches; I knew her mind was a million miles away. She paused in the middle of one, just staring off into space across the salon. I saw the beginning of a tear starting to form the corner of an eye. In the few months that I had known her, I had never seen her cry. I couldn't take seeing that, so I wrapped her up in a hug.

"It's going to be alright Linds. Everything is going to go great, and we'll have Murph back by morning. That kid is going to be so sorry he ever screwed with us."

Lindsay chuckled slightly.

I asked, "What?"

She looked at me and said, "You know he looks like he's only a year or two younger than me and Kari, right?"

Lindsay and I had had a conversation about my age difference with Kari before I went out with her. I had hesitated to ask Kari out because of it, and in the end, she was the one who did the asking rather than wait around for me to do it. Lindsay was a bit touchy about age thing, since Murph was even a couple years older than me. Some of her girlfriends back in Northern Virginia had given her a hard time about it, as well as about Murph's former reputation for being a bit of a "player" during his days back in South Florida.

I smiled and said, "Yep" as I released her. She hit me on the shoulder as I did. "Hey! Only Kari can abuse me like that!"

"I'm sure that had she been here she would have approved. And it worked, you got my mind off...things...for a second. You know, when you guys were in a tiff and I was trying to smooth things over for you, I asked her if you two weren't attached, and Murph and I weren't, did she think that you and I..."

That caught me totally off guard. "Really?"

She smirked, "Yes, really. As in, I said that, but I didn't mean it there stud, so cool your jets. It was just to get her thinking back along the lines of you being desirable to other women, so she didn't screw it up. She got mad, just like I wanted her to, then I started laughing. I told her I was kidding, that it would be like kissing my brother. Don't look so damn disappointed Marlin, you know we're both off the market for good." She paused a beat, "That's what you've become to me, you know. An older brother, and I like that, a lot. This is the second time since I've known you that you have jumped in to save me or Murph."

I smiled. "You guys would do the same if the situation was reversed. And Murph jumped in to help Kari save me when *Why Knot* exploded, so I owe him. You helped Kari and I get together, and I won't forget that, either. In fact, this helps even the score between us a bit. Oh, and for the record, I wasn't disappointed about you not meaning it." She shot me an indignant look for a second, until I smiled and winked at her and got a smile in return.

Chapter 5

By the time we all finished our late lunch, we were well onto the flats, headed straight for Great Sale Cay. Casey had throttled back to a slow cruise, because we didn't want to get to the anchorage too much in advance of sunset. We wanted enough light left to be able to scope out Timmy's boat, but not enough for him to watch us. We also needed Murph to be able to see and recognize his own boat, know that we were there, and that we had a plan to rescue him. But we also didn't want Timmy to see our boat's name, in case he could connect it to Murph.

Lindsey said, "I have an idea. The previous owner didn't use this boat a lot, and he really liked his varnish. So, he had a canvas cover made to protect the wood transom from fading when he wasn't using her. It covers the whole thing, including the name."

"Perfect! That was the biggest part I was worried about, that Timmy might recognize the name. This plan is gonna work guys, I can feel it." I said.

Casey had the radar on, and it showed Great Sale Cay about five miles ahead. He slowed to a fast idle, while Billy and Lindsay went down to the cockpit and dug out the transom cover. It was made of a heavy brown canvas, the type that was commonly used on more vintage boats. They attached it to the transom, then the two of them retreated into the salon where they drew the curtains over the windows. We couldn't risk Billy being seen by Timmy, since he would easily recognize him. And with Timmy having followed his father around, it was also possible that he might recognize Lindsay as well. So, we had all decided that the two of them would stay down in the salon.

Casey and I remained on the bridge as we entered the anchorage. Luck was on our side as there was only one other boat there; Timmy's. We idled past it, a little over a hundred feet abeam of them. Even at this distance, we could clearly see two people in the boat, and one was definitely Murph. We went about a hundred yards away from them before Casey swung us around and I went up on the bow to drop the anchor. I let out sixty feet of rode as Casey backed us down. The Danforth anchor bit deeply in the sand and marl bottom that lay a dozen feet beneath our hull. Casey shut off everything but the generator, then turned on the anchor light before we both went into the salon.

I looked at Lindsay, "I saw Murph. I'm certain he saw us and recognized both us and the boat. Timmy looked away, no doubt trying to hide his identity. But Murph knows we're coming Linds. Now, all we have to do is wait until it gets dark enough for those two to fall asleep."

The Merritt was loaded with more electronics than I'd seen on a sportfisherman before. One thing that came in very handy right now was a security camera mounted under the tuna tower platform. We could aim it from the salon and display it on the widescreen TV that raised up out of an aft cabinet like my new one on *Why Knot*. We focused the camera on Timmy's boat, zooming in until we could see both Timmy and Murph sitting on bench seats in the bow. They were eating, and we could see that Murph's hands were either tied or cuffed together in front of him. While it wasn't the most reassuring picture, at least he was alive and seemed to be unharmed. I looked over at Lindsay, who was glued to the screen. I knew she felt even more helpless than I did right then, but at least we knew a hell of a lot more this evening than we did this morning. And, we had a good plan of how to go about getting him back.

We watched the TV as the sun set behind them. Timmy was trussing up Murph with what looked like dock lines. I don't think this is what Murph had in mind about the old phrase, "sleep tight". As we were watching, the camera switched over to infrared,

45

meaning we would be able to keep an eye on them all night, but only in greyscale. Fortunately, the light breeze that was blowing was straight down our bow, so with the stabilization feature, the image didn't move much at all. The two of them apparently went to sleep sometime during the next hour, around 8 o'clock, since there wasn't a whole lot else for them to do on an open outboard. But this also meant that they would probably be awake before sunrise, which would be around 7 a.m.

We waited until 10 o'clock, making certain that they would be asleep. The light breeze and cool temperature would keep any flying pests at bay, so there shouldn't be anything to wake them up before morning. We shut off almost everything onboard the Merritt. The only light on the boat now came from the anchor light on the tuna tower, and the TV screen that was still displaying the infrared image of Timmy's boat.

The four of us went back into the fishing cockpit where I sat on the deck in only my boxer shorts, donning a pair of swim fins. While I was doing that, Billy and Lindsay undid enough of the canvas transom cover to be able to open the tuna door. That's a short door cut into the transom of the boat to allow the crew to haul in large fish. I was about to become the catch of the day.

So far, the only noise coming from our boat was the muffled exhaust from the generator which we intended to leave on all night. It was doubtful any noise from it or us would carry as far as Timmy's boat, but we were still being stealthily silent. I slipped three large dock line coils over my head and across my chest, then Casey handed me a flat-blade screwdriver that I stuck in my teeth like a pirate with a knife. I started scooting out the tuna door on my butt, and as I did I felt Lindsay's hand on my shoulder, patting it just before I entered the water. She couldn't see my face in the dark, but if she could have, she would have seen a ton of tension flow out of it then.

The seventy–two–degree water was calm enough that I had opted not to wear a diving mask, since it wouldn't be much help in the dark anyway. Slowly and quietly, I began the almost 150–yard swim from the back of the Merritt over to the triple engines of Timmy's boat. I knew my three friends would be following my progress on the infrared camera. I also knew that once I reached Timmy's boat, they would be my sentinels, watching for any movement from anyone on board. Casey was standing by on the airhorn to warn me in case that happened. I hoped like hell that it wouldn't, since we didn't have a plan to deal with that, and we'd be winging it again.

That 150–yard swim felt more like two miles by the time I reached the back of Timmy's boat. I took the looped ends of the dock lines and wrapped them around the lower units of the outboards. Then I pulled the bitter ends through the loops and wrapped them several times around each of the lower units and finally the hubs of Timmy's propellers before tying them back together. This left over 20 feet of line drooping down in a "U" under each engine, between the props and the lower unit housings. In reality, accomplishing this only took a little over a minute per engine, but it felt like an eternity. I kept stopping and listening for any noise from the boat, and half expecting to hear a horn blast from the Merritt at any time. Fortunately, neither happened. Then for the last part of the plan, I took the screwdriver and found the hydraulic trim and tilt bypass release screws on each engine mount. I was able to back out the ones on the port and starboard engines but the one in the center was stuck. At least now Timmy wouldn't be able to raise the two outboard engines, which meant he would have to get in the water to cut those lines loose from the propellers, separating him from both his gun and Murph. Which was the whole point of the plan.

I had done all that I could do, so I slowly and quietly started swimming back to the Merritt, taking my

47

time in order to be as stealthy as possible. We didn't want Timmy discovering he'd been sabotaged until it was too late to prevent the damage that was going to happen. I had just pulled up opposite the fishing cockpit when something grabbed my right fin. My first instinct was to yell, but I overrode that impulse, because I instantly realized doing so could easily screw up what I'd accomplished. Instead, I kicked with my left foot, which met something solid with very little give. I kicked again and again, my heel continuously connecting with something until it let go. I made my way over to the tuna door and hissed loudly, "Pull me in, quick!" Two hands grabbed my own hands as they yanked and dragged me up through the open door. Linds wrapped a towel around my shoulders as I removed the fins, bringing them into the salon as Bill and Casey closed the tuna door and secured the transom canvas.

Once everyone was back inside, I turned on the overhead lights and examined the fin. A good portion of the trailing edge had been detached by a large semicircle of perforations; a classic shark bite. A big one at that. There was a stunned silence between all of us until I said, "Murph is gonna be picking up one hell of a bar tab when we get home." I think Billy was the first one to chuckle, followed by Casey. Lindsay looked even more shaken than I felt, and she wasn't smiling nor chuckling.

I left that crew in the salon and grabbed a hot shower in the master stateroom. While the ocean had been in the low seventies, the air temperature was in the mid-sixties; late winter at its peak in the Bahamas, and the natives were all freezing. But I don't care where you are from, being soaking wet at night in those temps with even a light breeze is just plain cold. My teeth had started to chatter before I got in the shower. Then again, it might have been a delayed reaction to the shark attack, I don't know. What I do know is that I was glad I had pulled on a pair of new, dry, boxers before I walked out of the "head," because Linds was right there sitting on the bed, in the middle of a video call with Kari. The Merritt had come with satellite internet as part of all its electronics.

"Here's your hubby now." Lindsay swung the camera around, giving Kari a full view of me.

"If I didn't know you two better, I'd be jealous." Kari teased. Then she got her all-business look on. "You were really attacked by a shark?"

I looked past the camera and glared at Lindsay. "Jeeze, Linds, did you have to tell her about that right now?"

Kari didn't wait for Lindsay to answer, she did it for her. "Yes, she did! No secrets, pal! And I hope that you were only talking about the shark, right?"

I knew what Kari was up to, trying to distract Lindsay and help raise her spirits. But Lindsay is nobody's fool; she also knew what Kari was doing.

Lindsay looked serious. "Kari, you are marrying the bravest man ever. I don't know too many other people that would have made that swim in the dark tonight for a friend. Hey, I'm going to let you two talk now, and I'll call you again tomorrow after we have Murph back aboard. But before I go, I want you two to know I love you guys, both of you, and I can't thank each of you enough for your help today. Though it feels like it has been a week instead of really not even a day yet."

Kari replied, "Love you too. Promise me you'll be careful, and that you'll take care of Marlin, too."

"I've got his back, that's a given. Listen, you two talk." She handed me the phone with a smile, then closed the door on her way out.

Kari said, "Hey. Miss you. And promise me you won't take any unnecessary chances."

I nodded. "Miss you, too. I won't, I didn't, and we'll bring Murph home safe and sound."

"Linds and Casey, too."

I nodded. "Like she said, that's a given."

We talked about five minutes more, then said our goodnights. I walked Lindsay's phone up to her in the salon, finding that Billy and Casey had already crashed in the vee bunks in the crew's quarters. Everyone was planning on getting up at five a.m. There was no way that Timmy would be getting underway before sunrise, it was too easy to hit a coral head in the dark.

Lindsay had pulled the coffee table up to the couch that faced the TV so that she could stretch out with her feet up and was now under a blanket. I sat down next to her and passed her phone over. She was watching Murph sleep on the screen. She said, "You can have the big stateroom if you want. I'm going to be right here."

I shook my head. "Nope, I don't want it. I'm going to be right here watching with you." I lifted the edge of the blanket and slid in next to her.

She glanced over then looked back at the screen. "I meant what I said you know; I love you guys. If it weren't for you two, Casey, and Dawn, I'd be stuck back in Riviera Beach waiting for the cops to finally believe me that Murph was kidnapped, instead of preparing to rescue him. Thank you, Mar."

"Ah, don't read too much into this. I'm only here so I can tell the Beer–Thirty–Bunch that I slept with you after we saw Murph sleeping with another guy on a video." This was our regular afternoon marina group that meets after work for a beer or two. Tall tales were usually told there, as well as fishing reports that were usually based in fact, but at times stretched out of proportion.

"You are weird and annoying, just like a big brother. And, I don't know anyone else I'd rather have here right now with me other than Murph."

I said, "Don't make it creepy."

"Oh, like your description wasn't creepy?" She smiled for the first time this evening.

I chuckled. "Here's the deal. I'll take first watch, wake you in two hours, then grab two hours myself."

She replied, "Thanks, I'll take you up on that. See you in two hours." She rested her head on my shoulder and was asleep in no time.

I woke her at four-thirty, almost six hours later.

"Hey! You were supposed to wake me hours ago."

"You needed your sleep. You can make up for it by fixing breakfast though." I had been way too anxious to be able to sleep. This was all my plan, and if it didn't work it might get my one friend hurt or killed and break the heart of another. It would be my fault, my total responsibility. I wouldn't admit it to Lindsay, but I was scared to death right now.

"I was right, you are annoying." Lindsay gave me a fake frown.

While she got busy in the galley, I kept my eyes glued to the screen, watching for any movement. So far, neither Murph nor Timmy had even so much as rolled over in the middle of the night.

Lindsey came over with two cups of coffee and sat down next to me, passing over one of the cups. I needed this one and about twelve others just like it.

"By the way, just for the record, and I know I can speak for Kari also, we love both you guys too. I kind of figured that it went without saying that's the reason I'm here. And I know it's killing her not being able to be here to help. But, with her and Dawn holding down the fort, it made things a lot easier for Casey and me."

Lindsay looked over and smiled slightly. "I already knew all of that. But it's always nice to hear it too."

Chapter 6

By 5:15 a.m., the four of us had eaten our breakfasts, checked our weapons, and we were once again locked, loaded, and ready to go. We didn't have long to wait as the false dawn must have awakened Timmy. He stood up, relieving himself over the rail. I'm not saying that the camera was a good one, but it was still in infrared mode, and yet Lindsay was able to comment, "No wonder he has a boat with 'trips,' he needs to do a little compensating." Seeing the smirk on her face felt good.

He untied Murph, allowing him to heed the call of nature as well. Then Lindsay smiled and said, "That's my man! Even from here, you can see why he doesn't need 'trips'." Yeah, just when I thought the morning wasn't already creepy enough.

Casey doled out assignments. "Okay gang, it's showtime. I'll crank the engines and let them warm up. We wait until he goes overboard to cut the lines off his props, then we move up on him. Lindsay, you take the bow and handle the anchor. Billy, you get set up by the front corner of the wheelhouse, and Marlin, you have the cockpit and handle the Mossberg twelve gauge. If he tries anything funny, cover the water with buckshot, and we'll leave him for breakfast for your friend from last night. Nobody, and I repeat, *nobody* takes any chances on our end. We aren't going to put Murph or any one of us at risk. Period. Everybody clear on that?"

We all answered in the affirmative, and Billy added, "He beat the crap out of me because he's a weightlifter who knows some martial arts, and he's good at that stuff. If he tries to get onto either boat, trust me, you need to shoot him, we can't take any chances."

Billy, Lindsay, and I watched Timmy on the infrared while Casey stood by the helm up on the bridge. There were barely a few wisps of sunlight starting on the horizon. Timmy cranked up his engines then put them in gear without even letting them warm up. The extra twenty feet of loose three-quarter-inch nylon rope cranked right up on each propeller-like fishing line on a reel. All three reached the end of their slack and came tight on the loops around the lower units simultaneously, stalling and shutting down each cold engine. Timmy, still half asleep, tried restarting them in neutral, and of course, all three cranked right up. Again, he put them in gear, only to have all three stall and quit again. He tried raising the engines to see what the issue was, but of course, only the center engine responded. The other two remained in the down and running position. From his position up on the bridge Casey heard the cursing as Timmy thought he had picked up someone's lost anchor line.

I said, "Wait for it, wait for it..." We watched as Timmy stripped off his shirt and his pants, then he grabbed a knife and jumped over the side. He swam back to the engines and began hacking away at the rope on the center engine. I said, "Go!" We all filed out of the salon, heading to our predetermined posts. Casey started moving us up on the anchor line as Lindsay quickly hauled it up on deck.

Timmy hadn't noticed us moving yet. His back was to the Merritt while he was cutting away at the ropes on the center engine. Suddenly he became aware of a large dark shape looming over his shoulder in the dim pre-dawn light as *Irish Luck's* bow moved up alongside his boat. Too late he realized that this had been no accident. Even in this low light, he could see the outline of three armed figures that were now all aiming at him. I had left a shell out of the chamber on the Mossberg pump shotgun on purpose. I now racked a shell into the chamber strictly for effect; I wanted him to hear it and realize we were serious.

"Don't move Timmy, or you're dead. And drop the knife." I said.

"Wha...who are you, and what do you want?"

"Shut the hell up, you piece of crap, or I'll shut you up for good. And you heard the man, drop the knife, or I'll shoot." Lindsay's voice from up on the bow was like ice, and it had the right effect; Timmy dropped the knife and it sank to the sandy bottom.

Billy jumped over onto Timmy's boat with a spring line in hand, tying the two together, spring cleat to spring cleat. I knew that Lindsay wanted badly to jump over onto Timmy's boat with him to help free Murph, but I needed her here in the cockpit with me, and she started to make her way back. The fewer people that were over on the outboard, the fewer "friendlies" we would have in the line of fire if Timmy tried to climb back on board.

Lindsay climbed down into the cockpit with me, activating the laser on her Glock. She intentionally raked the light across Timmy's eyes. Just like my racking a shell into the chamber, this was all for effect. Then her laser was joined by Casey's, as he drew down on Timmy from the bridge, now that the boats were tied together. While this kid was definitely not the brightest bulb on the tree, he did seem to grasp the situation and stayed where he was, treading water.

Billy had taken a sharp knife along with him and had Murph freed in short order. He was never so happy to get back onto his boat in his life. Lindsay wrapped him up in a huge tight hug, embracing for several minutes. Meanwhile, Billy searched Timmy's boat, finding not only his hundred thousand dollars and TW's fifty grand, but an additional almost ten grand that Timmy must've brought over with him for expenses. He also found his passport, as well as Timmy's, plus a pistol, a shotgun, and Timmy's cell phone. He brought all of it back over to the Merritt.

Up until this point, Timmy had stayed quiet. That changed when he saw the money being taken off his boat by Billy.

"That's my money, Billy!"

Billy replied, "Like hell it is, you little son of a bitch."

"At least leave me the sixty grand; it's from my old man to me."

Casey spoke up, "Actually, your dad promised me fifty grand if I let you live. You had better be glad I'm a man of my word. And that other ten will barely cover my expenses. Here's the deal Timmy, we have you on video kidnapping Murph with a gun in his back in Riviera Beach." He held up his iPhone, "And we now have video of us saving Murph from you on this boat in the Bahamas. So, you could go to jail in both countries. If any of us ever sees your face again, that's exactly what's gonna happen."

Billy said, "Now hold on just a minute Casey. I've got a little bit of a score to settle with this asshole." Bill had put a fishing glove on his right hand which now held Timmy's semiautomatic pistol. He fired two shots into the cowlings of both the port and starboard engines, putting holes in their aluminum blocks. He then fired again, this time into the lower unit of each of those engines, putting holes in their cooling water systems, making each engine worthless except for their salvage weight. Then he shot one of the blades and the hub on the raised center engine's stainless–steel propeller which was sticking out of the water. This made sure that it would be unable to run at full speed because of the vibration it would cause. By leaving Timmy here like this, he was also making sure that he could still get home, but that it would be a very slow ride. Then he shot out his VHF radio and the other electronics, leaving him with only a functioning magnetic compass. "Well, that's not exactly even, but it'll have to do. And you listen to me you little bastard, maybe Casey's up for sending you to prison, but if I ever see your ass again there's not gonna be enough of you left to go there. You got off light today because there are too many witnesses. I even so much as hear of you stepping foot in these islands again, and believe me, I would hear about it if you did, then I will hunt you down. Have yourself a nice slow ride back to the states."

Billy jumped back over to Timmy's boat and untied the spring line. He hopped back aboard the Merritt as Casey put both engines in gear.

"You assholes have not seen the last of me! I'll get you for this! All of you." The rest of Timmy's rant was drowned out as Casey advanced the throttles connected to the huge MAN diesel engines, leaving Timmy bobbing around behind his now crippled "Johnson extender" of a boat.

We had been up at cruising speed for about five minutes when Billy tossed both of Timmy's firearms overboard, followed by his cell phone and Billy's fishing glove that was covered in gunshot residue. Then he and I took the canvas off the transom, folded it up, and stowed it. Murph and Lindsay had gone into the cabin and we wanted to give them some privacy, so we climbed the ladder up to the bridge to be with Casey. While the sun was now just barely above the horizon, we dug into the bridge refrigerator and pulled out three ice-cold bottles of beer. We toasted our success, and the reunion of friends.

Billy remained standing next to Casey, and the two of them were doing a bit of reminiscing. I went forward and sat on the bench seat, making a video call to Kari. She picked up immediately, looking concerned.

"All good, everything went as planned, everybody is fine." I was smiling my widest smile at her.

"Thank god. I couldn't sleep last night, partly because I was worried and partly because you weren't here. I can breathe again now."

I said, "It'll be a few hours before we get back stateside, and I'll call you when I get regular cell service back."

"Okay. Love you and tell Murph and Linds I'm so glad this turned out the way it did. I love them and can't wait to see them when they come back home."

"You already did," Lindsay said. She and Murph were now standing behind me on the bridge, also with beers in hand. Hey, this is the Bahamas, and it's always five o'clock here.

Murph took the wheel then ran the boat to West End where we dropped Billy off, not wanting to deal with the narrow canals at Bootle Bay again. He said he'd take a cab back to his house. He stepped off the boat with a hundred grand in cash in a grocery bag he found in the galley. I guess for a guy who once had millions stuffed in his furniture, this was nothing, but I'd have been a nervous wreck.

We headed back out, but this time instead of crossing to Palm Beach, we headed to Stuart. This was where *Irish Luck* is registered in next week's sailfish tournament and where Murph and Lindsay were scheduled to meet their next charter. Murph took the helm as we went out beyond the Bahama Banks into the clear blue indigo water of the gulf stream. Halfway across I pulled down the Bahamian cruising flag then tossed Timmy's passport overboard from the flying bridge, watching as our wake tumbled it before it finally disappeared beneath the surface and sank out of sight. Yesterday's west wind had died down; there was barely a ripple on the water, and Murph commented about how this was highly unusual for this time of year. It was like the gods had decided to cut us a break both in the weather and in getting our friend back safe and sound.

Casey handed Murph a second grocery bag with the fifty grand in it.

"It doesn't repay what you two went through, but at least it will buy some fuel."

Murph shook his head. "I can't take it. You take it, Marlin, put it against your new houseboat."

I said, "Fifty grand? You wish you were getting off that lightly. You get my next bar tab, fella. Besides, sleeping with Lindsay last night was more than enough reward."

Murph's eyes got big. "You did *what* with *who*?"

Lindsay scowled. "Never mind what I said about you being a big brother; you can be such a child!"

"Payback for telling Kari about the shark attack." I grinned.

"Wait, who got attacked by a shark? And, you seriously slept with Lindsay?" Poor Murph had had a rough and confusing thirty–six hours, and it didn't seem to be letting up.

"Guilty on both counts." I held up my hand.

A flustered Lindsay said, "We just slept on the same couch. Or, rather, I slept, he watched over you all night on the camera. Marlin hasn't even been to sleep yet, which had better be the reason he said it like that."

I just smiled widely.

"When did you get attacked by a shark?" Murph was still trying to sort everything out.

Lindsay explained the whole episode while Casey sat back on the navigator's seat, enjoying the show and laughing at Lindsay and Murph. I went over and lay down on one of the cushioned bench seats. The next thing I knew Lindsay was shaking me awake as we entered Stuart inlet.

"Wake up, Mar. By the way, you snore. Loudly."

I sat up. "Yeah, well, you drooled all over my shoulder last night, big time. You'll be getting my laundry bill as well as my bar tab."

"Kids, am I going to have to come over there and separate you two?" It was good to hear Murph laugh. A couple of times during the last thirty hours I had started to doubt I might hear it ever again. I looked over at him and matched his grin.

We had just finished docking at a marina in the Manatee Pocket when we saw Casey's plane pass overhead, on approach to Stuart airport. He and I repacked our "go bags" then headed over to the Twisted Tuna for a quick lunch with Murph and Lindsay. Our rideshare arrived just as the four of us walked out front.

"Thank you two for dropping everything to come help. I can't tell you what it means to have friends like you guys." The look on Lindsay's face told us what we already knew; if it had been one of us that had gone missing, she would have been there for us, too.

"Yeah, thanks, guys. Anywhere, anytime you need me, I'm there." Murph was as solemn as he gets right now.

"Yeah, well, I just need you to win and win big in this tournament. Remember what I said about that bar bill!" I got him to smile. Seeing Murph turn all serious on us just felt wrong.

Casey made us each a couple of vodkas on the flight back. What the hell, with only two hours sleep during the crossing, it wasn't like I was going to get any work done when I got back anyhow. He was in a rare chatty mood, and our in–flight subject was one of my favorites; boats. He had really been taken with Murph and Lindsay's "new" Merritt, and I had to admit, I was as well. She was about the most agile sixty–foot sportfisherman I'd ever been on.

I wish that we'd had more time to be able to get out and catch a sailfish or two while we were down there. But I was already planning on twisting their arms for some white marlin trips offshore on the Merritt this summer. And I had news for Murph, there would be more than just one bar tab involved. A LOT more.

*****

Timmy watched and continued to curse as the Merritt slowly disappeared off in the distance. Then he dove and retrieved the knife from the bottom, a dozen feet down. He finished cutting the rope off of his remaining operable engine and climbed back aboard. He cranked up the center engine and retrieved his anchor. Billy's aim had been dead-on, and the damaged propeller vibrated badly above twelve–hundred RPM. He would only be able to make about five knots without causing more damage. At this rate, it was going to take him about twenty hours to make it back to Palm Beach.

The first thing he was going to do when he got back would be to find his old man. He had to have been the one who pointed that crew at him. Timmy knew who Billy was, but he wanted to find out who those other assholes were. They were going to pay. They were *all* going to pay, *big time.* Nobody does this to him and gets away with it. But first, instead of his old man, he decided he would start with Billy. He knew those others, and he could easily be persuaded to tell him who and where they were. Plus, he wouldn't be expecting Timmy to show back up, at least not this soon. Then he'd deal with the others. One by one, he'd find and get even with all of them.

Now, instead of setting a course for Palm Beach, Timmy set it for Sandy Cay, an island just off of West End. He would hang offshore there almost until dark, then he could sneak back into Bootle Bay undetected. Since it was Saturday, hopefully Billy won't have had the chance to deposit that hundred grand, and he should still have it at his house. Then on Monday, he would force Billy to make a call to the bank to ensure that transfer wasn't canceled. Until then, he had plenty of time to get Billy to tell him who those others were, and where they could be found. Paybacks are a bitch.

Chapter 7

There's something so comforting about waking up in your own bed, even when it belongs to someone else. Remember that Kari and I were "boat sitting" the houseboat for Murph and Lindsay. I woke up at 5 a.m. as usual, even though it was Sunday. Also, as usual, Kari was already awake. I had slept like the dead for almost ten hours. Since I only had two hours of sleep in the previous thirty–six, I figured that wasn't too bad. I gotten home a little before Kari yesterday, and had just enough time to have another vodka, some dinner, and recount to her in detail the events of the prior thirty–six hours before quickly fading. Never even made it to a second drink. I don't think my head hit the pillow before I was asleep.

"Hey."

"Good morning, "I replied.

"What's up?"

"Figured I'd head over to Carlton's and check on the boats again. I wasn't there for long the other day before Dawn called, so I didn't have much of a chance to look over things." I was starting to make a mental list.

"That wasn't exactly what I meant, so let me try this again. Anything going on over there?" This was delivered in her sexiest voice.

"Better be if we're going to splash *Why Knot* on time." This was fun.

Now she sounded exasperated. "That's not what I meant, either."

I grinned in the dark, even though she couldn't see it. "I know what you meant, but I wanted to see how far you would go to get your point across." The same darkness that hid my smile also hid the punch that now connected with my shoulder.

An hour later we went up to the *Cove* restaurant and bar for breakfast. It was at the west end of the marina basin, behind the charter boat dock. As part of the whole Mallard Cove complex, it's owned by a group that includes Murph, Lindsay, Casey, Dawn, Kari, and two others. Another restaurant and bar, a hotel, a boat dry storage business and a three–story office building are all under construction here as well. Except for the office building, everything would be finished and open by spring, and that last building would be ready sometime in early summer.

Kari is overseeing this entire project as the head of M & S Partners, Casey and Dawn's marina management company. The third floor of that new office building is going to become the headquarters of M & S. At only twenty–five years old, at first glance, Kari would seem very young to have this much responsibility. But that would only be if you didn't really know her. Casey and Dawn had recognized the depth of her abilities and maturity soon after hiring her last year and they moved her up rapidly. Kari was also made a minority partner in Mallard Cove, ensuring that she would stay with them and help grow the business. Not that she needs the job, after what happened.

To make a long story short, a few months ago Kari and I accepted huge settlements in return for our silence about what was behind my boat exploding. This information would have landed some very wealthy and influential people in jail. When I say "huge settlements" I mean low eight-figures. Enough to retire anywhere in the world and do nothing. But neither of us are wired for that. We both like working and would be bored out of our minds sitting around just watching the stock market every day.

A very small group including Dawn and Casey know the details about what actually happened. They also know that as part of the overall settlement there was a multi-billion-dollar endowment created for the Mid–Atlantic Fisheries Foundation (MAFF) which, as its chairman and creator, is now my main focus in life.

Besides Kari that is. The foundation's purpose is simple yet complex; the protection of East Coast fisheries. Because it has this huge endowment, it is completely immune from outside political and donor pressure. I'm also the executive director, though very few people know anything about any of this. In fact, very few people have ever heard of the foundation. Our board is made up of several of my friends who are mostly anglers and business people. This group includes Kari, Murph, Lindsay, Casey and Dawn. It's our mission to help protect the fisheries for generations of anglers to come. MAFF's offices will be on the second floor of that new office building, and the first floor will actually be just covered parking. So, Kari and I will be working out of the same location.

I smiled as I looked across the table, watching Kari finish up her breakfast. Without a doubt, she was the most incredible woman I have ever met. 5'6" tall, mid–back length jet black hair, an amazing figure and hazel eyes that I love to get lost in. As I said, I had originally been hesitant about asking her out because of our seven–year age difference. By doing so I almost missed out on the best part of my life so far. Fortunately, she didn't care about age. And being such a strong-willed person, she was the one who actually pursued me. Why? I have no clue. I do know this; I'm never letting her near an optometrist. If she ever gets a good look at me in the cold, clear light of day, she'll probably run like hell.

"What?"

I replied, "I'm just thinking. About being so lucky."

She smiled. "Play your cards right, and you may get lucky again later." Her sly smile got wider.

"I wasn't talking about that. Well, not just that. Things have turned out so well for us. You've got your dream job, and now I'm not under a lot of pressure to take on new charter clients to make my slip rent, I can just fish my favorites. Plus, I'm going to go ahead and build the fleet without even having to take out a loan."

I already had a twenty–six–foot center console twin outboard, and an eighteen–foot center console flats boat that I used for my charters. I guide mostly fly fishermen, though at times my charter clients do use conventional rods and reels. It all depends upon the weather, the species we're chasing, and my anglers' abilities. But now with Mallard Cove expanding as much as it is, I saw great business potential here for parasail, eco-tour, and sailing tour boats. This would also give me more cover as to where my sudden increase in income was coming from. Though I wasn't planning on a lot of large personal expenditures beyond the new houseboat. My decade–plus old Ford Sport Trac gets me around just fine, and I don't have any expensive vices. But I have to admit, Murph and Lindsay's new Merritt really had me thinking about getting a larger offshore boat at some point down the way.

Kari said, "Yes, I'm lucky, mostly because you are back safe and sound, and because things are now back to normal. Want some company on your boatyard tour?"

"There, and everywhere else today. After all that's happened in the last two days, I'm up for a big giant dose of normalcy and you." I smiled across the table at her, getting the same back in return.

*****

Things were anything but normal back in Bootle Bay. Everything had gone according to his new plan for Timmy. He idled his crippled center console in through the inlet after dark without using his running lights. Anyone who might see his boat idling down the canals would figure that he was probably a drug smuggler, and they would look the other way. These kind of things weren't that uncommon at night in the Bahamas, and the best way to stay healthy was to mind your own business. But instead of taking a left at the connector and going directly to Billy's house, Timmy went down to the end of the first canal. There weren't any houses near there, so he was able to sneak undetected through the scrub, across the access road and up Billy's driveway.

After the events of the last two days, Billy had already relaxed with more than just a rum or two by the time Timmy showed up. It hadn't taken long with him in this condition and Timmy getting physical to pry all the information that he was looking for out of him. The hundred grand was in Billy's desk drawer, right where the fifty had been. There was a pistol on top of the money, which he pocketed. Billy had a phone call to make Monday morning, and after that, Timmy wouldn't need him anymore. He planned to be back home late Monday night, with three hundred grand more than he had in hand right now.

*****

"Earth to Marlin, are you there Marlin?" Kari was looking at me sideways as I drove us back from the boatyard.

"Sorry. I've just been thinking about an idea for the foundation. You know how one of the things that bugs me about fishing tournaments is how some still promote killing the largest fish for prizes? The problem with that is the largest fish are usually females. Take blue marlin for instance. All of them that are over 400 pounds are female. Meaning that the ones which are killed and brought in for weighing are all females. And the larger they are, the more eggs they produce.

A full-grown blue marlin female can release over a million eggs every time she spawns, up to four times a year. Those eggs have to drift in the water column and come in contact with some free-floating marlin sperm in order for them to become fertilized. Even then the odds of a fertilized egg making it to adulthood as a marlin are slim.

So, the idea of continuing to kill these big females for sport is just insane if we want to maintain a healthy and sustainable fishery. I know they usually study the ones that are brought in, and that some of the meat from those makes its way to food banks. But so many of the really large ones just spoil, all in the name of sport. It's bad enough that the almost 4,000 longline boats worldwide will kill 40,000 blue marlin and 50,000 white marlin over the next three years. If they were to get wiped out, those guys would just move on to catching the next species. But as anglers, we should be the ones that are dedicated to protecting these fish. At least the longliners utilize the entire fish and don't waste any of it like what sometimes happens in tournaments."

I had Kari's full attention now. She asked, "So, what's your idea?"

"We announce a cash bounty for existing kill tournaments to switch over and become exclusively release tournaments. I mean yes, there is a small element of ego involved in putting the biggest fish on the dock. But the main point to a lot of these teams is the prize money. Pictures with those jumbo-sized checks are just as impressive as the ones with a dead fish, maybe even more so. By increasing the size of the purse, we're helping incentivize conservation by the very people who should be the most concerned with it; billfish anglers."

I could see the wheels turning in her head as she thought this over. "I like it. Not only will we be helping to save the fishery, we will be setting a precedent for other generations to follow. Lots of tournaments are already in the planning stages for this summer, so the sooner we can announce this the better. Let's do a conference call today with the other board members and get it approved. Then we can do a press release tomorrow morning and get letters out to the tournament committees right away."

I nodded. As an attention-getter this could be huge. Just how many marlin it will save remained to be seen, but it's certain to have at least some impact. I couldn't wait to get started.

*****

The next day, Ronnie "Ron" Sanders re–read the social media post that had been shared by the US Fishing Association, a group that he had once been involved with. The one whose board he had been appointed to because everyone there had adored his late wife and owed her favors. She had been the real angler in the family but had wanted him to gain some status in the sportfishing community. Ronnie had created a false public persona for himself; his whole life was about putting on a huge front. To hear him tell it he had been an executive who had risen rapidly through the ranks of a national soda company, finally leaving corporate America after discovering that he had a tremendous talent for investing. And if you were anywhere near him, he made sure you heard that story. But the truth was about as far from that as it could be.

In reality, just as she was the talented angler, his late wife Caroline had also been the provider. Or rather, the oil business founded by her late father was. Not that anyone would have cared, except for the fact that Ronnie put up that false front and lied about it, thinking everyone else was gullible enough to believe his line of bull. That was the part which was insulting, and what really rubbed people the wrong way when they saw through it.

It was a mystery to those around her as to why she would've ever married Ronnie, who now insisted upon being called just "Ron." It's true that he did dote on his wife while she was alive, catering to all of her whims and desires. And it was because of her they had built the hundred sixty–foot mothership and the

67

successive string of sportfishing boats that had accompanied it. This was part of why they both created the illusion of Ronnie being an investment genius. The angler in her wanted to be seen as having landed a trophy, rather than merely marrying a servant. And he wanted to appear to be a success around all the wealthy sportfishing crowd.

But it was Caroline that everyone loved being around; the champion angler, the life of the party, and the great storyteller. This was also because most of her stories were true. Those that weren't, were the ones that involved Ronnie. And it was Ronnie that everyone else dreaded seeing approach them. Unbeknownst to him, he had been pegged as a huge braggart, and a total BS artist. But worst of all, he thought that everyone believed the load of crap he was shoveling out. Which is why he was stunned not to have been re–nominated for the board of the fishing Association after cancer finally took Caroline.

He had thought his reappointment would've been almost automatic. It really humiliated him, and briefly he considered selling Caroline's sportfisherman and the mother ship. Being bounced off that board had really stuck in his craw, but instead of just moving on, finding a way to get back at the other board members had become an obsession with him. He followed everything the organization did on social media, looking for an opportunity to belittle or poke fun at both the Association and the people behind it.

Even after being bounced off the USFA, Ronnie still received invitations to a lot of non-fishing related Palm Beach cocktail parties. Mostly this was because of his donations to several strategically chosen charities; donations that came from the huge fortune left to him by his late wife. These charities all had certain things in common; connections to "A List" stars and/or national politicians. But another reason the invitations kept coming was the fact that he was now engaged to

Marguerite James, a very pretty and outgoing strawberry blonde socialite in her mid-forties. She had been Caroline's good friend, though it had been almost common knowledge to everyone except Caroline that Marguerite and Ronnie had been more than just friends for quite a while, even well before Caroline had been diagnosed. She was also a somewhat competent angler, not nearly as gifted at fishing as Caroline. Then again, so few were.

"What's so interesting, dear?" Marguerite asked Ronnie.

"There is a new, very well-funded east coast fishing group called the Mid–Atlantic Fisheries Foundation. It just came out of nowhere, and according to their press release, it has a three and a half billion–dollar endowment. And get this, they are trying to convince several of the existing kill tournaments to convert over to being catch and release. Depending on the size of the tournament, they will match the prize money, up to a million dollars. And they are super-secretive about the members of their board. I'm going to get on that board, and then those clowns over at the USFA can shove it."

"If they're so secretive about their board dear, how are you going to become a member?"

Ronnie smiled at her. "Because I'm going to enter every single tournament that they're trying to flip. They are also the chief sponsor for the high–dollar inaugural Mallard Cove White Marlin Tournament, so I guarantee that all their board members will be there. The foundation's address is also located at Mallard Cove Marina, on Virginia's Eastern Shore. So, that's where we're going to base my mothership and sportfisherman this summer."

*****

"Billy, there's still three million missing." He held up an open ledger found under the false bottom of the desk drawer.

Billy was in bad shape after being tied up for so long with no food or water and having been "worked over." He opened the one eye whose lid wasn't glued shut with dried blood. "Screw you, it's gone. Everything that's left is in the real estate, and the businesses."

"I don't believe you; these numbers don't lie. Where's the rest of the money?"

Billy took a deep breath, knowing this wasn't going to go over well. "I spent it. I forgot all about that book and stopped keeping track of everything ten years ago."

"That's crap! You've got that money hidden, and one way or another you're going to tell me where. It'll go a lot easier for you if you just come clean."

Billy knew there would be no reasoning with him. He'd already told the truth; the money was gone. Over the past ten years, it had been spent travelling, drinking, gambling, and womanizing. He also knew that he only had one way he could come out of this alive. "Casey, Murph, Lindsay, and Marlin took it with them back to the states for me for safekeeping. I was afraid you might come looking for it. It's up in Virginia."

Chapter 8

On Wednesday evening, Kari and I were relaxing after dinner when my phone rang. The caller ID showed it was Casey.

"Hey Marlin, I need to give you a heads up. A friend of mine down in Palm Beach called me, knowing that I'm an old friend of Billy's. They found his body this morning in his house at Bootle Bay after he didn't show up for a meeting with his marina manager. He said that Billy had been tortured and stabbed to death sometime yesterday."

I was totally taken by surprise at this news, though I guess I shouldn't have been. Timmy had already beaten up Billy once, but now he had finished what he started. And I had heard Casey when he was serious before, but I never heard him use this grave tone of voice. It could've been because he was quietly furious over the death of his friend, or maybe nervous about Timmy possibly coming after the rest of us. Or, both.

Casey continued, "So, you need to keep your eyes open, and be very aware of your surroundings. Since Billy was tortured by that son of a bitch before he died, we need to assume that he knows for certain who and where we all are. Remember the last thing Timmy said to us; that we hadn't seen the last of him, and that he would 'get' us all. We need to keep our guard up in case he tries to carry out that threat."

I said, "I'm really sorry about Billy, Casey. But do you really think that Timmy would follow us all the way up here just for revenge? I mean, I'm assuming that he must have been able to clear out Billy's bank account this time. That's probably part of why he tortured him; forcing him to transfer the money. After all, it was Billy that shot up his boat and ruined those two engines, so his revenge would probably be directed at him." I felt kind of bad, speaking so matter-of-factly to Casey about his dead friend. But I really did doubt that Timmy would come this far north, especially if he now had Billy's four hundred grand.

Casey said, "We can't take any chances. I've already brought Rikki into the loop on this. She's got feelers out now to see if we can get a location on Timmy and find out if he is headed in our direction. I'll let you know what she finds out." Rikki Jenkins was another board member of MAFF. She was the majority owner of ESVA Security, a very well-connected national private security firm based at Bayside. I know that a lot of those connections stem from some arms–length work that her firm does for some high–profile government agencies and people. I didn't want to know beyond that. But if anyone could find out what Timmy was up to, it was her.

I said, "Thanks. If it's still active, I'll pull up Timmy's social media page and show his picture to Kari. We can make copies and leave them with Barry the dockmaster and the bartenders. If anybody spots him around here, I'll give you a call."

Casey said, "Good idea, I'll do the same here at Bayside and also over at the Bluffs." The Bluffs was another marina and restaurant combination that Casey, Dawn and some partners owned, over on the Atlantic side of ESVA. "I have a friend over in the Bahamas in their customs department, and I'll let him know that their police should be looking at Timmy for Billy's murder. Unfortunately, we can't turn over that video footage or tell them exactly what happened, because we weren't in their country legally then. But at least we can point them in the right direction."

After I hung up with Casey, I wondered if we had made the right decision by taking things into our own hands. Hindsight is always 20/20. It had sure seemed like the thing to do at the time. And the more I thought about it, the more I realized that we had indeed done

72

what was needed, when it was needed. Things might not have turned out well for Murph if we had left it up to the local cops in Florida and the Bahamian Defense Force. If they had even found him in time, they probably would've gone full speed up to Timmy's boat instead of using a stealth approach like we had. And now knowing what Timmy had done to Billy, I doubted that he would've shown any mercy to Murph.

Billy's blood was not really on our hands; he had known what he was dealing with in Timmy. It was his past that finally caught up with him. He should've been more vigilant, especially knowing that Timmy wasn't going anywhere very fast. He had to know that he might come back after the money. No doubt Timmy would've quickly found that the sixty grand was missing, and he could easily figure out where it had gone. Would that be enough to make him want to come up and take us all on here on our own turf? I just didn't think so, but Casey was right about us needing to keep alert. Like I said before, this kid isn't the brightest bulb on the Christmas tree. But if he did come this way, he'd find out that he made a mistake. A big one. We would be ready and waiting.

*****

Captain Max Johnson sat at the bar of the Palm Beach Marlin Club, chatting with a very attractive and somewhat recently unattached woman. Max was a handsome man in his mid-thirties, with the rugged look of someone who enjoyed the outdoors. He was obviously enjoying this woman's company, and from the look on her face, it was mutual. She was somewhere around his age, blonde, and with a natural beauty that most women long for. The Marlin Club wasn't a pickup bar, it was a private waterfront club with both a restaurant and bar that was frequented by many prominent Palm Beach sportfishing anglers and boat owners. His

73

cocktail companion had been married to one of this group up until a few months ago.

Usually, captains and crews were only guests here on special occasions, and it wasn't that uncommon for members' ex-wives to fight to retain their own membership in a divorce. In Max's case, he had received a fully paid membership as a parting gift from his last boss after he had sold his boat. It was a testament to how Max had been both revered by his ex–boss as well as accepted by most of the owners and anglers around the Palm Beach sportfishing community, and beyond.

He was a little irritated when they were interrupted, until he recognized who it was that had walked up to them and butted into their conversation. The man was Stuart Lieberman, the legendary investor who was one of the wealthiest people on the island. Max had instantly recognized him after having seen his picture in many financial articles, but he was surprised when Lieberman called both he and the woman by name. Especially because, as far as Max knew, Lieberman didn't even own a boat, so he didn't have any reason to know who he was.

"Carissa, it's so good to see you. And Max, if I can call you Max, it's good to finally meet you. Are you both here for dinner?"

Carissa spoke up first, "I was hoping so, Stu, though Max and I just met. But he is a very interesting man." She looked from Lieberman back to Max.

Max smiled, "I was just about to ask her if she would like to have dinner with me, and yes, I prefer Max."

"In that case, I insist that you two join my wife Debbie and me. This will give us a chance to get caught up, Carissa, and for Max and me to get acquainted as well." Lieberman said.

Carissa Lockton looked at Max who smiled and nodded like this sort of thing happened every day. Then the trio made their way over to the best table in the dining room where Stu's wife was already seated.

What followed was a great dinner, drinks, and conversation. Max had instantly recognized it though as what it really was, a job interview.

At the end of a very relaxed and enjoyable evening, the four of them walked out together. Lieberman asked Max, "Do you have time for lunch tomorrow, Max, just the two of us? I have something I'd like to discuss with you."

"Sure. I'd love to."

"Great. How about noon at my house? Do you know where it is?"

"Noon works. And everyone knows where your home is." Max chuckled, because Lieberman's home was one of the most famous and historic estates on Palm Beach.

"I'll see you at noon then," Lieberman replied as he and Debbie climbed into their car that the valet had brought up to the club's entrance.

Carissa smiled as she hooked her arm through Max's. Looking at the valet she said, "Pete, look after my car, would you please? I'll pick it up tomorrow. We'll only need Mr. Johnson's car tonight."

The first thing that Max noticed as he was led into the Lieberman estate the next day was the fact that the staff were all dressed in resort wear rather than the stereotypical uniforms which were required in the majority of the households on the island. It gave the huge estate a much more relaxed feeling, and it told Max a lot about Stu and Debbie, and how they liked to live.

"Max! Thank you for coming. Please pull up a chair." Stu indicated the seat across the table from him. He was sitting out on a lanai that overlooked a huge manicured lawn and finally, the Atlantic Ocean.

"What a beautiful place, Stu. Quite a view."

"Yes, I never get tired of it. Though I haven't gotten to enjoy it as much as I'd liked. My work has kept me on the go my entire adult life. But I'll be sixty-five next month, and I've decided it's time to slow down a bit. Look out toward the horizon Max, all of those sportfishing boats are out doing what I wish that I had been doing all along. You know Paul Levine?" The question felt more like a statement.

Max nodded. "I used to run into Paul a lot more when he lived down here. I actually fished with him one day last fall at the mouth of Chesapeake Bay, chasing stripers. He's got a great guide up there named Marlin Denton. It was a heck of a fun day."

Stu smiled. "I'm jealous. I wish that I had been there as well. Which is part of why Paul suggested that I talk to you, Max. He said that you have more contacts in the fishing world than anyone else that he knows." Stu paused to judge Max's reaction. What he saw was only a slight nod, a confirmation of that fact. He also noted that it wasn't followed up by any statement bragging about those connections. It was exactly what Stu had hoped for. "I went fishing with Paul on his boat a few years back, and if you'll pardon the pun, I was hooked. But I didn't have the time to devote to it then. Now I'm about to, but I don't even own a fishing rod. I have a lot to learn, and I want to learn it in a very short time. Are you up for a challenge?"

Max leaned back in his chair, quietly studying Stu's face. "So, you're looking for a captain and a boat?"

Stu shook his head. "Not a captain. More like a professional fishing partner; a marine coordinator. Someone who has his finger on the pulse of the fishing not just here, but around the globe. I have the resources to get us out in front of the best fishing on a moment's notice, no matter where it is. Knowing that it's happening and where it's happening would be where you come in. Then we fish it together. I told Paul what I had in mind and asked him for a recommendation.

Yours was the only name that he would give me. So, I found out as much about you as I could."

"Then your showing up at the Marlin Club last night wasn't just a coincidence." Max looked intrigued, not angry, even though he must have been professionally investigated if not outright followed.

"No."

"And Carissa, was she part of all this?"

Stu laughed. "Absolutely not. She's a lovely woman with very discerning tastes in...company. Seeing how interested she seemed to be in you also told me a lot. The conversation at dinner told me the rest of what I needed to know. You didn't brag, exaggerate, or try to dominate the conversation like so many men would have in order to impress her. And believe me, there are a large group of men who would have given a lot to have been in your shoes last night.

Our dinner was all about conversation and compatibility. I wanted to make sure that you were someone I would like to fish with, who wouldn't drive me crazy after spending a week together in a fishing cockpit. You won't. I also wanted to make sure that you were someone who could be responsible for both a sportfisherman, a mothership, and their crews. I think you are. The only question that remains is whether you are interested in doing this."

Max knew that there are basically two different types of sportfishing boat owners. Ones that treat their crews like domestic servants, and then there is that very rare breed who treat their crews like members of their extended family. It looked like Stu would fit in the latter group. It also looked like this could be Max's dream job.

"You know that's a two–way street, Stu. The part about driving each other crazy. It's not just you, that goes for both of us. But last night was a ball, and I think fishing together would be a hell of a lot of fun. And yes, I can oversee the boats and their crews, making sure that they are pre–positioned where we need them to be in order to be ready at the drop of a hat in the hot fishing areas. I just need to have a free hand to send them wherever they need to be, or to line up local operators and charter if we need to be somewhere quicker than we can reposition our own equipment."

Stu nodded. "Agreed. This exactly what I hoped you'd say. My free time is going to start coming in longer periods as we go along, but for now, it'll be sporadic. Less long–range planning, more spur of the moment. Knowing that all I have to do is get on my plane, and wherever you say to land will be where the fishing is good at that time, is exactly what I'm looking for."

"Let's do it, Stu."

*****

Timmy Wilton was hanging out at his idea of paradise; a beach bar in Costa Rica where the drinks were as large as the bikinis were small. He was doing his best to impress a well–endowed young occupant of one of those tiny bikinis, in the hopes of talking her out of it in the not too distant future.

"Yeah, I'm really well known in sportfishing circles. I got my own boat back in Palm Beach, and in another month or two I'll be headed up the East Coast, fishing high dollar tournaments all summer. Maybe you should think about coming with me." Of course, he had no intention of taking the girl anywhere beyond his room at the resort; this was all about saying whatever would get the job done. He was only hiding out in Costa Rica long enough until things cooled down for him back in Palm Beach. The one truth in that line was that he did plan on making a run up the coast after he got back; he had people he needed to catch up with, and he was going to fish along the way.

Chapter 9

A few weeks later...

I had just gotten onto the first bridge section of the Chesapeake Bay Bridge Tunnel, or as we like to call it, the CBBT, when my phone rang.

"Marlin? It's Casey. I just talked to Rikki, and she said that Timmy is still down in Costa Rica and doesn't seem to be in a hurry to come back to the States. The Bahamian police still haven't definitively linked him to the murder, and since Billy had dual citizenship and the crime happened there, they are the ones who would have to decide whether to try to extradite Timmy if he is ever charged."

I could hear the frustration in Casey's voice. I knew one of Rikki's teams had been keeping tabs on Timmy after following his trail to Central America, to give us ample warning whenever he headed back. I also knew Casey wanted vengeance for his dead friend, but I was more interested in keeping the rest of us safe. Not that I wouldn't be happy if Timmy got what was coming to him, but I had barely known Billy. However, I had gone through so much with our crew before I ever even heard of him, they had become like family to me. I'm prepared to do anything, and everything needed in order to make sure that none of us got hurt.

"Thanks for taking point on this, Casey. Good to know where that son of a bitch is. I hope that if he was going to come after the rest of us, he would've already done so. Maybe if he gets his fill of rum and beach babes, he won't want to chase that sixty grand he didn't get, and he won't feel like he has anything left to prove."
I really hoped that I was right.

"Maybe." Casey didn't sound convinced. "But I don't want any of us to take any chances. You know, it's so ironic; this all started because a couple of guys decided to run grass twenty years ago, and none of the rest of us would've ever had anything to do with that. But we did what anyone would do, or should do, to save a pal and now we're in it up to our necks." His voice softened a bit. "And to think, all you wanted was a better deal on dockage when you moved into Mallard Cove last year. Well, my friend, you got a lot more than you had bargained for."

"Yeah Casey, I did. I ended up with a bunch of new friends that look after me as much as I look after them. And if you ask me, that's a hell of a good trade-off."

Twenty minutes later I pulled into short-term parking at the Virginia Beach International Airport and hurried inside. I was just in time to meet up with Max Johnson. My old friend and client, Paul Levine, had called in a favor asking that I pick up Max and show him around. I was happy to do it because Paul and I go way back. Also, because I had heard he was looking for a summer home base for a fleet of three boats that his new boss had just acquired. Mallard Cove was at the top of his list. While I don't own any part of Mallard Cove, as I said before my fiancée Kari does, and of course, my growing fleet is based there. So, I have a vested interest in the place becoming more and more popular and successful. But even more important was the fact that we had fished together before, and I liked the guy. He would fit in perfectly.

I spotted Max coming out of the "Arrivals" security area, a carry-on bag in hand. "Marlin, thanks so much for picking me up. It's always nice to see a familiar face when you get off an airplane."

Now I remembered why I liked fishing with Paul and him so much that day last fall. The guy made you feel like you've known him his whole life, and that it was the highlight of his day to talk to you. Not in a phony kind of way, but like he really meant it. The truth is, I think he does mean it. Max is also a walking encyclopedia of both fishing and boats, and a lot of fun to be around.

"My pleasure, and it's great to see you again, Max. Good flight?"

"They're all good if they are on time and it's a landing you can walk away from." He grinned.

I chuckled, "Very true." As I led him out to the truck I said, "So, Paul tells me that you just landed the job of a lifetime. It's true that your boss bought three boats in the last two weeks?"

Now was his turn to chuckle. "Stu doesn't let any grass grow under his feet. He's been running me ragged. We found a hundred–forty–foot Benetti mothership in Texas, a sixty–six–foot Viking sportfisherman up in Stuart, and a new thirty–two–foot center console in Miami. They're all in different boatyards right now getting customized, and I've been in the middle of hiring crews and overseeing the upgrades. Bear in mind that I didn't know Stu a month ago, and he didn't even own a fishing rod at that point. So, he and I have a lot of water to cover and a very short time in which to do it. His goal is to be a consummate angler by the end of this summer. And part of the reason he's so successful is because he always meets or exceeds the goals he sets for himself. This means we will have to follow the fish, and this area is the perfect place to be based, from spring until we head back to Palm Beach at the end of fall. This is the closest spot to the hot white marlin fishing at the canyons offshore, and the center of the great tuna fishing between Long Island and the Outer Banks. Not to mention, the fall striper fishing in the Chesapeake like you, Paul, and I did that day."

"Don't forget the mahi fishing up here. As good or better than Palm Beach in the summer. There's a reason everybody bugs out of there after Easter. It's cooler up here, and the fishing is great. Everybody just thinks about Ocean City or Hatteras for fishing, but we have more of a variety of species than both of them; we even have tarpon and grouper."

"So, how long have you been working for the Virginia Tourism Bureau, Marlin?" Max smiled as he ribbed me.

I replied, "Hey, I love living here. Fishing is a big part of why."

Max said, "The last time I was here you were based out of Lynnhaven. Now you're over on the Eastern Shore? What changed?"

"The ownership of both marinas changed. The new owner of my old one jacked his rates up to the stratosphere. At the same time, this couple bought what was then an old decrepit marina at the southern point of the Eastern Shore. They brought in some heavy hitter partners, rebuilt the marina, they've added one restaurant and have another on the way, plus a hotel, and an 'in and out' boat storage facility. The food is off the charts, and they just opened a brand-new beach bar which has become a much anticipated 'happening' place for this season. But their main focus was to turn the marina into the mid-Atlantic mecca of sportfishing."

Max asked, "Good boats and crews?"

"Absolutely. And we're adding more each month. Plus, we're going to have a huge offshore tournament this summer too. At the rate they're going, the place should be full this year. They have an unreal rate of progress considering that they only started renovating the place last summer. The ownership group is really good at marketing as well as managing. It helps that they all fish and own boats themselves. They knew coming into it exactly what they wanted in a marina complex."

Max looked confused as I turned off of the feeder for the CBBT. "Where are we going? Isn't this the way to Lynnhaven?"

"Yeah. I wanted to show you something while we're over this way." Two minutes later I pulled up to a huge scrub and swamp property on the river, right next door to the marina that I left when I moved to Mallard Cove. "The same group that owns Mallard Cove just bought this property. There's going to be a big marina complex with restaurants, shops, and condos going in here. I didn't know if this would be an option for you down the way or not."

"I haven't even seen Mallard Cove, and you are already trying to get rid of me?" Max laughed.

"Just trying to be helpful since you mentioned Lynnhaven. Truthfully, I hope you and your fleet do end up over at Mallard Cove, I think you would fit in with all of us there perfectly. They're trying to attract more active sport fishing boats and crews."

We took the CBBT over to ESVA, and Max got his first look at Mallard Cove from the top of Fisherman's Inlet Bridge.

"Wow. That's quite a complex over there. Nice to have a straight shot out to the fishing with no bridges. Though this one seems to be plenty high. What's its clearance?"

I replied, "About forty feet. So, unless you have a skyscraper of a tuna tower on that Viking, you should be able to clear it." I could see Max taking in all the details of the area. As we pulled into the property his head was "on a swivel" like a pilot, checking everything out. That included Kari, since she was making a beeline for where I was parking. "Max, meet Kari Albury, the head of M & S Marina Partners, and my better half."

He gave an almost imperceptible nod to me, acknowledging the "better half" part as he turned and smiled at Kari, shaking her outstretched hand. "Nice to meet you. Heck of a marina you have here, and a heck of a guy, too."

She smiled as she dropped his hand. "Thanks, on both counts. Each of them is a handful." She winked in my direction. "So, your email mentioned a hundred-forty–footer, a sixty–six–footer, and a thirty–two-footer? Quite a group you're responsible for."

Max nodded. "I was just telling Marlin, all three boats are new to me, though I've known most of the crewmembers for several years. And I'm more on the logistics side of things, keeping up with the best fishing locations and making sure that our equipment gets pre-staged and is ready to go whenever our boss Stu is. For the next couple of years, he'll be popping in and out with little or no notice. When I checked the charts, this seemed like a logical place to be in order to accomplish what we want to do in the summer. And now that I'm here and can see what you've created, I'm really impressed. What slips do you have available for us?"

Kari led us over to the center dock, and out onto the end. "I was thinking this would probably be the best setup for you. Mothership on the outside of the tee, closest to the breakwater inlet. We can put the other two on either side of the dock just inside of the tee. Easy access to fuel one dock over, and right across from the breakwater's inlet, the easiest in and out for your mothership. Plenty of shore power available for her, and the fuel dock also has high-volume pumps, so you won't be waiting all day for a few thousand gallons."

Max nodded. "Perfect. And the rates you quoted me work as well. Done deal. Hey, since the sun is already over the yardarm, how about letting me buy you two a drink? Then after that, if you could point me to a hotel, I'll get out of your hair."

Kari shook her head. "Our hotel isn't quite finished, and we didn't want you to have to stay off-site. So, we made up the guest berth for you on the houseboat we are staying on. I hope you don't mind bunking here. We wanted you to spend time around Mallard Cove instead of in some strange hotel, and I hope that you'll have dinner with us at our *Cove Restaurant*. By the way, all your food and bar tab is comped this trip, too."

"Thanks, I'll take you up on all of that."

I could see that like us, he was happy to be around the water and the marina. If the crews he picked are half as good as I think they'd have to be to work for him, they will be good additions to Mallard Cove. And we had a surprise coming up; he was about to meet the Beer–Thirty–Bunch.

We collected his bag from the truck and got him settled on the houseboat, then grabbed two six packs and headed over toward charter boat row. I could see Max taking inventory of the boat types, including my center console and flats boat. We ended up in the far corner where Kim Collier's fifty–five–foot orange hulled Carolina built *Kembe* lay next to the last boat in the row; Bill "Baloney" Cooper's aging yellow hulled forty–eight–foot New Jersey built *Golden Dolphin*. Her ancient Johnson Towers diesels put out almost as much smoke as Bill's huge and ever–present cheap cigar. Fortunately, Bill's wife Betty laid down the law years ago, and Bill is only allowed to smoke those putrid things out on a charter and can only light up after he clears the breakwater.

"Isn't the bar over there?" Max asked, pointing a thumb back in the direction from which we had come.

I nodded. "Yes, and we'll get there soon enough. But we thought you might like to enjoy seeing the captain's lounge and meeting some of the gang first. There is usually an informal meeting in the afternoons where a lot of us compare notes on the fishing conditions, and swap scuttlebutt."

"Nice to know. Most of the info on the up and up?"

Kari spoke up. "For the most part. Back when Murph and Lindsay took over the place, everyone realized that it was in all of our best interests to work together to make Mallard Cove the 'go-to' choice for charter fishing. Now that has spilled over to the private boats whose owners and crews recognized the value of being here and mixing in with the pros. You'll see more and more of them in here as the weather gets warmer and the fishing gets hotter."

Max asked, "Is Baloney one of the regulars?"

I was surprised. "You know Baloney?"

He shook his head. "Not yet, but I'm sure I will before long; I saw that he docks his boat here. I remembered hearing him on the radio when Paul and I went out with you, and that he runs the *Golden Dolphin*. He was hilarious."

"Still is. And speak of the devil..." I pointed him out as we walked through the door marked "Captains and Crews Only" into a comfortable room that looked out over charter boat row. It was filled with couches and overstuffed chairs, and on the wall that the room shared with the restaurant was a large flat screen tv permanently tuned in to the Weather Channel. Under that was a small refrigerator we used to keep the afternoon's beer cold. But no one in their right mind would ever leave beer in it overnight; all unattended brew was fair game.

"What did I do now?" Baloney looked up questioningly as he heard my comment, his reply spoken with a thick New Jersey accent.

"Nothing but the usual," I replied. "Bill Cooper, meet Max Johnson, our latest addition to the fleet."

Baloney started to giggle uncontrollably. "Max Johnson? For real? Nah, we'll just call you Big. You know, 'Big Johnson.' That's your dock name." The giggle morphed into a belly laugh, as the handful of others in the room just smiled. Everyone was used to the sophomoric "Baloney Humor," and his habit of hanging a nickname on most of the regulars. "So, Big, what's your favorite beer?"

"Whatever you brought," Max smiled. Baloney was already living up to what he remembered.

"Hey, I like this guy! He's a man after my own tastes. By the way, Marlin..." He held out his hand.

I gave him a can as he grinned. Baloney never brings beer with him, preferring to mooch off of everyone else. Nobody really minds; it's expected, and kind of like paying the court jester's fee. Seriously though, Bill is a good guy who would give you the shirt off his back if you needed it, and if you were dying of thirst, he'd share his water with you. Just not his beer.

Kari said, "Max is in charge of a private three-boat fleet that will be based here half the year."

"Great! Welcome home, 'Big.' So, I'll get to find out what your favorite beer brand is after all!" Baloney then took charge like he normally did, introducing "Big" to everyone in the room. Kari and I looked at each other and she winked at me. Max had fit in just like I hoped he would. Baloney had taken to him like a long–lost brother. It was easy to do.

At dinner that night, Max did indeed look like he was "home." He no sooner walked through the door before he was recognized by the *Cove's* newest bartender, Mimi Carter. She was a very pretty strawberry blonde in her early thirties who had been hired to manage the bars. She came out from behind the bar to race over and give him a hug.

"Max! What are you doing here? This is a long way from St. Johns!" It was obvious there was some history here between these two that Kari and I weren't privy to. Mimi was "lit up like a marlin on a bait."

"I'll be working out of here half the year, 'Memes', starting in a couple of weeks. Did you track me down or what?" His eyes had a twinkle as he teased her.

"Yeah, it was easy. I just followed the trail of broken hearts." She smirked.

Apparently Mimi could dish it out as well as take it. I could see that they were going to be fun to watch this season.

Max replied, "I could say the same about you."

"And you'd be right, except for yours."

He shook his head slightly and smiled. "I don't break easily."

She laughed. "Don't I know it! But then again, neither do I. Hey, I need to get back behind the bar, but I hope that we can catch up later."

"Count on it when I get back. This is just a quick trip up to get situated, but I'll be back in a few weeks."

Mimi went back to the bar as Max turned back to us. "Sorry about that. Mimi's an old friend."

"We got that part." Kari chuckled. "What are the odds of you running into each other here?"

"Better than you might think. Mimi loves to fish, and she's darn good at it. She bartends to pay the bills. If she could afford her own boat, I'd hate to run up against her in a tournament. You know how some people can instinctively know what a fish is going to do even before it does? That's Mimi. I saw her pull in a six hundred plus pound blue marlin down in St. Thomas in under twenty minutes. The fish was so green that when we got her to the boat, she left half her bill broken off in the transom."

I whistled. "Better in the boat than the mate!"

"Exactly."

Kari said, "Maybe she and I can fish together at some point. I'd like to see her in action."

Max nodded. "I know she would like that. To tell you the truth, if she and I were the kind to settle down, I'd love to team up and fish with her from now on. But we're both kind of free spirits. Not that several boat owners and captains I know haven't made a run at her, trying to tie her down. But that's just not her style, at least not now. I guess that's why we've gotten along so well through the years."

I asked, "You two have known each other for a while then?"

"Since we were teenagers, hanging around the docks in South Florida. Bumping into each other up and down the islands, wherever the fishing was good.

Lots of great memories, and not all of them about fishing. But enough of this history lesson. What's good to eat here?"

As the conversation evolved over dinner, we found out that Max's ideas about the conservation of fisheries mirrored Kari's and mine. Meaning that he also thought along the same lines as the rest of us on the board of the fisheries foundation. We didn't tip our hand about its existence and our involvement just yet, but he told us about a program that exists in south Florida that I think we might like to replicate here. A fishing foundation in Palm Beach County takes hundreds of kids fishing on drift fishing boats and charter boats, all in one day, up and down the county's coastline, out of several inlets. The kids are all either "at risk" or have disabilities, and they have to be nominated by a police officer, teacher, or social worker. For many, it's their first ride out on the water. They learn not just about fishing, but about the importance of protecting the fisheries through conservation methods like catch limits as well as catch and release. Max had been involved in the program since its inception. He moved up another notch on my "list of favorites."

He told us, "A couple of years ago I called some guy's office and gave my name to the young woman who answered the phone. She asked if I was the same Max Johnson that was involved with the Kid's Fishing Day. I said yes, then launched into my spiel, about how if we just get one of those kids hooked on fishing, what a difference it would make in his or her life. She said that it really had. I didn't understand until she told me that she had been one of our "at risk" kids; put up for it by a neighborhood police officer. She said it literally changed her life and given her a new focus. She even met her future husband one night while bridge fishing, and they had worked hard and saved up until they could afford an old center console boat. They had just bought it and were as excited as ever. Then she thanked me.

You know, I've won more than my share of tournaments, I've fished with a lot of famous and interesting people, and I've caught some record fish. But nothing, and I mean nothing, compares to that feeling on that day. And I guarantee she'll be someone dedicated to preserving the fishery and passing it along in good shape to the next generation. There's no bigger accomplishment that I'll ever make in this lifetime. I wish there was some way I could do more of it."

His gaze had drifted, and suddenly he snapped back to reality, refocusing on the two of us. "Sorry, didn't mean to get on my soapbox, but I guess Mimi still pours a heavy rum drink." He looked sheepish.

"Our rule here is that we never want to get accused of having watered down drinks. So, she's right on point, and don't worry, you are among people with 'like minds' who loved that story." Kari smiled.

I was busy texting. I know, it was rude to do at the table, but I had a plan and I figured that Kari would approve of it. Three minutes later, I looked up.

"What time is your flight tomorrow?"

He gave me a questioning look, "Just after noon, but I can catch a cab if it's an issue."

I shook my head. "That wasn't where I was going with this. How about cancelling your flight, and riding back down with our friend Casey on his plane after lunch? He's one of the partners here. He has a meeting in West Palm late in the afternoon. He and a few of his marina partners would like to meet you and show you around their other resort which is a chip shot north of here. And on the way up we can stop by Kari's cousin's boatyard so that you can check it out and get to meet him as well."

"Can his yard handle something as big as a hundred forty feet?"

Kari replied, "Without even breaking a sweat, and it's only a few miles north of us."

"Perfect! That all sounds like a plan, thanks. The way that this is all coming together, it sounds like it was meant to be."

Chapter 10

Back aboard *On Coastal Time* Kari and I were lying in bed, talking.

"You know where I'm going with this." I wasn't really asking a question, because I already knew that she did. I was really looking more for her agreement.

She answered, "I like it, he said he wished that he could find a way to do more along the lines of that kid's fishing day event. If he's willing to be part of MAFF's board, I think he'd be great at it. I get the feeling that he can talk to either the town mayor or the town drunk; he's quite a conversationalist. He thinks along the same lines we all do about protecting the fisheries, and with his knowledge, having his input on creating a kid's fishing day here would be fantastic."

"I texted Murph and Lindsay, and they are trusting it to the rest of us to decide if we want to invite him to join us. They still have two weeks left on their schedule before they head home. Hopefully, Dawn, Casey, and Rikki will like him as well. Tomorrow will be interesting. Nice to have something positive to think about instead of continually worrying about Timmy showing up."

She nodded in the darkness, and snuggled in closer to me, her arm going across my chest, and one of her legs going over mine. "Yes it is so, let's forget about Timmy for a while. If you know where I'm going with this."

That wasn't a question either, I sure did know.

The next morning Max and I drove up to the boatyard where Carlton's crew was putting the finishing touches on *Why Knot*. He and Max were soon engrossed in conversation, almost forgetting that I was there, too. I hoped the same thing would happen with Max, Casey, Dawn, and Rikki, and I was pretty sure it would.

Back in the truck headed up to the Chesapeake Bayside Resort, Max was in a talkative mood. He had been impressed with Carlton's yard and the work they had done on both of my boats. "Having that facility nearby is a huge plus."

I nodded. "Trust me, I know. Nothing worse than losing a cutlass bearing or dinging a prop and not having a yard close by that can haul you out and do repairs. Plus, Carlton is reasonable as far as his prices go."

"So far so good. I'm hoping that Stu likes the area, though when he's here it'll be all about the fishing."

I asked, "What about his wife?"

Max shook his head. "I don't think that she's going to be up for fishing. And nothing personal, but I don't think there's anything around here to hold her attention. She's just a few years older than you or me. And only one of her pals in Florida is into fishing. So far I haven't seen much for her here."

"I don't know, Max, I still have a few cards up my sleeve."

He looked at me quizzically, "Like what?"

"You'll see."

Half an hour later we were pulling through the gates at the Chesapeake Bayside Resort. We drove down a long tree-lined drive where workers were busy prepping flower beds for spring plantings. Ahead to the left was the marina, straight ahead down by the water was their Beach Café, and ahead and to the right was the boutique hotel that also housed two fantastic restaurants. Across from the hotel and sharing its circular brick paver driveway was a low single–story office building. Like all the rest of the buildings at the resort, it had a green metal roof with gray composite faux cedar siding. A glass door at the southern end was lettered with ESVA Security, and another at the north end read McAlister & Shaw. I pulled in next to it.

Max looked around after he got out. "This is nice. Again, nothing personal, but not what I expected up here."

Bayside was more along the level of what you would expect to see in Palm Beach, but with a Nantucket design and feel to it.

"This isn't even all of what I was talking about, as far as those sleeve cards. But I'll leave the rest of those up to Casey."

We walked into the office as Casey and Dawn came out to the reception area to greet us. Dawn McAlister is a statuesque thirty–year–old just an inch shy of six feet tall with long red hair, blue eyes, and a great personality. While I introduced everyone, Rikki Jenkins also walked in. Rikki is in her early thirties, a few inches shorter than Dawn, with short natural platinum hair and ice blue eyes. Having literally grown up in the security business, she knew how to quickly assess a new person.

I could see that Rikki was already taking in what she could about Max, from his appearance to his mannerisms. I also knew that Casey and Dawn depended a lot on her opinions in addition to their own. I have a tremendous amount of respect for her, and of course, them as well. The fact that she was here told me that Max had already passed a quick dive by her associates into his background. The last thing that we wanted to do was bring someone onto the foundation board if they had any issues in their past which might end up biting us in the butt in the future.

Casey led us all outside where Rikki said she'd join us later for lunch. Then the four of us climbed on a golf cart for a tour of the property, including the Bayside Club and Bayside Estates development. Casey was driving with Max next to him, and Dawn and I in the rear seats. I leaned over by Max and said, "These are some of those cards I was talking about."

We drove through an electric gate at the far end of the hotel's circular driveway, past a huge thick stand of evergreens that shielded from view another set of buildings set on the shore of the bay. The view of the Chesapeake from each facility was stunning. The first will house a private spa, and the second is going to be a large private club with interior and exterior pools as well as enclosed squash and tennis courts. Both were nearing completion, and landscaping crews were hard at work making them blend in with a "manicured low country" feel.

After a quick tour of the buildings, we were back on the cart, following a winding asphalt lane. We passed several vacant lots that bordered the grassy shoreline and finally came up on a large house that was also nearing completion. It was set on an oversized corner property bordering the bay on one side and a large, wide creek on another. The road paralleled the creek and wound up at the site of a large, new, and secluded marina which was set in a natural bay. A crew on a barge was busy assembling floating docks.

Casey explained that it had been designed to take advantage of the pre-existing depth while utilizing the natural grass edges, making it as eco–friendly as possible. We continued the tour, passing a concrete heliport and finally making our way to another set of electric gates that opened back out onto the resort's entrance drive. We drove up to the hotel and went into its Rooftops restaurant, which overlooked the other marina on the property. Even though it was well before the start of the season, this public marina was already more than half full of everything from center console outboards to a few large yachts, weeks before the official start of the season.

Since it was still quite cool outside, the restaurant windows, which were normally open in season, were closed. But they still provided a beautiful panorama of the marina, the hotel's beachfront café, and the Chesapeake beyond.

We sat at a table next to the windows. Rikki joined us as Max was taking inventory of the boats in the marina.

"Beautiful Hargrave and Trumpy yachts over there."

Dawn replied, "Thanks. The Hargrave is our home, and the Trumpy belongs to our friend and partner, Eric Clarke."

Max's eyebrows raised almost imperceptibly. Eric Clarke was a northern Virginia billionaire, almost as wealthy and even arguably a bit better known than Max's new boss. "I see what you meant by having a few cards up your sleeve, Marlin. I think Stu's wife Debbie and her friends would love this place. Think there's room and depth for our mothership here, Casey?"

He replied, "Plenty, on both counts and in either marina."

Max nodded. "I definitely made the right choice, picking this area for home base. This place is also a plus if Stu wants to lure Debbie and her friends up here; it hits all the right notes. It would be a good thing if she viewed the mothership as something more than just floating fishing equipment."

Then the conversation did shift to fishing, and Max's involvement with that foundation back in Florida. Everyone else was busily peppering him with questions throughout lunch as I just sat back and took it all in. He gave me a few curious side glances, but never missed a beat in the conversation. Finally, after lunch was over he looked straight at me.

"Marlin, you're being awfully quiet, and this feels a bit like the second 'clandestine job interview' that I've had this month."

I looked around the table at the others, each of them giving a small nod of approval. I knew I already had Kari, Murph and Lindsay's votes, so I launched in, explaining about MAFF's goals, funding, and how intrigued we all were with the idea of an event to introduce more kids to the sport we all love. "So, that's it in a nutshell. We know that you have your hands full with your new gig, but we aren't into too many formal meetings, and you can always attend by phone. Interested?"

He paused for a moment as he thought it over. Giving us all one last glance, he replied, "I'm honored, and yes, I'm in."

Later, their conversation on the flight down to Florida just reinforced to Casey that Max was a good choice, as they compared their thoughts and innovative ideas about fishing and protecting fisheries. They made plans to get together and go tuna fishing after Max got his new fleet settled in and situated at Mallard Cove.

After saying goodbye to Max at the North Palm Beach County Airport, Casey drove to the lawyer's office where his meeting was scheduled. All he knew was that it had something to do with Billy's will. As he pulled up in front of the office he saw TW walking out. When he got out of his car, the silent glare he got from Wilton could have melted steel; even at this distance, he could see it was unmistakably pure hatred. TW turned and kept walking. While he figured that TW wouldn't have been happy about Timmy's boat being shot up, he should have been relieved that his son had been left unharmed, just as Casey had promised. It wasn't Casey's fault that the kid was unhinged and out of control, and that this had led to the death of their friend.

He shook off the uneasy feeling from the encounter and continued into the office. The estate's lawyer started their meeting by explaining that Billy had no close relatives. He had left the bulk of his estate including the house at Bootle Bay as well as his share of the additional Bahamian properties and businesses, to

97

TW. But he had left his Piper Aerostar airplane to Casey, knowing well his love of these increasingly rare and out of production high-performance aircraft, as well as their joint history in aviation. This was totally unexpected, and Casey was touched by the gesture. It was also welcomed, since Casey had lost his own Aerostar in a crash during takeoff several months ago after it had been sabotaged. He missed that aircraft, which he had flown for several years. Billy's had just been completely redone including new paint, interior, and engines, and was undoubtedly the best one left anywhere around.

"I guess Tim Wilton was upset that Billy didn't leave the plane to him."

The lawyer looked surprised. "No, he was quite happy to receive the bulk of the estate. He never said anything about your having been left the aircraft."

Now Casey was left wondering what had set TW off. For the second time today, as he left the lawyer's office, he shook off that same bad feeling.

Chapter 11

Costa Rica, two weeks later...

As he had now for too many afternoons in a row, Timmy walked in under the thatched roof of the open-air beach bar. This place was getting stale, and it was time to get back to the states. But he still had this afternoon and evening to kill. He headed for a seat at the corner of the bar where he could easily scope out any new arrivals as they approached the bar front. Then he slapped a hundred-dollar bill down to get the barkeep's attention. What he didn't know was that he was about to find the tables were turned on him, as the hunter was about to become the hunted.

She came up from behind, taking the seat next to him. She was the most stunning woman he had seen on this trip so far. She looked to be in her late twenties, with long blond hair, green eyes, and an unforgettable body. And most of that body was on display instead of tucked into the three tiny patches of material that barely passed as a bikini. A slow tilt of her head coupled with an equally slow, sly smile communicated volumes before she ever uttered a word.

Timmy, accustomed to being the hunter, was totally taken aback in the presence of this seasoned huntress. "Uh, hi. I'm Timmy." He mentally kicked himself for such a lame start, but at least it was a start.

A slow bat of her eyelashes again kept him off guard. "Well, hello, 'I'm Timmy.' Are you going to offer to buy me a drink or not?"

"Uh, sure. And you're..."

"Thirsty." The way in which she said it conveyed much more than desire for just alcohol. "I'll take a Gran Patron Platinum tequila shot, for starters." She smiled at him. "Then we'll see where we go from there. *If* we go from there."

Timmy nodded at the bartender in his usual confident and cocky way, having quickly recovered his composure and gotten back on his game. His chest was out, his chin was up, and a "get lucky grin" along with a knowing look had now replaced his confused one. He was so fixated on the girl he didn't notice that the bartender filled her shot glass with water as he filled Timmy's with the expensive tequila. They each picked up their glasses and downed the liquids at once. She put her glass back on the bar and shoved it toward the bartender. Timmy slowly did the same, again nodding at the bartender to signal for refills.

"Don't you think drinking partners should know each other's names?" Timmy asked.

"I like the way you said that, 'partner.' I guess so. You can call me Sam, that's short for Samantha." She picked up her shot glass and held it aloft while indicating his, and he followed suit. "To partners...and maybe even playmates." After clinking the glasses together, she emptied hers and was followed shortly by Timmy. Her smile had gone from noncommittal to more of a teasing, almost evil one. She now looked more like a cat playing with a mouse.

"So, 'I'm Timmy,' what do you do when you're not shooting tequila? And why are our glasses empty?" She asked with an air of someone used to getting what she wanted.

Timmy again nodded to the bartender before turning back to Sam. "I fish. I've got my own boat back in Palm Beach, and I'm really famous on the tournament circuit." Which of course was a lie. The truth was he'd never even been on the tournament circuit; he was merely a boat bum. But he planned to use Billy's money to start fishing tournaments. He'd heard about the big money ones in the mid–Atlantic and the northeast, and they sounded like easy pickings to him. Plus, it sounded like a great direction to head this summer until things in the Bahamas and Florida cooled off.

She feigned being impressed and picked up her glass as he picked up his, both downing them. Again, she shoved her glass to the back of the bar for a refill. The bartender came over and looked at Timmy, who nodded. Then the bartender picked up the hundred and said, "You're a bit shy."

Timmy, now irritated at being interrupted turned to him and said, "That's a hundred, pal."

"Yeah, and those shots are fifteen bucks apiece. The lady didn't ask for the well brand."

Timmy was shocked but then dug into his pocket, taking out a fifty and slamming it on the bar. Sam looked over and gave him a disappointed look. "Running low already? And here I had such a nice evening all planned out for us with dinner, dancing, more drinks and later maybe some...celebrating." The cat was batting the mouse around again.

"Don't worry, I've got plenty of cash back in my room safe." He held up the keys to his room and the lockbox. "Like I said, I'm famous."

The lopsided grin he gave her started to show a bit of the effects the potent tequila was already having on him. A short time later after two more pairs of shots, they were weaving arm in arm back to Timmy's room. Just inside the door, Sam was all over him, finally stripping him and pushing him down on the bed.

A few minutes later a spent and very buzzed Timmy lay next to Sam who told him, "Oh, that was just an appetizer, babe. Now go take a shower and get dressed so we can go out. I promise we'll have both the main course and dessert later." The promise was punctuated by that teasing smile and a finger that traced lightly down his chest.

Timmy got up and wobbled to the bathroom thinking that if this had been the "appetizer," he might not survive long enough to have "dessert." But what a way to go. He jumped into the cold shower to clear his head, then quickly switched it over to warm. Suddenly it hit him that there was room enough in the shower for both of them. He left the water running as he went back into the room to fetch Sam, only to find her back in her bikini, kneeling in the closet in front of the little lockbox, pulling out his cash.

"What the hell?" He yelled.

She jumped up and spun toward him, stacks of bills in each hand. "Now wait, babe, I was just making sure you weren't lying about having enough cash for us to go out to dinner." The teasing smile was gone, replaced by a desperate and fearful look.

"My ass. You're just a cheap whore out to roll me!"

"Hey! I'm no whore, and who are you calling cheap?"

His head was clearing even more as the sudden adrenalin rush he was feeling had a countering effect on the tequila. His eyes narrowed as he replied, "If the shoe fits bitch... now put down my money."

Sam gave a side glance at the door, but Timmy was already moving over between her and it. Then her shoulders drooped resignedly. "If I don't come back with this money, he'll beat me. Or, worse."

"Who will? And who says I won't?"

Her chin came up. "I do. I know how to read people, and you aren't into beating up women."

"Yeah, well, I don't mind beating the crap out of anybody who steals from me. Trust me, I've done it before. So, who is this guy you're afraid of?" Timmy's anger had dropped a notch.

"Jimmy, the bartender. My boyfriend dumped me here two months ago, leaving me with no money after he took off with some chick on her yacht. I don't have anyone back in the states I could call for help, and no way to get home. Jimmy took me in and was really nice to me at first. Then he hid my passport and forced me to start robbing tourists that he picked out at the bar. He bribes the local cops to look the other way and says that he can have me thrown in jail in a split second if I don't do what he says, and I believe him. If I don't come back with your money I'm in deep trouble."

Timmy weighed what she had told him as he looked into her pleading eyes. He wasn't buying the whole story, but he felt that there was some kernel of truth at the center of it. Not that he trusted her, but she definitely had some talents that might come in handy when he headed up to Virginia to get his money back. Plus, there was more fun to be had in the meantime, starting back up where they had left off a few minutes before.

"Must've been a hell of a yacht for him to want to leave you behind." He watched for her response and wasn't disappointed when she suddenly exploded.

"That bastard only left me a note telling me he was sure I'd have no problem finding a way to get home!" She composed herself as she looked down at the money in her hands which was maybe five grand. Timmy knew what she was thinking, that if she only had her passport, this was more than enough money to get her back to the states and a fresh start.

"Think that's a lot of money?" He asked.

"Don't you?"

"It's not even a down payment on a score I've got planned up in Virginia. I'll give you twice that much if you want to come along and help."

Sam shook her head, "I told you, Jimmy hid my passport. I can't get back into the states without it."

"I'm really good at getting people to tell me where they've hidden things." It was Timmy's turn to wear an evil smile. "I'll take care of getting your passport back tonight and get Jimmy off your ass at the same time. Tomorrow I'll get us up to Palm Beach, then we can head north in my boat to take care of some business. What do you say?"

The look of relief on her face said it all. "If you can do all that, I'm in."

Half an hour later, Sam walked back into the bar, catching Jimmy's eye. Then she went around behind the back where he appeared two minutes later.

"How much did he have?" Jimmy asked.

Sam handed over the cash, which was all that Timmy had been willing to trust her with. "Just a few hundred. He's headed back tomorrow. Hope he wasn't counting on having cab fare to the airport." She made the joke because she knew Jimmy would be angry, expecting much more cash than this.

"I knew that musclebound moron was lying about being loaded! Damn it, we should have hit him two weeks ago when I first saw him before he ran through it all. And why the hell did you insist on the most expensive tequila we stock?"

She frowned, "Because that's what he would've expected from me! Plus, you got to pocket half of that anyway."

"So, where is the idiot?"

She grinned. "Snoring away, passed out in his bed. And I'm gonna take off before he wakes up and finds his money missing then comes down here to get it back. I'll be at the house."

Jimmy nodded while counting the money she had given him. What the heck, the idiot would be gone tomorrow, and any police report he might make before that will end up getting "lost." Then they could get back to picking out better marks. He hurried back to the bar.

"Where is she?" Timmy was at the bar an hour later, about as Jimmy expected.

"Where's who, pal?"

"The blond that I left with two hours ago! She ripped me off while I was asleep." Timmy raged.

"If you mean that hottie you were sitting with, I don't think I'd have been sleeping. But she's not here."

"Do you know her?"

"Never seen her before, she must be a tourist, not a local." Jimmy lied.

"Damn it! Well, if she comes back in here, call and leave a message at my hotel. I'll make it worth your while."

Jimmy took the slip of paper with the number Timmy offered as he watched him leave. Make it worth my while? With what? He knew that Sam was thorough, if nothing else. She would have taken his last dime. He tossed the paper in the garbage and went to refill another tourist's beer glass.

A little after one a.m., Jimmy walked through the front door of his completely dark bungalow. He flipped the switch next to the door, but nothing happened. He cursed as he stepped inside and closed the door then saw a sudden burst of white before lapsing into total darkness again.

"Hey. Hey!" Timmy splashed water on Jimmy's face, and after he started to come around he slapped him a couple of times for good measure.

As Jimmy's eyes began to focus, he saw Sam sitting in a chair across the room with all her clothes and gear packed in bags beside her. That musclebound idiot from the bar was crouched down in front of him. That's when he realized he was bound, gagged, and lying on the floor. He also realized about the same time there was only one way this guy found his house; Sam had to be working with him now.

Timmy was grinning. "So, you've never seen her before, eh? It's not smart to lie to me, Jimmy. See, I already found your stash of cash and all that stolen jewelry, so thanks for all that, I'm taking it off your hands. But first I took some nice pictures of the jewelry piled up on you while you were still out. Pics the cops might love to have. Or, not. I know you have some pals on the local police force that might try to cover your ass, but there's limits to everything, Jimmy. And if these pictures get sent to the tourist bureau, or if they happen to find their way onto social media back in the states with a story about this place, I bet your pals will forget really fast that you were ever friends. So, Jimmy, if you are a smart guy, you'll tell me what I wanna know. If you don't, I'm gonna get it out of you anyway, it'll just take a little longer, and it's gonna hurt. Either way, I'm good with it. Now, I'm gonna take that gag out, and you're gonna tell me where you hid Sam's passport. If you try anything stupid, that hurting part I mentioned is gonna start. Nod if you understand me."

Jimmy nodded slowly, looking into Timmy's eyes as he removed the gag.

"Help! Policia..." Jimmy screamed as Timmy stuffed the gag back in place. Then he punched him repeatedly in the stomach then rolled him over and kicked him viciously several times in the kidneys. Tears were running down Jimmy's face when Timmy rolled him onto his back.

"Jimmy, I'm starting with the places where the bruises can still get covered up when you're at work. I really don't want to have to get all the way up to your face, because that might make for some embarrassing explanations when you go back to the bar. Explanations that neither of us wants you to have to give. So, be a smart guy and tell us where Sam's passport is, and we'll leave you alone. Stop being stupid. See, I've got plenty of time, and I can do this all night. Do you need a little more convincing, or are you ready to tell me now?"

Jimmy nodded, and Timmy removed the gag again. This time he quietly told Timmy about the loose baseboard in his bedroom. Timmy replaced the gag as Sam went to check. She returned with not one but two passports, and more cash. She handed the second passport and the cash to Timmy.

"What's this? Reginald Shalhoub? And it has your picture. Why do I think that somebody must have been a bad boy back stateside and is down here hiding out? Hey Sam, I think we just got some more insurance."

Timmy could see the panic in Jimmy/Reginald's eyes. He had hit the nail on the head; there was a lot more to his story. Jimmy/Reginald started shaking his head.

Timmy said, "I bet your cop friends don't know your real name either. And I wonder if you're wanted back in the states and if there's a reward for catching and returning you? I bet they could find out really quick. And, I also bet you went by Reggie back home." He laughed. "So, Reggie, if you do anything dumb after we leave, we'll make sure the cops back in the good old USA know where to find you. Do we understand each other?"

Reggie nodded.

Timmy added, "Okay, here's what we're going to do. After we get back stateside tomorrow, we'll call the bar and tell them to send somebody over here to cut you loose."

Reggie started shaking his head violently, total fear now showing in his eyes as he fought against his bindings.

"Easy there, Reg. See, you don't get a vote in this. You just have to trust me. If you keep struggling, it'll just make things worse for you. So, now I need you to do two things. First, I need you to come up with a good story about how you got tied up, and it better not have anything to do with me or Sam or anyone who looks like us, got it?"

Reggie had stopped fighting the bindings and his eyes were now fixed on Timmy. He nodded slowly.

"The second thing is, you better start praying that our plane don't crash. Hey Sam, grab your stuff and let's go."

Back at Timmy's room, Sam asked, "Won't they be able to trace your call tomorrow?"

Timmy grinned wickedly, "What call?"

Chapter 12

Angler's Marina, Eagle Island, NC

It was a little before dusk, and Murph and Lindsay were hard at work in the fishing cockpit of *Irish Luck*. They were going over all the tackle, checking for sticky drags or frayed line and rigging the next day's trolling baits. A whiney, slightly reed–like voice came from the dock beyond the transom.

"So, I see your boss is from Mallard Cove. How does he like it? I'm docking my fleet there for most of the summer." The guy's voice was irritating enough, but his attitude seemed even worse; he sounded really condescending. Lindsay and Murph had been running north for almost ten hours, arriving just in time for the Eagle Island Tournament's captain's meeting, and they were bone tired. They had purposely skipped the kickoff cocktail party, leaving that to their charter anglers, and opting instead to pay attention to all the finite details of their preparations. This attention to detail was a large part of what made *Irish Luck* one of the top boats on the tournament circuit.

Lindsay looked up and found that the voice was attached to a short semi–scrawny guy with white-blond hair. He was wearing the latest in fishing fashions and had an entourage of similarly attired guys with him, all with "to go" cups from the party. Something about them really rubbed her the wrong way, this short guy in particular. But if what the blowhard said was true, he was going to be a customer, and she was willing to overlook a few things if that was really the case.

"Actually, we own this boat, and we are partners in Mallard Cove as well." Lindsay hoped that he would hear the tired edge in her voice and move along. He looked surprised, but unfortunately took this news as an invitation for introductions and conversation. He came down the finger pier with a big fake and goofy grin on his face.

He stuck out his hand across the teak covering board and next to the portable rod holder mounted cutting table where she was working. "Ron Sanders. I guess then we're going to be neighbors as well as competitors." The grin got even wider. It soured slightly as she turned from the table and without wiping off the fish slime from the mullet she was rigging, then took and tightly gripped his outstretched hand.

"Lindsay Davis, and that's Murph."

She pointed in the direction of the cockpit bench seat where Murph had the faceplate off a fifty–pound reel and was in the middle of installing new drag plates. He looked up and nodded. She turned back to the cutting board, leaving Ronnie's hand suspended in midair, still covered in fish slime. He still held his cocktail in the other hand, and now wore an unhappy look on his face. Ronnie motioned to one of his group to take his cocktail while he found a hose behind a neighboring boat to spray off his hand. Lindsay was hoping he'd continue on down the dock, but she wasn't that lucky today as he came back, again standing behind their stern.

"Since you two own the place, can you fill me in on that Mid–Atlantic Fisheries Foundation? I just retired from the US Fishing Association, and I'd like to talk to them; I have a lot of experience that would be useful to them."

Yeah, this pompous ass was really starting to get to her. He could see that they were both busy, but obviously thought that his time was a lot more valuable than theirs, even with the tournament starting in just under ten hours. Fortunately, she had dealt with his type before, and having his pals with him gave her just the audience that she wanted.

"Gee, Ronnie, I don't think they're hiring yet." One of his group chuckled, earning him a frosty glare from Sanders.

"That's Ron, and I'm certainly not looking for a job, I was on the *board* of the association, and I'm going to offer to serve in that same capacity with them. Unfortunately, I haven't been able to find any contact information other than a mailing address at Mallard Cove, and I'd prefer to deal face to face with whoever is in charge. So, if you'd just give me that information, I'd appreciate it." He sounded like he wouldn't appreciate anything; more like it was expected because of who he thought of himself as being.

Lindsay again stopped what she was doing and turned toward Ronnie with a very tired expression that wasn't a put on. "Well Ron, I'd love to help you, but they are a very private organization. One of their conditions for being based out of Mallard Cove was that we keep anything and everything to do with them completely confidential. Right now, until they name a spokesperson, the only way for you to get in touch with them is by US mail."

It wasn't what Ronnie wanted to hear, but he did pull one "ah hah" tidbit out of it. "So, they are physically based at Mallard Cove?"

She sighed, wanting this conversation to be over. "Again, we respect their privacy."

Now Murph looked up, irritated that this bozo couldn't catch a hint. "I'm sure they have a full board. If you are as connected as you say you are, then you probably know or have met at least one of their board members and they know who you are. If the phone didn't ring, then they have decided to go in other directions. Being at Mallard Cove this summer, you'll no doubt be running into a few of them, and they'll be able to get a closer look at you. So maybe down the way if someone drops out they might give you that call."

Not if Murph had anything to say about it, but he wanted to pacify this jerk so that he'd leave them alone and let them finish up and get some sleep. Unfortunately, this didn't come close to pacifying Ronnie.

"Look, if you want me and my fleet as a customer, then you'll need to make some introductions when I get up there. They need my expertise and connections, and when they find out that you two stood in between me and them, they aren't going to be happy about it, I can guarantee that. So, I'll be expecting those intros when I arrive." With that, Ronnie turned on his heel and stormed down the dock with his pals in tow.

"What a tool," Lindsay said.

"Ass wipe is more like it. I know we want to fill the marina, but if he's like that when he gets up there, I'll toss him out myself. And I don't care how many boats he has, or how much fuel they use. By the way Linds, how many boats *does* he have?" Murph asked.

"No idea. I've never heard of him before; Kari must be handling him. But he and his crew just boarded that big sucker at the end of the dock. Must be a mothership of some kind."

Murph grumped, "That ugly thing? That isn't a 'mothership,' it's a 'mutha–ship.' What a POS. Matches his attitude; overbearing and totally out of scale."

"Yeah. I want to check the scoreboard and find out which sportfish is his. I want to beat this guy more than anything."

Murph nodded. "Me, too."

Ronnie's rig turned out to be a Dutch designed and built seventy–five–footer named *Gusher*. And it would take a gusher of an oil well to feed that pig. The builder was better known for their large yachts than for their sportfishermen. Which meant the interior woodwork was impressive; performance and speed though, not so much. Murph especially enjoyed passing them and leaving them in the Merritt's wake on the run offshore. Almost as much as he enjoyed passing them on the way back, his outriggers loaded up with twice the number of fish release flags than theirs. Even better, he saw Ronnie climb down the bridge ladder and go into his salon when he saw them coming. Murph smiled, knowing this was no coincidence as he realized how fragile Ronnie's ego was. This summer was going to be fun.

Chapter 13

Kari and I had moved the last of our gear over to *Why Knot* last night, since Murph and Lindsay were due in today. We were excited to have our pals back home, and anxious to hear all of their fishing stories. We left a bottle of Papa's Pilar Lost Cask Blonde Rum on the salon table as a "thank you" for letting us stay aboard, and also as a hint that we'd love to sit and chat. Nothing like a little limited-edition, ninety–one–proof liquid lubrication to grease the wheels of conversation.

The Merritt arrived late that afternoon, just ahead of the *Kembe* and the *Golden Dolphin*. I caught the lines from Lindsay, attaching them to the dock cleats. She adjusted their fenders and then took up the slack in the lines, snugging *Irish Luck* against the floating dock in her new slip. We had just finished when Baloney passed by.

"What the hell is that? Youse two win the lottery or what!" Baloney shouted from the flybridge of his boat.

Murph yelled back, "You water 'em and they grow. You know, like the fish in your stories!"

I smiled as I stood on the dock. It was great to have everybody getting back together again for the season. During the cold months, the docks had been mostly empty and quiet, but this was a good indication of how raucous things might soon be, and I liked it. And despite having seen her just a few weeks prior, Lindsay hopped over onto the dock and wrapped me up in a hug like she hadn't seen me in years.

"I missed you, my annoying older brother! And, where is your better half?"

As I have said before, we aren't related, it just felt like that at times. Like right now.

"Right behind you." Kari beamed and held her arms open as Lindsay dropped me like yesterday's news. Her view of Kari had been blocked by *On Coastal Time* as she had walked up. Its slip was on the other side of the finger pier, eight feet away. And I couldn't blame Linds, since Kari hadn't been with us when we rescued Murph; she hadn't seen her in months. The two of them had even more catching up to do.

Murph stepped onto the dock, grabbed my hand and gave me a "bro hug;" no words were necessary.

"I hope you brought beer back with you!" Baloney was just now coming into sight from behind *OCT*.

"Yeah, I missed you too, Bill." Murph chuckled as he took Baloney's outstretched hand. "Already iced down in the bait box because I figured you'd be over."

"Course you did. I wanna hear all about how you left with a Rybo and came back with a bigger Merritt! But first..."

Murph laughed, "I know, I know, you need a beer." He pointed to a beautiful varnished cabinet next to the rear facing padded cockpit bench.

Baloney made the round trip to the bait box and was drooling over Murph and Lindsay's new ride. "Wow! She's a beaut! Just as nice as the ol' Rybo, but so much bigger."

Murph said, "Newer, faster, and with much lower time on her engines than the Rybovich." He told the story of how they ended up with her.

Baloney just shook his head, amazed. "You named your rigs right; you are the luckiest Irishman I've ever known, and that's sayin' somethin'!"

Murph and I each grabbed beers and joined Baloney sitting on the gunwale and transom covering boards, trading stories about what had happened since Murph headed south. However, Murph and I omitted anything and everything to do with the Bahamas, or the TW and Timmy debacle.

While we were busy yakking, Kari and Lindsay grabbed armfuls of clothes and gear, starting the move over onto *On Coastal Time*. Once onboard, Lindsay looked around and said, "I had almost forgotten how spacious she is. It's good to be home!"

"Thanks again for letting us borrow her; you guys were lifesavers," Kari replied.

"Not at all. *Why Knot* looks great, but you didn't need to rush her, you could have still stayed here in the guest quarters."

"Thanks, but Carlton ran ahead of time, and I really wanted to get back aboard her. And it won't be too much longer before *Tied Knot* is finished. I can't wait, she's going to be great to live aboard, just like *OCT*."

"Even better, I envy you two the third deck and hot tub," Lindsay said wistfully.

"You shouldn't, because it's yours to use, too. We designed that deck to be big enough to hold all of us on nice days and moved the tub up there with the bar and outdoor kitchen. The idea was to have a private place where our gang could hang out. Not that the Captain's Lounge isn't nice, but the Beer–Thirty–Bunch is already getting a lot bigger than I thought it would with all the new people docking here. The Captain's Lounge is getting used night and day, and we aren't even into the summer season yet. So, problem solved." It was easy to see that Kari was looking forward to entertaining in her new home.

"Hey, speaking of new people, what do you know about a guy named Ron Sanders? We bumped into him down at the Eagle Island tournament, and he said he's headed here."

Kari saw the look of concern on Lindsay's face and said, "Yes, and he's bringing three boats with him. Is there a problem there?"

"The guy is a major butthead. You know how they say that five percent of your customers create ninety-five percent of the problems? He's going to fall into that

116

five percent." Lindsay told her the details of their encounter.

"Maybe he won't be that bad once he gets here. Maybe he was just showing off for his fishing buddies and they won't be travelling with him." Now Kari looked worried.

"Maybe, but don't count on it. On the other hand, it sounds like Max Johnson's group is going to be a dream to handle."

Kari nodded. "He's a sweetheart and a real pro. Wait until you meet him; he's going to be a great fit for the foundation. I think for our gang as well. He's a fisherman's fisherman, and he seems to know everybody." She told the story about him remembering Baloney, and how he already knew Mimi, who Lindsay had yet to even meet.

Lindsay sighed. "You know, we did really well with the Florida leg of our run, but I wouldn't be all that upset if we shortened it a bit next year. I'm tired, I missed you guys, I missed this place, and apparently we missed some fun 'goings on.' I can't believe that Bill nicknamed Max Johnson 'Big.' Then again, yes, I guess I can." She chuckled. "But it wouldn't hurt my feelings if we dropped a few of those tournaments off our schedule next year and stayed here longer."

"It would be great to have you guys around more. Everything here will be open year 'round then, so a lot more will be a lot more happening next winter. To tell the truth, it was kind of quiet and dull this year without you two." Kari hoped that Murph would be up for a shortened schedule as well.

I saw the girls coming back for another load, but they saw several others had joined the group which was now spilling into the salon through the open doorway. We'd all pitch in and help with the move later, but this was the time to kick back and get caught up.

Bobby "B2" Smith, Baloney's mate, was here along with Kim "Hard Rock" Collier, the captain/owner of the *Kembe,* and his mate, Fred "Mad Gaffer" Everett. She was actually the *Kembe II,* the replacement for the original which had ended up on top of one of the CBBT's rock islands after a steering system failure. It was this mishap that had inspired Baloney to brand Fred with his nickname. Rounding out the group was Timmy "Spuds" O'Shea, the hard drinking, fun loving, slightly rotund, and Fu Manchu mustachioed bait business owner. He used to operate solely out of his thirty–foot bait skiff, the *Rum Runner,* but had recently leased space next to the new dockmaster's building by the in and out boat storage. This was what he and Murph were now discussing. Spuds looked worried.

"I swear, Murph, I keep *Rum Runner* clean and smelling good these days. The shop, too! I'm buying that green eco–friendly cleaner stuff by the case." Spuds looked sincere.

In the past, the running joke was that you could smell *Rum Runner* before you could even see her approach. A few days every year in the summer when the wind was right and the bait fishing good it wasn't actually a joke. The boat had been a fixture around the marina back when it had other owners who had let the place deteriorate. They didn't care about the smell. But after Murph and Lindsay bought the property and started fixing it up, they told Spuds in no uncertain terms that *Rum Runner* had to be kept clean too, or she would be banned from here. Since she wasn't only for catching bait but also had been his primary source of transportation to the Beer–Thirty–Bunch meetings, it was a threat Spuds really took to heart.

Kari said, "It's in his lease, Murph. All premises and equipment shall be kept clean and odor free."

I jumped to Spuds' defense. "Murph, '*Runner*' has been clean as a whistle while you guys were gone, and Timmy has now started his own frozen bait brand called

118

'Splittails.' Wait until you see how he's fitted out the Splittails shop with display freezers, his own branded tee shirt line, and even has twenty–four–hour automated frozen bait and ice bag vending machines outside. It's impressive!"

Spuds looked over and shot me a grin, and I could see he was thankful for the support and compliments. But they were earned; he had put his heart into this, as well as all of his savings. I'm betting on him to make a go of it, and I was willing to stand up for him while he did.

Murph looked thoughtful for a minute before saying, "Way to go, Spuds! Sounds like your place is a good fit with what we're doing."

A visibly relieved Spuds raised his beer in thanks to both Murph and me before getting up and going on a tour of the Merritt's cabin. Murph turned to me.

"You know the story of how Casey and Dawn talked Lindsay and me into letting their group come in on Mallard Cove, both buying it, running it, and adding the new businesses. It was the right move for all of us, me and Linds especially. But the absolute best part of it was having Kari come oversee the management as well as the development, not to mention also getting to know her. Without her here, Spuds' place wouldn't have happened. And I can't wait to see what she comes up with for the Lynnhaven project."

Casey and Dawn had seen that Kari had a natural eye for real estate, both promotion as well as development. It was her plan that had removed a decrepit boatyard and commercial docks from the property, replacing them with the hotel, more recreational boat docks, the *Cove Beach Bar*, the second restaurant and bar called the *Steak & Fin*, and the in and out boat storage. Casey and Dawn added our new office building to the plan later. But Murph was right in that Splittails wouldn't have happened, at least not here, without Kari's vision and her confidence in Spuds.

I looked beyond Murph to where Kari was standing in the salon doorway. She had overheard the last part of our conversation and was both smiling as well as blushing slightly.

So, this had ended up becoming an impromptu meeting of the original core of the Beer–Thirty–Bunch. But after a while, one by one, they all drifted back to their boats or headed home, leaving just the four of us remaining. Kari and I helped Linds and Murph make quick work of their move over to *OCT*, as they would be taking *Irish Luck* over to Carlton's boatyard tomorrow to get hauled out for her annual maintenance. Then we all went to the *Cove* restaurant for an early dinner since they were both worn out from their trip, and nobody really wanted to cook. And tomorrow promised to be busy.

Chapter 14

For the second day in a row, Kari and I woke up on *Why Knot*. She had stayed aboard with me some before the explosion, but that was before we were engaged, and before things became more...permanent. I had lived aboard by myself for years, so this had a totally different feel to it because right now until *Tied Knot* is finished, she's our home. Together. Honestly, it felt kind of weird, but also very good.

And, for the second day in a row, we were expecting the arrival of a boat. Only this one was coming by land, and not sea. She was the first addition to what has been dubbed the "Pelican Fleet", which was my newest endeavor. This next boat is a thirty–five–foot Ocean Pro parasail rig. I got her from an operator down in Myrtle Beach, she has very low hours and was at a "fire sale" price. The guy and his wife were getting a divorce which forced the sale; I hoped it wasn't an omen about this business. But she was due to arrive this afternoon on a flatbed marine transport over at Carlton's, where we'll lift her off and launch her with the strap hoist. She already has her new name installed on the stern: "*High Flier*." There's a flying pelican in the center between the two words; it's the logo for my working boats.

High Flier will join my twenty–six–foot Gold Line, *Marlinspike*, and my eighteen–foot Maverick flats boat, *Bone Shaker*, in my expanding fleet here at Mallard Cove. Yeah, the name *Marlinspike* is pretty self-explanatory, but *Bone Shaker* comes with a Baloney story. See, a few years ago, I carried more than just a few extra pounds, ones that I have since shed. But on a particularly low tide, back before the new floating docks were installed here, I stopped by to visit Bill. There was a long drop from the dock to his teak covering boards, and then down to his deck. I hit the gunwale a bit off balance and continued on down to the main deck. Some parts of me stopped faster than others, leaving Bill to exclaim, "Take it easy on the teak there, Shake and Bake!" He quickly shortened it to "Shaker," and it has since stuck like epoxy in August. So, when I bought the Maverick, he, of course, came up with that name and it stuck as well. It's not like I really had a choice. No matter what I named her, Baloney would have still used *Bone Shaker* over the VHF radio. Sometimes you just have to pick your battles.

Anyway, I'm hiring a crew for *High Flier*; I'm not planning on running her myself. I've even cut down on my own charter work since the settlement hit my bank account. Not that I'm thinking about stringing up a hammock under some trees and sleeping all day. But ever since my windfall, I'm no longer worried about where my next meal is coming from. So, now I just take out my valued and long–time customers like Paul Levine, and I still write the occasional fishing article for a few of my favorite national magazines. But MAFF has been my main focus for the past several months, figuring out new and innovative ways to use the money from it to help protect the fisheries, and to educate people about how important that mission is.

You're probably wondering, then why not just sit back and enjoy life? Why add to the fleet and all the headaches that can come with running a business? Because as part of the settlement agreement, neither Kari nor I can say anything publicly about it. Meaning, I need to have a visible and logical source of income. And when parasail boats are run professionally, they make a ton of cash throughout the season. A typical flight is about ten minutes long. Each flier pays ninety bucks, we can fly up to three at a time, and the boat will hold up to fifteen passengers on a run with two crew. Non-flying friends can ride for $25 each if there are seats left open, and many of them end up coming back to fly. When you do the math, you'll see that I wasn't kidding;

these can make a TON of money. I just happened to be lucky enough to have fallen into the perfect location and have great landlords.

I also want to add a sailboat and an eco-tour boat to the fleet too. Eco-tours are hot right now, and sailing tours are always popular. They all will be nice draws for Mallard Cove, and I have an exclusive agreement for all of these activities here. Since I love the water and I love boats, this is all a "no brainer" for me, providing a nice income stream and cover. For Kari, with as hard as she works and her involvement in M&S, Mallard Cove, and the Lynnhaven project, no one would think twice about her having a big income.

But I wasn't the only one who was looking to capitalize on the increasing traffic at Mallard Cove. Baloney has been looking at several used sportfish boats, wanting to pick up a bargain for his mate Bobby to run. B2, as we call him, had earned his captain's license at the end of last year. Baloney knew it was only a matter of time before he would end up running a boat of his own, so he decided to partner up instead of losing him outright.

It won't be long before the word gets out that there are lots of "freelance" opportunities for mates around Mallard Cove. See, it's not as easy to get into marine-based businesses as you might think. Typically, teenagers hang around the docks in the summer hoping to pick up jobs washing private boats. Then maybe they can snag a "fill-in gig" as a mate on a charter boat, finally working their way up to a full-time job. With all the new private and charter boats moving into the Cove, it meant a lot of opportunities for Shore kids looking for a start. This place was really getting a great reputation around crews on the other docks up and down the Shore, as well as over in VA Beach.

I called Carlton and found out that the truck was going to be there right after lunch, about the time that Murph and Lindsay were scheduled to haul the Merritt.

123

The three of us decided to ride up together on her, then bring *High Flier* back. The timing ended up working out perfectly. I was able to help Lindsay handle the lines to position the Merritt over the cradle as the ways hauled *Irish Luck* out of the water. Then the yard crew got started pressure washing her bottom in preparation for a new coat of anti–fouling paint and hull waxing. As that crew got busy, the three of us walked over and toured *Tied Knot*. Murph and Lindsay had both seen drawings of her, but we had just started the build as they headed south. I think they were almost as excited as Kari and me.

We finished up and saw Carlton headed over to the slab where the truck hauling *High Flier* was just backing in. The boat had a bright red hull with white interior. There was a side console with a captain's seat, large raised landing deck flush with the gunwales aft, anodized aluminum inflation arch similar to a radar arch, and bench seating on each side of the bow.

"You really believe in advertising, don't you?" Murph chuckled as he spotted the new giant white–letter vinyl stickers spelling out "PARASAIL" down each side of the red hull.

I replied, "A business with no signs is a sign of no business. And you haven't seen anything yet, just wait until you see the new parasail."

"What did you do now?" Lindsay asked, sounding worried.

"You'll see soon enough. Let's just say they won't have any trouble finding us." I was enjoying leaving the two of them in limbo.

The seven–mile run from Albury Boat Works back to Mallard Cove was a nice short shakedown cruise for my new rig. We extended it a bit, running around a flat calm Magothy Bay for a while with each of us taking a turn at the wheel. We wanted to see what the Cummins diesel powerplant was capable of, and how well *"Flier"* handled. She cruised right about thirty mph, and wide open she'd do thirty–five. With her diesel she was a dependable workhorse, but we quickly found out that she was a lot of fun to run too, very quick to respond to her helm. After half an hour I headed toward Skidmore Island and the narrow Virginia Inside Passage, a channel cut into the lower point of ESVA. It was similar to a lot of areas along the Intracoastal waterway to our south, and it would spit us out right at the entrance to Mallard Cove.

As we made our turn through the cut in the breakwater, we had a surprise waiting dead ahead. Quite possibly the ugliest, most ungainly yacht I'd seen in a long time was tied up on the end of the dock where Max Johnson's group was supposed to dock their mothership. On top of this boat's totally out of scale design, someone had the brilliant idea to paint the hull gray and the superstructure white, emphasizing its top–heavy look. I couldn't believe that Max would have advised his boss to buy this thing. Despite its length, it was so tall that it looked as if a stiff breeze would cause it to capsize.

"Oh, crap." Murph's mood had just soured.

Lindsay added one word which relieved and concerned me at the same time: "Ronnie."

Kari had relayed the story about the guy and his run in with Murph and Lindsay, forewarning me about his comments regarding MAFF. And as we passed, I saw Barry Rolle the dockmaster standing next to Kari. She was now in what I recognized as her arguing stance, squaring off with some guy on the dock who I figured was Ronnie Sanders. He had a slight build and was shorter than average height. His chinos were topped off with a long-sleeved angler's shirt, a sun mask bunched down around his neck, wraparound sunglasses and golf visor. His wardrobe screamed that he was a real "sport," and already I didn't like him. Kari was gesturing to the next dock over, and he was pointing straight down.

Murph said, "Let me off at the next dock, Marlin."

125

I pulled in against the tee that Kari had been gesturing to, and Murph and Lindsay hopped off, hurrying over to Kari's side. I wanted to go with them, but I needed to get *High Flier* tied up in her own slip a couple of docks farther down. I didn't have any standing here, not owning any part of the business, but I wasn't happy seeing that guy getting in Kari's face. Besides, if I went over there, it might look like I felt she needed her boyfriend to bail her out, and that wasn't the case. So, I stuck with taking care of my own boat. My slip was on the first dock east of the charter boat docks, all the way in at the base next to the parking lot. My bow faced the *Golden Dolphin's*. I backed in, positioning my fenders against the floating dock in order to protect the vinyl lettering from chafing. By the time I finished and was admiring *"Flier"* from the main dock, Kari arrived, followed by Murph and Linds.

"What an egotistical jerk!" She was still steaming.

"I may have my moments, but I don't think I'm that bad." I smiled at her, trying to lighten her mood.

"What? Oh, ha, hah. You know I was talking about that Ronnie Sanders guy. He assigned himself Max's slips, then went ahead and tied up even after Barry had directed him over to the next dock. What a total jerk. He said he wanted to be closer to the inlet, but I think he really wanted to be the first boat that anyone saw when they pulled in. And it's the ugliest thing around. Doesn't look like a mothership, it looks more like an oil rig tender."

I had found that in situations like this, it was best to let her vent. You know, like a volcano. After the big eruption, things tended to calm down. You just needed to drop the subject. Fortunately, Kari didn't get mad often, but when she did it wasn't pretty. Unfortunately, Murph didn't have the benefit of my hard-earned knowledge, and he plowed ahead.

"That's because it was built by a company that specializes in oil rig tenders, they were the low bidder.

Some of the guys down at Eagle Island clued me in." He shook his head.

Kari looked at Murph then me. "That figures. He doesn't want to listen to anyone but himself. I was just telling him to either move or leave when Linds and Murph showed up and they backed me up. Apparently, he really wants to be here so that he can try to meet the MAFF board, so he swallowed his pride and he's moving over to where he was supposed to be. Good thing too, because Max's boats are supposed to start arriving tomorrow."

I put an arm around her shoulders. "Then you'll have someone pleasant to deal with, and you can forget about this bozo."

"Oh, I doubt he'll leave me alone. This is going to be one long summer."

Lindsay said, "Just let Barry handle him. He's a dockmaster problem."

Kari shook her head. "Until he won't listen to him, just like today. Trust me, this guy won't want to deal with Barry. If anything, he'll want to deal with you two even more than me now since he knows that you're the biggest partners in the place. He'll see you as his intro to MAFF. And, I was right. Here he comes." She sighed, looking down the dock where Ronnie was now making a beeline for our group. He zeroed in on Murph and Lindsay, just like Kari figured. He put on his best huge, fake smile as he approached.

"Hey there. I think the three of us got off on the wrong foot down at Eagle Island, and I'd like to make it up to you. How about letting me buy you two a drink at the bar?"

I saw a funny look blossom on Lindsay's face, and she tried to suppress a grin. I'd seen this look before, and I knew this was going to be good.

"As much as we'd love to Ronnie, we have an informal meeting that we have to go to in a few minutes.

We promised the chairman, er, I mean Bill, that we would bring the beer."

Ron brightened on hearing this. "Well, if it's an informal meeting, would you mind if I tagged along and got to meet him? I'd be happy to bring the beer myself. Since I'm going to be here half the year, I'd like to meet as many of the...regulars as I can." He was so excited at the prospect of meeting "the chairman" that he ignored her use of his longer name.

Lindsay looked dubious, then glanced over at Murph. "Gee, I don't know."

Murph had seen this coming and was ready for it. "Oh, what the heck, Linds. I mean, he's going to meet our group soon enough, it might as well be today rather than at a formal meeting. This way they can all get to know him before we decide to add more members."

Sanders couldn't believe his luck, getting invited to an informal MAFF meeting. "What does the chair...uh, Bill like to drink? Heineken, Stella Artois?"

Lindsay shook her head. "Bill is kind of funny, he hates beer snobs and prefers the lower–end beer brands. His favorite is the generic stuff from over at the ship's store. Oh, hey, look at the time. We have to be there in five minutes, and he hates it when we're late."

Sanders looked slightly panicked. "Wait for me! I'll be just a couple of minutes while I get the beer." He took off down the dock at a good clip while Kari fist bumped Lindsay.

"Remind me never to get on your bad side," I said to Lindsay.

"You should already know that by now," She retorted.

Kari asked, "Think we should give Bill a 'heads up?'"

Lindsay laughed. "Oh, hell no! That would take away half the fun. Let this jerk hang himself with Baloney, then maybe he'll end up leaving us alone after all."

Five minutes later we all headed to the Captain's Lounge, with Sanders casting disapproving sideways glances at both Kari and me like we were crashing his party. But there was no way the two of us would miss out on what was ahead.

A few of the regulars were already there, and as usual Baloney was holding court while waiting for a beer handout, his unlit cheap cigar in the corner of his mouth. He looked over disapprovingly at Murph's empty hands. "You on the wagon now or what?"

"No, our new friend here offered to buy. I think he's looking to join up with our crew, Bill." Murph looked over at Ronnie who moved up beside him. He pulled out a can from the twelve pack he was holding and offered it to Baloney. Murph spoke back up, "Bill, meet Ronnie Sanders."

Sanders looked cross for a split second before recovering and saying, "Actually, it's Ron, Bill. I'm glad that we finally have a chance to meet, I've heard a lot about you, and the work that you're doing. I'm going to be around most of the year, when I'm not in Palm Beach for the winter, and I was hoping that we might get a chance to fish together. I've got my fleet here, including my big sportfisherman, *Gusher*, my center console, *Roughneck*, and I'll be staying aboard my mothership, the *Toolpusher*."

Baloney gave Murph a sideways glance, figuring there was a backstory that he'd get later. "Well, if you wanna fish with me, you'll have to get on the schedule like everybody else." He looked down at the beer he was holding, then back up at Sanders. "The top–heavy sonofabitch that just came in is yours? Bet she rolls like a barrel in a beam sea. And it looks like you got the same taste in beer as you do in boats."

Ronnie briefly looked confused before deciding it must have been meant as a compliment since the beer was supposed to be Bill's favorite. But he wasn't at all what Ron had been expecting. "Uh, thanks. She did have a few issues at anchor when we first launched her and before we added ballast and a gyro system."

"Ballast, that's it! We're gonna call you Sandbags!" Bill exclaimed.

Sanders now didn't know exactly what to make of this "meeting" and Bill. One thing he was sure of is that he didn't want to be called "Sandbags."

"I'd prefer Ron, Bill." He was starting to use the same annoyed tone of voice that he had used on Eagle Island with Murph and Lindsay.

"Yeah, well, if you wanna be part of our little group here, it's gonna be Sandbags." Bill still didn't know what was behind this, but he knew that he was already starting to not like Ronnie.

"I know this meeting is supposed to be informal, but this is ridiculous. I'd like to join your board, but I'd also appreciate your using my given name, and showing me a bit of respect."

"Yeah, well, that *is* the name I gave ya, so go respect that! And, whattaya mean, 'board?'" Baloney was standing firm.

"The fishing foundation board, of course. The one that you chair, and that this is also a meeting of?" Sanders was getting exasperated.

"Well, I've heard that there's one of those around here, but nobody knows who runs it, and it sure ain't me. This is our usual meeting of what we call the Beer–Thirty–Bunch, and yeah, I guess I do run these."

Sanders spun and glared at Lindsay. "You said you were going to a fishing foundation meeting, and that you were bringing the beer for the chairman."

"No, you *assumed* it was a foundation meeting. And 'the chairman' is one of Bill's nicknames, just like Sandbags is now one of yours. You said that you wanted to meet 'the regulars' and that would be us. The Beer–Thirty–Bunch regulars. We have this little informal get together almost every weekday afternoon." Lindsay's "sweet and innocent" look wasn't helping Ronnie's disposition.

Slowly, it began to dawn on him that he had jumped to the wrong conclusions by being totally played. He was no closer to knowing who the members of the foundation board were, and he had now shown his cards, letting them all know that he was so anxious to be part of it. He set the box of beer cans down and walked out without a word, but not before glaring at Lindsay.

Baloney looked over at the box and directed B2 to put the leftover beer in the refrigerator. "It's junky beer, but it's free." He turned to Murph and Lindsay. "You two mind tellin' me what that was all about?"

Lindsay said, "A bit of revenge. For us as well as Kari." She went on to tell the story of their encounter at Eagle Island and Kari's run-in with him this afternoon. There were chuckles around the room, and outright laughter from Baloney.

"Hah! Sucker got what was coming to him. Maybe now he'll steer clear of the rest of us," Baloney said.

Murph shook his head. "Unfortunately, it may just make him that much more determined to 'big–shot' his way around here. If he starts importing his Palm Beach pals to fish with him up here like he did at Eagle Island, he's only going to get worse."

Kari and I had been sitting back, silently watching it all unfold, and I was finally about to jump in, "Well, right now we can't do anything about that. So, I'm not going to worry about something we can't control. But what we can control is the level of the beer in some of those cans he left; how about passing two over."

131

Chapter 15

We didn't see Sandbags again yesterday; he must have gone back to that floating monstrosity to sulk, which was fine by Kari and me. Maybe Baloney might have been right about him steering clear of us now, but somehow I just didn't buy it. Not that it mattered, because today Kari was busy with the commercial interior design firm that was doing both of our new offices. And I was interviewing a couple of people for the parasail crew; Ron Sanders was the last person on either of our minds today.

My first captain candidate ended up not having the depth of experience I was looking for. I wanted to run the safest parasail operation around, and that meant hiring the best, most experienced captain available. My second candidate was a guy named Chris Wagner, and he had the right credentials. He had started as a mate but had been running a parasail boat up in Atlantic City for several seasons, and now wanted to get out of there. In addition to his experience as an operator, he also had a great marine maintenance background. We ended up talking for an hour over lunch, and I was pretty sure I had found who I was looking for. Now, I wanted to see his skills firsthand. As we left the *Cove* restaurant, we ran into Lindsay out on the charter dock, and I introduced the two.

I asked her, "Ever been parasailing, Linds?"

"Uh, no. Never wanted to, either."

"Well, we need some deadweight." I grinned.

"Excuse me?"

I laughed at the way she sounded so insulted. "We need a 'flier' to do a test run. By law, we need a mate onboard with the captain."

"Good, that'll be me. You can start flapping your wings because I'm staying down on the water. Let's go."

Chris hit all the points I was looking for by first checking out the boat, the motor, the winch, and line as well as my new parasail before we ever left the dock. He set me up in the harness, double-checked the rig then the three of us were off. Out beyond the breakwater, Lindsay took the wheel as Chris attached my harness to the rig. As he utilized the inflation arch to hold the lines as he filled the parasail canopy with wind, Lindsay glanced back and started laughing. The parasail had a giant Mallard Cove logo printed on the fabric; it was the surprise I had been holding back the other day. Now there was no mistaking where *High Flier* was based, and it could be seen all the way over on the CBBT bridges next to where we would be operating. You couldn't ask for better advertising.

Chris let out a thousand feet of line, and my view from above was stunning. I was using my phone to take some pictures and video of *High Flier* when I spotted a beautiful emerald green hulled yacht in the distance, on a course for Mallard Cove. Chris was back at the wheel by this time and Linds was now the spotter. I pointed at the yacht and I saw her give the "okay" sign. Chris headed for it as I took more video.

As we got closer I recognized Max standing on the uppermost deck. He must have recognized me at the same time because he started waving as he looked up. Chris circled the yacht then headed back to Mallard Cove. He reeled me in to a couple hundred feet then slowed down, letting me lose altitude almost to the point where my feet were in that extremely cold water. At the last second as I was about to raise my feet he gunned the engine and I ascended again. This time he reeled me all the way back in to the landing deck, still completely dry.

"That was amazing, Chris!"

He nodded. "You had a beautiful, clear day for it. And this is one great winch boat. I wanted to show you how fast she responds with that 'dip drop' at the end. When the water is warm enough, a lot of fliers like getting their feet wet on the way back in."

I looked at Lindsay. "You missed a great ride."

"No, I didn't! I had a great ride right down here on the surface, thank you very much. And I got a great view of Max's mothership. What a beauty!"

I knew she was changing the subject so I wouldn't keep ribbing her about not flying, but I was willing to let it go. "She is. Not your typical mothership, since she isn't rigged for carrying other boats on deck, but still a gorgeous rig. I can't wait to see his other two boats."

Chris asked, "Who is this Max guy?"

I brought him up to speed on Max and his fleet as we ran back in. Then I offered him the parasail captain's job which he quickly accepted. I knew his maintenance abilities would come in handy as well, especially in our down season, doing preventative work on all of our boats. Then I told him to go ahead and hire a seasonal crewmember, leaving the interviewing and choice up to him. This weekend was supposed to be warmer than normal for this time of year, and we wanted to be ready to go.

I walked out to the tee on the center dock, watching as the one hundred–forty–foot Benetti pulled in. I was glad that Kari had kept this spot for her, as she was so stunning. As I pointed out, Sanders' *Toolpusher* looked more ungainly with her gray hull and white superstructure. But the dark green hull of *Deb's Emerald,* as the Benetti was called, only served to accentuate her sleek hull lines and Matterhorn white superstructure.

The crew was obviously very experienced, coordinating well and making the huge job of docking the yacht look like child's play. I glanced over at the next dock and saw an unhappy-looking Ronnie Sanders checking out the new arrival.

"Hey, Marlin! Come on aboard." Max was on the side deck and had that same look he wore when I picked him up from the airport. The one that made you feel like him seeing you was the highlight of his day. I climbed the gangway that had just been put in place and took his outstretched hand when he met me at the landing. "Do you always greet incoming boats with a fly by?" Even his eyes were smiling as he said it.

"Only special arrivals, Max. And remind me to send you the video I took of this boat. The view from up there was great."

"I bet. Hey, aren't those Ronnie Sanders' boats on the next dock?"

With all of Max's connections, it didn't surprise me that he might know Sanders. It also wasn't a surprise that his welcoming face had disappeared, replaced with a frown. "Yes. You know the guy?"

He nodded. "Yeah, I know him."

He wasn't happy, and he also wasn't more forthcoming. I wasn't going to press him on the issue, so instead, I changed the subject. "Hey, these sure are much nicer digs than where you stayed last time you were here."

"Let me give you a tour. I'll be moving over to the Viking when it arrives tomorrow, since I'll be spending most of my time on her. And the houseboat was really comfortable on the last trip, thanks for both putting up with me and putting me up as well. Hey, do you happen to know how long Ronnie will be here?"

With the way he almost spat as he said the guy's name, I knew there was a back story to this and it sounded like it wasn't a good one. He almost scowled when I told him that he was going to be based here all summer. Before that, I hadn't seen Max scowl.

As we toured the Benetti, Max returned to his normal relaxed mood. While he preferred fishing boats, his depth of knowledge of all boats was impressive. He was able to point out several unique features of the yacht that I otherwise would have missed. Stuart Lieberman was indeed lucky to have found Max. That, or very smart. I suspected it was a combination of the two.

I liked Lieberman's taste in boats as well as fishing directors. The Benetti was elegant, but also comfortable at the same time. Its polished and varnished wood interior gave off a warm vibe that would lend itself to a formal cocktail party in Palm Beach, or an informal fishing group in the out islands. And back in the "toy garage" in the stern, Max showed me some of what had first caught their attention. She had been fitted with a small walk-in bait freezer for long trips, a separate gasoline storage tank, and oversized diesel tanks with pumping systems so that she could act as a refueling station for both fishing boats. Only, unlike *Toolpusher*, she didn't look like a floating fuel dock. I loved it.

Max explained, "We can tow the outboard, and this rig doesn't even feel her back there. While this is no speed demon at only fourteen knots cruise, she'll go 4,000 nautical miles at that speed. The Viking can only go 725 miles when she goes that slow. Her normal cruising speed is thirty–five knots, with a 540 nautical mile range. So, depending on where we are headed, they can either leapfrog this one and meet up, or stick with her and refuel en route."

It was a slick setup. They could fish anywhere on the east coast, the Antilles, Central or South America, following the fish migration with relative ease.

"Have you had your boss out on either of the fishing boats yet?"

He shook his head. "No, he's been too busy. We're scheduled for next week, fishing from here for tuna. Oh, and he doesn't like to be referred to as 'boss,' he prefers 'Stu.'"

"Got it. But starting him off with tuna? Don't you want to break him in gradually on something smaller?" Tuna tend to pull like a freight train, whether it is the giant bluefin or the smaller but still sizable yellowfin, bigeye, blackfin, or longfin.

"Ordinarily, yes. And we still might do some inshore fishing, but I've been watching the water temps, and it has gotten warm early this year. The giant bluefin are already off Long Island, and the yellowfin should be almost here. It's still a new job for me, and he's spent a ton of money. I don't want to take a three million dollar rig out just to catch a few mackerel or redfish. I want him to feel the excitement of pulling in a tuna first with the heavy tackle, then we can branch out and start using light tackle as he learns."

I couldn't fault his reasoning, I just hoped that he wouldn't scare his boss, er, Stu off with such a strong fish right off the bat. But Max was a pro, and he should know what Stu is capable of, and what he would be looking for.

As he was showing me through the accommodations, he picked up a small box from the stateroom where he had been staying during their cruise up to ESVA. He asked, "Are you going to the Beer–Thirty meeting this afternoon?"

I replied, "I'm planning on it, why?"

"Didn't really want to go by myself. Kind of hoping to meet Murph and Lindsay, if they are going to be there."

I nodded. "They were planning on it, so I'll be glad to introduce you guys."

*****

In West Palm Beach, Timmy had been keeping Sam on a short leash. Back in the states with her passport back in hand, she could have taken off, except for the fact that she had no money, nor anywhere to go. At least with Timmy, she knew she had the promise of a decent payoff after their trip up north. In the meantime, he was covering the bills and showing her around the

137

area. The short-term tradeoff was sex with Timmy, but she still had a much better situation than she had back in Costa Rica with Jimmy and his marks. For now, she could put up with Timmy.

The really surprising thing had been meeting Timmy's mother after they arrived. She seemed to want to buy into the façade of Sam being Timmy's actual girlfriend. She treated the two of them to nice restaurants and took Sam shopping while Timmy was busy getting his boat repaired and preparing for the trip north. Timmy had explained that his mom's current boyfriend was loaded, and she was just bored while he was out of town. Sam was taking a load off of Timmy by keeping his mom occupied instead of letting her bug him all day. Meanwhile, he had three new engines mounted on his boat as well as all new electronics installed, and he was busy with the engines' break-in period. He and Sam would be taking off for tournaments in a few days in Florida, the Carolinas, then finally Virginia, and he didn't want any problems with the boat along the way.

Sam was already thinking ahead about the Virginia trip. Yes, Timmy had promised her ten grand after they got the money back he said was stolen from him. However, he hadn't shared any of the money he took from Jimmy, and she didn't trust him to keep up his end of the bargain when they finished up in Virginia. But at least in the meantime they should be rubbing shoulders with some very wealthy people on the fishing circuit. And, you never knew what opportunity might present itself. The good thing was that Timmy was so overconfident in himself it wouldn't occur to him that she might "jump ship" before they got the money up in Virginia. And he hadn't even come up with a plan yet as to how to get it back. Meaning, she didn't know just how far he might be willing to go in order to carry this out. As it was, she hoped that someone had gone over to Jimmy's place after he didn't show up for work for a day or two, but she couldn't be sure. For all she knew, he might have died there on the floor. And she didn't know if Timmy was willing to get even more violent with whoever had taken his money. Right now, she wasn't an accomplice to murder; at least she wasn't sure that she was. And she wasn't going to become one willingly. So yes, if a better opportunity knocked, she would be ready and would leap at the chance to get away from Timmy.

Chapter 16

Baloney greeted Max as he came into the Captain's Lounge, "Big! Glad to see you back. That huge green beauty that just pulled in yours?" Then he looked at Max's hands with a disappointed face when he only saw the small box he picked up on the boat instead of beer.

"Good to be back, Bill. Yes, she's one of the ones I look after. The other two will be here tomorrow. Hey, I brought you some upgrades." He stuck the box in Baloney's hands, which turned out to be filled with Connecticut leaf tobacco cigars. Then I followed up behind Max and handed him a bottle of Kalik beer. His face lit up.

"Damn! What a great way to close out the day. Thank youse guys! Big, I don't think I've had as nice a box of cigars as this in years. These are so good Betty might even let me light one up in the marina!"

Max laughed, "I did a friend a favor and he gave them to me. I figured you might like them."

"Love 'em. Remind me to put you on fish the next time we're both out. And Shaker, you've got much better taste in beer than Sandbags." Baloney took one of the cigars out of the box and admired it.

I had to hand it to Max, he sure knew the way to get on Bill's good side, and I had no doubt that he would pass along that fishing info. And maybe, just maybe, that Kalik might rate me some of that the same info. Max then gave me a quizzical look, no doubt about the "Sandbags" comment. I replied simply, "Sanders." Instantly Max looked disgusted.

Murph and Lindsay arrived, and I was finally able to introduce them to Max. After talking for five minutes you'd swear they had been friends for years, which is what I had both hoped and expected would happen. Kari joined us a few minutes later, and the five of us ended up outlasting everyone there. Then we moved over to the *Cove* for real drinks and dinner. Halfway through our first post-dinner drink, Ronnie came in and made a beeline for us.

"Max! I thought that was you out on the dock. How've you been? I haven't seen you in ages." Ronnie never gave any of the rest of us so much as a sideways look.

"You mean since I caught your girlfriend's son stealing things off the boat and blaming the members of my crew that you fired for it? And after I defended them, you fired me as well in order to cover the kid's ass, then tried to blackball me on the docks? I'm good, Ronnie, or should I call you 'Sandbags,' how are you?" This was delivered in an icy tone.

Ronnie didn't seem the least bit put off by Max's words nor tone. "Ah, that was just a little misunderstanding, and it was so long ago. Let's just let bygones be bygones. And It's Ron now." He stuck out his hand.

Max left the hand hanging in mid-air, and his eyelids lowered until they were slits. "Go. Away." It sounded more like a threat than a direction.

Some color was rising up into his cheeks as Ronnie slowly lowered his hand and turned toward Murph. Ronnie's brain raced as he tried quickly to come up with a way to save face. Unfortunately for him, he picked the wrong idea. "I meant what I told you, Murphy. I'm expecting introductions to that foundation's board or I'm going to pull my fleet out of here."

Murph smiled. "Yeah, well, if the phone doesn't ring, it's probably them. Let me know what time you're leaving; I'll meet you on the dock and toss you your mooring lines."

Ronnie froze for a second, not quite believing what he had heard, before turning on his heel and storming off. He headed for the packed bar, and a whole new audience that had yet to hear any of his usual bull.

I looked at Max, surprised. "You worked for that guy?"

He shook his head. "I went to work for his late wife, Caroline, who was a great person. She was a natural born angler, a lot like Mimi." He motioned over toward the bar where Mimi was working tonight. "But I try to make it a habit not to tell tales out of school."

I could see that there was a lot more to the story, and I wanted to hear it.

"But as a member of the MAFF board, if you have information that might be useful about someone that we are considering adding, don't you think that might take precedence? And since it is MAFF business, whatever you might tell the rest of us would just stay here." I winked as I picked up my drink.

Max looked shocked. "Please tell me that you aren't serious about involving him in MAFF!"

I shrugged. "What I know about him is that he has experience in similar organizations, and beyond having a really high opinion of himself, I don't know much more about his character. I need more information." I really didn't, but I needed to give Max enough cover so that he would feel comfortable while bending his own rule.

I could see that he was weighing his options. Finally, he smiled at me and returned to where he left off. "Right. Like I really believe that you would want him around. Okay, I'll tell this story if the rest of you will all agree to keep it just to yourselves."

We all nodded then he continued, "So, Caroline bought an old Bertram 25 Bahia Mar to try her hand at fishing without dumping a ton of money into doing it in case she decided it wasn't really her thing. I was in between boats at the time, so I picked up a few days with her, freelancing as a captain and a fishing mentor. That boat was small enough to fish with just the two of us, but big enough to handle most days off Palm Beach. I quickly saw how good she was, that she had a natural ability, and that we worked well together. She ended up hiring me full time soon after that. It was about fifteen years ago, and I was really just starting out.

Then Ronnie jumped into things, showing up to the dock when we came back in and sucking up to the owners of some of the bigger rigs. He snowed the owner of an older forty–foot Rybovich that was for sale, peppering him with all of his bull crap. The guy was headed over to Walkers Cay in the Bahamas the next day to meet some friends and invited Ronnie and Caroline to tag along in the Bertram. I was supposed to run the boat. I knew there was a front that was going to be coming through then, and I tried to talk her out of the trip. But Ronnie heard me and went ballistic. He said that if we didn't go, it would make us, meaning *him*, look bad around the docks, like we were a bunch of wimps. With Caroline now pleading with me to run the boat over so that Ronnie could save face, I finally gave in.

We met up with the Rybo at Lake Worth inlet early the next morning. The wind was out of the west, blowing about fifteen knots. I tried one more time to talk Caroline out of making the run, but Ronnie went nuts again. So, I tucked in behind the Rybovich as she hooked up. She had those huge and heavy old Ford Seamaster gas engines and was no racer by any stretch of the imagination. On any calm day our Bertram would blow right by her at cruise. But I throttled way back, staying a hundred yards off her stern in a three-foot following sea. Fifteen minutes later, as we were getting farther away from the protection of land, the wind had gone to twenty knots and the seas were now over six feet. Ronnie was leaning over the side, already losing his breakfast. Really, it wasn't that bad. Yet. Those little Bertrams can handle a sea nicely, and six-foot is nothing for them, especially down sea. But the morning was still young."

Max paused for a minute to take a long sip of his drink. Nobody else at the table said a word, waiting for him to continue.

"Finally, half an hour out of the inlet, the wind had increased to just shy of thirty knots. The seas were now over ten feet, fortunately spread out a bit. But the tops were blowing off of them, and while the prudent thing would have been to turn back earlier, that was no longer an option. We'd be heading right back into that mess and it was really questionable as to whether we could make it. We had no choice but to surf all the way to the flats, now almost fifty miles ahead of us. Ronnie was totally spent, lying on the deck getting thrown around after puking his guts out. Caroline had to wedge him back in the corner of the cockpit using their dive gear bags in order to keep him from getting hurt. I couldn't even leave the helm to help; I was working my butt off to keep us up with the Rybo.

The wind was still increasing, as were the seas. I don't even want to guess how big they were, but I can tell you this; I couldn't see the flybridge on that Rybo very much anymore. At times I could barely even see the buggy top on their tuna tower. I was now getting into the throttle more and more just to keep the waves from breaking into the cockpit and swamping us. Every time I had to go to wide-open throttle, our carburetors poured gas into the engines by the bucketful. In the middle of all this, I glanced over at Caroline and she was grinning, giving me a look that told me she had the utmost confidence in me and that I'd get us there safely. Something I had started to have my doubts about before that point, but she gave me confidence, too.

Usually, we made the crossing to the flats in two hours at our standard cruise. Slowing down to match that Rybo's speed even in a usual sea, it should have been three. It turned out to be five hours, and it was all I could do to keep up with the Rybo at that. As you guys all know, the Bahama Banks come up steeply right

144

before you hit the flats, and the waves were still large enough at that point to be breaking over Memory Rock as we passed by. But then we quickly went from over twelve–foot seas to a two–foot chop in less than a mile. I was exhausted, Caroline was happy, and Ronnie was still stuffed in the corner, completely soaked and unable to move or talk. It was the first and only time I've ever felt sorry for the guy.

We still had two more hours to go, but the Bertram didn't even feel that short chop. That's when I realized the guys on the Rybo's flybridge were all in foul weather gear. She had been digging her bow into the waves and taking spray over the bridge for most of the trip. The tower's buggy top was even covered in salt. I looked at Caroline and said, "Don't you even think about buying that Rybo." She looked over at me nodded and said, "We're going to need a bigger boat."

"She ended up buying a sixty–five–foot fiberglass production boat after that trip. But back to that crossing. Like I said, the next two hours might as well have been glass as far as the Bertram was concerned. It was smooth enough for Ronnie to recover somewhat and almost look like he hadn't been sick, at least until you looked closely at him. He came over and stood next to her seat and I told them both that the next time I said we aren't going somewhere, the boat either stays at the dock or I quit. Ronnie started to run his mouth, but Caroline stopped him and said, 'Agreed.' I meant it, too. If he had kept up his yammering, I'd have hopped the next flight back to the states, and she knew it. We fueled after clearing Customs at Walkers, and I ended up putting more gas in the boat than I ever had before, just three gallons shy of its stated capacity. So, we had been literally on fumes when we pulled in, on a day where we had no business being out there. I swore that was the last time I would ever let an owner override any safety concern I had. And it was."

Again, he sat back, taking a big draw of his drink. The rest of us sat there silent until I spoke up. "So, a guy who was on the board of one of the most prestigious fishing associations is prone to getting seasick?"

Max chuckled. "He can get sick just looking at a glass of water. He has to load up on prescription seasick pills before he leaves the dock. He's a total fraud, it's all just about phony prestige with him. I don't know why he doesn't find something else to do that doesn't involve water." Max looked at the rest of us again, obviously making up his mind about something. In the end, he decided to trust us to keep his confidence. "He was heavily involved with the design and construction of *Toolpusher*. That should tell you a lot about that boat. From the first minute it was launched there were problems with its stability, especially at anchor. Not a good thing for someone so prone to seasickness. By the time we got those things worked out, Caroline had already started to get sick. The trips that she had planned and dreamed of were all shelved, permanently. She went back to her home in Texas for treatment, but Ronnie came back and stayed on *Toolpusher* several times when she wasn't there."

I sensed there was more to that, too. I said, "I'm guessing he wasn't alone." It was more of a statement than a question.

Max picked up his drink without saying a word. But his silence spoke volumes. There are certain lines that professional crewmembers never cross and discussing the "indiscretions" of a previous boss was the biggest one. That is, if they ever want to get hired again. Max was a pro's pro, and he would keep silent on this even though it was obvious he completely despised Ronnie. It was also obvious that he had really liked working for Caroline, and that's why he had been willing to put up with Sandbags. I was guessing the incident with the girlfriend's son must have come shortly after Caroline's passing. Then again, maybe it had come even before. I wouldn't put anything past Ronnie, and I sure wasn't about to ask Max. But I knew he already would have had his eye on the door before he was fired.

I cleared my throat. "All those in favor of banning Sandbags from anything to do with MAFF and keeping this entire conversation confidential signify by saying 'Aye.' The motion passes, five to zip." I hadn't even waited for their replies.

"Just tell me that you weren't seriously considering adding him to MAFF." Max looked at me suspiciously.

"Heck no, but I love sea stories and I knew you'd never tell it without a little shove, and that story was a doozie." I caught Mimi's eye and circled my finger in the air, signifying another round for our table. I had a feeling that I'd be making that same motion on many more nights in the future as well. Between the five of us, there were a lot of stories yet to be told. Probably more than a few to be made together, as well.

*****

He knew that Murph, Lindsay, and Casey Shaw would probably all be fishing the Mallard Cove White Marlin Tournament at the end of next month. They would be there for the captains' meeting on the eve of the tournament. The timing would be perfect; their guard should be down, and there would be a lot of strangers around and loads of confusion. If everything came together he could grab them all at the same time, forcing them to cough up the location of the money. He thought, "Paybacks are a bitch."

Chapter 17

Max's two fishing boats arrived the next day, and we heard later that Ronnie had been bragging up at the bar about still having the largest boats in the marina. The guy was a total tool, but he was also paying the largest monthly dockage bill as well. So, Murph and Lindsay took the position of just ignoring him as much as possible, though I'm pretty sure that Murph's offer to help with his docklines if he left still stood.

Ronnie was quickly becoming a fixture at the bar in the afternoons, having decided that none of the directors of a group as well funded as MAFF would stoop so low as to associate with the Beer–Thirty–Bunch. As happy as we all were about not having him hang around us, the rest of the marina partners were just as happy with the business that Ronnie was now generating at the bar. He figured that the MAFF members probably used this as their watering hole, so he decided to cast a wide net in order to snag one or more of them. His plan centered around buying a lot of drinks, shaking a lot of hands, and telling a lot of his stories, most of which of course were total fiction. He succeeded in doing two things; the first was alienating a lot of the regulars that had their own boats or boating connections, and the second was that he created his own group of followers. Like the cobia that follow large stingrays, picking up food exposed by the disturbance in the sand from their large "wings," these suck–ups followed Ronnie for the free drinks, appetizers, and hopefully a shot at fishing with him in the white marlin tournament.

The even better by-product of Ronnie's efforts was the fact that he now unknowingly left most of the members of MAFF alone. He steered clear of Murph and Lindsay because of their earlier conflicts at Eagle Island, as well as here. He also avoided me because of my connection to Kari, and he was still upset with her for making him move over to his actual assigned slips. That, and the fact that she was only a junior partner in the marina complex made her not worth the time and effort to talk to, in his opinion. And he openly started mocking Max to his pals at the bar. While this really ticked me off, Max could have cared less, and he ignored this as much as he ignored Ronnie.

I guess that's another part of why I like Max, he's about as even-keeled as they come. And, I was excited to have gotten an invitation to go fishing with him tomorrow. As part of his deal with Stu, he had unlimited use of the fishing boats. The thing about professional fishing crews is that the good ones hate sitting around at the dock. As Stu's fishing coordinator, Max wanted the crew happy but also on the top of their game. The only way to accomplish that was through practice, meaning lots of fishing. These guys wanted to be ready when their new boss showed up, so they wanted to go hunt some tuna. And, so did I.

*****

Timmy and Sam had a farewell breakfast with his mother and then climbed aboard his boat for the first leg of their trip. Today's destination was Merritt Island, about halfway to Jacksonville, their first tournament stop. His mother's parting words as they cast off were that she would see them in a few weeks. As they idled out of the marina, Sam pondered the comment.

"What did your mom mean by that?"

Timmy asked, "What?"

"That she'd see us in a few weeks."

"You'll see." With that, he pushed the two throttle levers forward and the digital system took over, controlling all three engines as if they were one, their combined roar now drowning out casual conversation. The auto trim system also kicked in, positioning his engines for maximum speed and fuel economy. He had to pay a lot more than the insurance settlement for all this but upgrading to the latest in outboard engine and electronics technology was so well worth it. Two seventeen-inch touchscreens now replaced all of his bullet damaged electronics, making his console look more like something out of the cockpit in a jet. Looking at those screens, he saw that the digital system was suggesting a much lower throttle setting on the digital tachometers, but Timmy ignored it. He had paid a lot of money to be able to go fast, and he wasn't about to have some computer now tell him to slow down.

*****

The following day a little before six a.m. I boarded *Timeout*, Stuart Lieberman's 66-foot Viking, and Max's home for the season. Joey, the captain, had the engines already warming up as I stepped into the cabin. Max and Mimi were just cleaning up the galley after having finished breakfast. I didn't know if Mimi had just gotten there, or if she was just leaving. It turned out that since it was her day off she was coming with us, and she had indeed been an "overnight guest" of Max's. Like I mentioned before, these two have a lot of history.

"Good morning, gang! Looks like it's going to be a great day ahead." I said as I sat on one of the built-in barstools at the galley island's granite counter.

"Any day fishing is a great day, but you already know that, Marlin." Mimi was obviously eager and excited to go. Can't say that I blamed her; I felt the same way.

Max said, "It should be a great day, period. Joey is a born fisherman; I've known him since he was washing boats at the Marlin Club as a kid. He can smell tuna a mile away. And don't let Jeff's size fool you, he can wire and handle fish several times his size." This was high praise, coming from Max. Jeff, the mate, was somewhat short and slight, and looked like a tuna could pull him

150

over the side in a heartbeat. But looks can be deceiving. Like Max had said about Mimi, anticipating what a fish is going to do before it does is what makes for a hall of fame angler. The same goes for being a mate. I was looking forward to seeing both of them in action today.

I felt the boat go in gear, and I guess I looked surprised. When you are used to running your own boat, it felt kind of unnatural to still be down in the cabin when you were leaving the dock. Max smiled at me, knowing exactly what I was feeling. This was his first job where he wasn't the captain.

"It's hard to let go of the helm, Marlin. But Joey is one of the best. Outside of you and me, of course." Max smiled as he grabbed the countertop edge. We had cleared the slip, and Joey had put one gear in reverse while hitting the bow thruster to spin and aim us at the marina basin's inlet. The three of us were now subconsciously leaning into the turn. At the same time, Mimi poured three travel mugs of coffee without spilling a drop, handing one to each of us. This wasn't her first floating rodeo either. Then we all headed for the flybridge where Joey had his three, twenty-two-inch data touchscreens in the console up and running. Max stopped next to him, taking in all the data. In addition to the usual engine readouts as well as radar and a sidescan sonar/fish finder, one screen was also set up with a GPS plotter and real-time satellite water temperature overlay. Joey started explaining what he had already discovered.

"See out beyond the hundred-fathom line, that dark red is the gulf stream. I was thinking of running out to Norfolk Canyon at first but then I saw this." He pointed to a sharp color contrast only twenty miles out. "That's a six-degree temperature shear in a current eddy by this rise. Just a little too interesting to let pass by, and since it's so close we can go give it a shot. If it doesn't pan out, we can always run offshore to the canyons."

I nodded at Max; Joey was indeed good. A lot of people would have missed that little detail. A small current eddy like that can trap bait in it, attracting predators. In this case, I was hoping it would turn out to be a tuna magnet.

Jeff climbed up through the access hatch, "We've got company."

We all turned and saw green and red navigation lights about two hundred yards behind us. Jeff continued, "Pretty sure it's that Sanders guy in their center console. I was at the bar last night but left early, telling some new friends that we were fishing in the morning. I'm willing to bet that guy heard me; he looked like he was trying to listen to my conversation." Jeff then moved to each side of the bridge, lowering the aluminum outriggers into their fishing positions.

I commented, "Pretty choppy to be out in an outboard for someone who gets sick easily."

I could see Joey's smile from the muted light coming from the screens. "You say that guy gets sick easy? Well, if he wants to follow us, let's make him pay for it." With that, he advanced the throttles and made a hard turn away from the eddy, and directly into the five-foot seas.

If it was indeed Sanders' center console rig, *Roughneck*, the twenty-six-foot outboard would have a tough time keeping up with the Viking at this speed. They would be bouncing around badly while we had a nice smooth ride. Sure enough, the lights changed course to follow us, and they were now moving up and down erratically. Whoever was running the boat was pushing hard to stay up with us.

"Leading him away from that eddy?" I asked.

Joey shook his head. "No, we'll make our turn when we're abeam of it. But I wanted to shake 'em up a bit first. Then we'll slow down and ride in the trough the rest of the way at trolling speed. I want to time it so that we get there right after sunrise, and still give them a little time rolling around first."

Mimi laughed, "Joey, remind me to never get on your bad side!"

Joey grinned. We all knew that some of the biggest things that can bring on seasickness are motion in darkness and rolling in the trough, or beam sea. Putting both together would make things miserable for Sandbags. Thirty minutes later Joey altered course again, this time heading straight for the eddy. He throttled back, and once again the outboard matched our direction and speed. Even from this distance, we could see their navigation lights bounce and rock in the swells. Max smiled as he patted Joey on the shoulder.

Joey hit the cockpit floodlights as the four of us went down the bridge ladder, leaving him alone on the bridge. The large LED lights lit the cockpit like daylight and even spilled out a bit beyond the transom. Jeff had rigged several 50 and 80-pound rods. I also noted that he had stocked up on some of Spud's finest splittail mullet and horse ballyhoo, some of which were now sporting blue and white sea witch lures ahead of the baits on their leaders. We ran out all six lines, two on each outrigger and two flatlines off the stern, then Max, Mimi, and I settled in on the aft-facing padded bench seat on the cockpit mezzanine level.

"Max, why would Sanders follow us? I mean, he has all the right equipment and a professional crew, what does he need us for?" It made no sense to me.

Max sighed and paused before answering. "His reputation has gotten around, and I don't know a decent seasoned crew that will work for him. His crew are all young green kids. They don't have the experience that all of us have on this boat, and Ronnie knows that. He also knows we'll find the fish, and he doesn't have much of a clue himself. He'll probably follow some of the other boats too after the marina fills up for the season, but until then we're probably going to be stuck with him in the meantime."

I looked back beyond our wake, but the floodlights had now made it tough to see anything beyond the baits. I knew Sanders was no doubt still back there, and if Joey had the radar set on close range he could still "see" him. But those of us in the cockpit wouldn't begin to make him out until after sunrise, another ten minutes from now. At least we had a comfortable ride. He had no doubt opted to use his center console boat because there was no way his pig of a sportfish could keep up with our Viking.

For a production boat, Vikings are "the machine" when it comes to sportfishing platforms, and their prices reflect that. Sleek, fast, comfortable, and thanks to their width and built-in gyro, extremely stable. Those are the words most often heard used to describe their performance. Today's Vikings are a far cry from the ones they built forty years ago. The interior woodwork and finishes are as luxurious and similar to what you'd expect to find in a private jet, and the accommodations are as comfortable as anything else afloat. And Viking wasn't the least bit bashful about charging top dollar for it all.

As I mentioned before, the flybridge is well-appointed with its cutting-edge electronics, and there is also comfortable seating for the full crew and angling team up there. But the real nerve center of any sportfisherman is the fishing cockpit. Viking's attention to detail extends down here as well. Every edge or corner is radiused, because if you are going to take a spill on a boat in rough weather, chances are it will be in the open space of the cockpit. Landing on a sharp corner or edge could lead to a real medical emergency far from shore. The fishbox and livewell hatches as well as the storage lockers under the covering boards all have recessed hardware so as not to catch or tear any fishing line, clothing, or skin that's softened by extended salt water exposure. Viking has thought of pretty much everything, which is why they are a favorite among professional crews. Today, *Timeout* was a new favorite of mine, as she might as well have been a barge in this beam sea, she was that stable. While our coffees were in travel mugs, we wouldn't have spilled any even in regular open mugs.

As the sun peeked over the horizon, we now had visual confirmation that it had indeed been Ronnie who was shadowing us. We also could see that his outboard was rolling badly, just as Joey had planned. I sipped my coffee and smiled. I know, it's bad form to delight in another person's misery. So, sue me.

Joey leaned over the bridge rail, "Coming up on that eddy in two minutes. It's gotten longer, and the temps are holding steady. This should be good."

The three of us got up and took positions around the cockpit. Mimi took up station behind the fighting chair, ready to cover either side. The gunwale rod holders on each side were loaded up with two 50-pound rods on the outriggers, and an 80 on the flatline. I took the port, or "right" side. I know, it seems wrong to call the lines on the port, or left side of the boat the "right 'riggers" and "right flat," but remember, the captain, the mate and the anglers are all supposed to be looking back at the baits. So, to avoid confusion, many years ago someone named them this way and it stuck.

We hit the eddy long after Joey had killed the floodlights. However, the sun still wasn't high enough or at the right angle yet for Joey or any of us down in the cockpit to be able to see any fish coming up on the baits. But there was enough light for the tuna to see them, and a transom clip snapped right before one of the 80-pound reels started screaming. At the same time, one of my right 'rigger clips snapped, and one of my reels also started screaming. I grabbed the 50 and yelled for Mimi to get the flatline. Simultaneously, Max's two left 'rigger clips snapped, and we had two more fish on.

The 'rigger clips hold the line out away from the boat and also give a small amount of slack before the line comes tight, fooling the fish into thinking it killed the bait. Max grabbed one rod, as Jeff reeled in the other two rods that hadn't been hit. We were using circle hooks, so you don't "set the hook," you just keep even pressure on the line and the fish should get hooked in the corner of the mouth, every time. Joey kept us moving slowly forward, keeping tension on that fourth rod's line until Jeff could get over to it and start fighting the fish.

At that point, Joey was trying to figure out which direction each fish was headed, pivoting the stern as needed to help gain back some of the line that had been stripped from the reels. The good thing was no two fish were sticking that close together, which also meant that the lines shouldn't tangle and chafe each other causing a line to part and us to lose a fish. But it also meant that Joey had to watch all four lines closely, to make sure that none got under the boat. He had his hands full, too.

I had no doubt that these fish were in the tuna family; all were peeling off line as they sounded. That, and the fact they hit almost simultaneously told us that they were in a school, which is how tuna travel and hunt for food. Jeff, Max, and I were making gains on our fish, fighting while standing up using gimbal belts. These have built-in receivers for the rod butts protecting our, well, the more vulnerable parts of our anatomy. Mimi was in the fighting chair, the curved butt of the big rod seated in its gimbal, with a harness now clipped to her 80-pound reel. This allowed her to keep pressure on the fish while giving her arms a break. Max was right, she really is a talented angler. I could tell by how she was already finessing the fish; applying just the right amount of pressure to wear it out without losing it. And I could tell by the bend in the rod, this one was a real "hoss."

Both Max and Jeff's fish turned out to be keeper yellowfin tuna, each around fifty pounds. Jeff's came up first, with Max reluctantly putting his rod back in the holder just long enough to gaff the tuna and haul it over the side, dropping it into the refrigerated fishbox that was built in below the deck. His was next, with Jeff now on the gaff. That left Mimi and me still fighting our fish. Hers was showing no sign of tiring, and I was slowly starting to gain on mine. Twenty minutes later, I brought my hundred-twenty-pound bigeye tuna close enough for Max to get a shot at it with the harpoon. Big tuna can spook easily when they get close to the boat and before you can reach them with a gaff. At this most crucial point when you think they have "run out of steam" they can get a sudden burst of energy and break the line if you aren't both careful and aware. Getting a harpoon dart in them with a few hundred feet of heavy nylon line attached helps ensure that if this were to happen, you still have a good chance of retrieving and boating the fish.

I backed up, still holding the rod as Max manned the harpoon line and Jeff moved in with the long gaff, stroking the big hook into the tuna high on the shoulder. I backed the drag off so that we could pull more line as needed and then opened the transom door after raising the gunwale cover. I used a shorter gaff, hooking the tuna through the jaw, and with Max's help the three of us hauled it through the door and dropped it in the refrigerated fishbox.

Just as we were about to start congratulating each other, a string of expletives came flooding down from the flybridge.

"What the hell does that idiot think he's doing?" It was the first time that I'd heard Joey angry.

I looked out to see Ronnie on a course to pass by us with his baits only about thirty yards off our stern. Even if Mimi hadn't been fighting a fish, there was no excuse for this. I heard Joey on the radio, telling him to back off, as Jeff made a beeline for the tackle center. We had a speaker mounted under the cantilevered part of the flybridge deck that allowed us to listen in on Sanders' response. I knew it wasn't going to sit right with Joey, as Ronnie told him to just relax, he didn't own the ocean. I was right, Joey exploded over the radio, calling him a complete idiot with no business being out on the water.

What came next surprised me the most. So far, my impression of Jeff had been that he was extremely quiet and very mild mannered, almost to the point of being shy. That all changed when he raced back to the transom with a handful of large lead sinkers, launching one after the other at the outboard as it passed directly astern, scoring some direct hits. Sanders went nuts on the radio.

"Damn it, stop! I've got every right to be here the same as you, and your fish has sounded so I'm not interfering. The school is still here, and I still need a shot at getting a hookup...oww!"

Jeff had scored another hit, this time nailing Ronnie in the shoulder. Joey radioed Sanders, "If you are close enough for us to hit you with a sinker, then you're way too close you moron!"

Ronnie seemed to get the message and finally turned his boat away from ours. Yes, he had the right to be on the same ocean as us, but at a distance that not only kept his boat out of range of our fish, but also any fish that he might catch that could get tangled up in our line. That acceptable distance might vary a bit, depending on where you were on the east coast, but not by much. It sure as heck wasn't this close anywhere I'd ever fished.

Ronnie still wanted to get in the last shot in, "This isn't over!"

I could tell that Jeff felt the same way. If I were Ronnie, I'd tread lightly back at the dock. Some of the toughest guys I had met were short, quiet, and once their trigger was pulled, explosive. I had yet to see Jeff go off, but I had an idea that was coming in the not too distant future.

Through all this, Mimi had kept silent, totally focused on her fish. I was starting to understand why Max said he'd love to team up with her and fish together from now on. You know how so many times watching another angler fight a fish can be really boring? That's why those "reality" tuna fishing shows focus on fake interaction between the crews, the initial strike, and the fire drill as they try to subdue and land each fish. The fight part gets condensed down to a few minutes of video. Well, they didn't have Mimi. There was something about her and the way she fought this fish that was like watching a conductor direct an orchestra. But she also had a comfortable and confident intensity. Something I'd love to have, but I knew I never would. Don't get me wrong, I'm a decent "rod jockey" if I do say so myself, but what Mimi had was a quality that so very few anglers possessed, and those that did were born with it. This wasn't something that could be taught nor learned.

I watched as Max now used the chair back to swivel the fighting chair to keep her facing the fish. Despite the coolness of the morning, she was working up a sweat. Max took a towel and wiped the beads that were forming on her brow, keeping them from running down into her eyes. I saw the quick glance back and small smile of thanks she gave him, and I could tell this wasn't the first time he'd done that for her. But there were no words that passed between the two, and no verbal encouragement nor direction from Max. None were needed. He knew she had this, and nothing he could say would make the situation better. I knew I was watching something special as I took out my phone, snapping a few pictures as well as taking a few minutes of video in addition to the video from the camera mounted on the aft flybridge rail.

159

I was getting an idea for another article, and hopefully this fish would end up being bigger than mine, though there was little doubt of that. If it was another yellowfin or bigeye, it had to be seventy pounds or better to earn a state citation. With the way that 80-pound test had been screaming off her reel every time the fish made a run, I knew Mimi's was probably a lot bigger than my fish; a citation for sure. But first, we had to get it into the boat.

Forty minutes later Jeff announced, "We've got color!" This meant that he was getting his first glimpse of the fish, a flash of silver against the deep blue backdrop. But it was still down deep, enough that neither the swivel nor the leader was yet above the surface. It was, however, a milestone in the fight and a signal for the rest of us to get ready. Again, Max would be on the harpoon, Jeff would "wire" the fish, and I'd back them up with the long gaff. I also set out a tail rope. With the way this fish had been pulling, I had little doubt but that we would need it.

Jeff stared down into the water then turned and looked up at Joey. "She's huge. Might even be a bluefin."

Max and Mimi exchanged glances as the excitement over the confirmation of the size of the fish showed on their faces. I knew that despite using the harness, cranking on a fish this size for three-quarters of an hour was exhausting. And also exhilarating. Then Mimi got back into her focused zone. We all still had work to do.

Two minutes later, Jeff had the leader, and was taking wraps of it around his gloved hands. Max waited for the right moment and threw the harpoon. As he pulled on the dart's line, I stroked the fish with the gaff just ahead of the tail. Jeff was right, it was huge. The shaft of the gaff looked like a toothpick next to it. Even with the dart and the long gaff in it, the fish still had some fight left, and it was all I could do to hang onto the gaff handle. It was thrashing around, that powerful tail trying desperately to propel it away from the boat. I still don't know how he did it, but in the middle of that pandemonium, Jeff managed to get a tail rope on it, cinch the loop down and then that fish was ours. Mimi was now out of the chair, pulling on the tail rope with the three of us. Joey backed the boat quickly, forcing a little wave of water through the open transom door, which helped lift the tuna up to the cockpit deck. Once onboard, we all stood in stunned silence as we took in the size of the fish and realized that it wasn't a bluefin after all. It was another bigeye tuna; the largest one that any of us had ever seen. At 84 inches long with a 59-inch girth, we knew we might possibly have a new state record. The old record had stood for over a decade at 311 pounds. We wrestled it into the vacant second refrigerated fishbox, where it just barely fit. Joey had come down from the bridge to help, and Max looked over at him.

"Home, Jeeves, and don't spare the horsepower! Refrigerated or not, that fish is dehydrating and losing weight. I'd hate to lose a record by an ounce or two."

Joey grinned. "Aye, aye, commodore! I'll get us there in a jiffy!" He turned and shot up the ladder.

I looked at Max and chuckled. "Commodore?"

"Hey, he can call me whatever he wants, so long as he gets us back before this fish dries out."

Chapter 18

I called Kari on our way back in, so there was a local news crew and a few photographers waiting as we pulled into the scale dock. She doesn't miss a trick when it comes to promoting the marina, and if this was indeed a new record at the beginning of the season, it would be a huge PR coup. She, Murph, and Lindsay were among the growing group on the dock. Kari made sure that the word spread quickly throughout the fishing community on ESVA.

Barry the dockmaster swung the scale's boom over the cockpit as we opened the hatch on the fishbox. There was an audible murmur among the crowd. We attached the scale's tail rope to the fish, and hoisted it up, then swung it over the dock. After letting the scale settle down, the digital readout read 322 pounds, 8 ounces, breaking the old record by eleven pounds. It still had to be certified, but it was without a doubt a new Virginia state record.

Mimi let out a "whoop," then hugged Max followed by the rest of us on the crew. Barry filled out a four-foot–high chalkboard with the Mallard Cove logo at the top that had species, weight, angler, boat and date categories permanently painted on it. Next to the weight he added an asterisk and put "New State Record" underneath. By nightfall, a framed picture of all of us standing next to the fish and behind the chalkboard would be hanging on the wall in the *Cove Restaurant's* bar. One with just Mimi and her fish went up in the outside *Cove Beach Bar,* which was now packed on the weekends. Right next to it went another picture, this one of me with my citation weight bigeye tuna. This wall was now reserved for photos of citation sized fish caught on boats out of *Mallard Cove Marina.* Like I said, Kari doesn't miss a trick.

Ronnie and crew came back late in the afternoon with several smaller tuna; nothing even approaching the citation threshold. I wasn't there to see it, but Barry said that he went nuts when someone on the dock told him about Mimi's new record. He and his two-man crew came charging into the bar where Mimi, Max, Joey, Jeff and I were eating over on the bar side in the *Cove* after dealing with the last of the photographers and reporters. Murph, Lindsay, and Kari were over by what would become the gallery wall, hanging a large flat screen TV in the middle.

"Nice try with this state record crap." Ronnie wore a smug grin as he stared at Max and Mimi.

"Read it and weep, Ronnie. Beats the old record by eleven pounds." Max said it in a dismissive tone.

Ronnie shook his head, the grin getting wider as his voice got louder, enough volume to ensure everyone in the room would hear what he said. "It would if you had never touched that rod. But I saw you pick it up and set the hook then hand it off to her. It's not a legal record unless the angler is the only person to touch the rod. So, you're a liar and a fraud, and so is your record." He made air quotes with his fingers as he said the word record, then crossed his arms looking really satisfied with himself. No doubt in part because everything in the room had stopped, and every patron was now staring from him to Max.

Jeff started to get up to head over to Sanders, but Max forcefully put a hand on his shoulder, keeping him in his chair. Max replied, "Nice try there, Ronnie. But there are a few things wrong with your story. No, make that *everything* is wrong with your story. As usual, and like all the rest of your tales, it's a total fabrication. First, I never touched that rod; Mimi had it from strike to landing. Second, we only use circle hooks on our boat, to cut down on the mortality rate of the fish we release. If I had 'set the hook' like you claimed, I'd have yanked it right out of that fish's mouth; they hook themselves when you keep a nice steady tension on them. Third, there's no way that you could have even seen into our cockpit because we kept you rolling in the trough for half an hour, so I know you were too busy puking your guts out to be worried about what we were doing."

One of his two crewmen started to chuckle, earning him an icy stare from Ronnie, who by now was starting to lose some of his smugness.

Max looked at the same crewman, "It may seem funny now, but you see what he's trying to pull. It's not so funny when he blames you and tries to ruin your name around the docks like he keeps trying to do with mine. Trust me, your day is coming, and there's a bus ahead with your name on the bumper that he'll throw you under when it suits him. This is about your livelihood, too. You want to be very careful about signing onto his lies, for the sake of your own reputation." Max looked back and forth between the two crewmen. "Because now everyone in this room is waiting to see if you're going to back up what your boss is saying. There's no room in fishing for cheating, and lying about another angler is even worse. Once that happens, no one will ever believe anything you say in any tournament or about any record you ever set, and the word will get out of this room really fast. So, you need to think long and hard about saying something right now that you'll end up regretting for the rest of your lives."

Both young men stayed silent, obviously uncomfortable. Ronnie exploded, "Well, speak up! You saw what I saw, right?"

Max said, "Before you answer that, you should know that we had the cockpit video camera running the whole time." He looked over at Kari, who nodded and pressed a button on the remote control she was holding. Suddenly the view from the flybridge of the *Timeout* started playing on the new screen up on the wall. A little over a minute into it we were all scrambling for our rods, and it was clear that Mimi had handled her rod by herself from the start and without anyone else so much as being near her.

"That could've been taken on another day!" Ronnie Sanders was now scrambling as all eyes in the room were on the screen.

Kari spoke up. "Could have been but it wasn't. We will edit it down a bit as we add more clips of other fish to the loop, but right now it runs completely from hook up to landing. Oh, and it has a clear view of that stunt you pulled, getting so close to them while they were hooked up. They should probably thank you for the verification. The video captured the audio from the VHF as well. By the way, nice arm, Jeff!"

Jeff seemed to have calmed down a bit now that Ronnie was clearly on the ropes. I did feel bad for Ronnie's crew; they were young and inexperienced, and they were just standing behind their boss, literally. Neither one had actually said a word, it was all Ronnie up to that point. From the looks on the faces at the bar, he was going to be the subject of a lot of conversations here tonight. The same thought seemed to hit him at the same time.

"Well, that video's a damn fake, and so's your record." Ronnie was nothing if not consistent.

Jeff looked pleadingly over at Max, who shrugged. With that approval, Jeff was up and charging Ronnie at full throttle. Ronnie grabbed the nearest one of his crew and shoved him into Jeff, who was now being backed up by Joey and me. Yes, me. I can only take so much of my friends and me being wrongfully accused. Ronnie's guys put their open hands out in front of them showing that they weren't up for a fight, as Ronnie bolted out through the front door.

I knew what was up next; the "ESVA Telegraph" was going to be in full swing, starting in the next few seconds with some texts from several of the bar patrons.

165

A few had even videoed the confrontation with their phones when they saw it start, it would be up on social media sites in minutes. I also knew that no matter what, Ronnie's bunch of mooching hangers–on would at least pretend to take his side, and the rest of the patrons in the future who watched this video and the ones that were here in the bar today wouldn't.

*****

TW walked into his Probation Officer's office, only slightly surprised to find the lead investigator from his case in there as well.

"Detective Raymond, what a surprise. I didn't know that you and Parole Officer Dodson knew each other." TW sounded almost sincere, as he tried his best to hide his distaste for the detective.

"Siddown, Wilton. Hand me your cell phone but unlock it first." It was obvious that Raymond didn't like even being in the same room as Wilton.

TW complied, smiling as he handed it over. "If you can tell me what this is all about, maybe I can help."

"What name do you have your son's number listed under in your contacts?"

TW first looked over questioningly at his PO who just stared at him, then turned to Raymond. "Told you I could help. I don't have Timmy's number. In fact, I don't know where he is, nor how to reach him. If you check the records you'll see that neither he nor his mother ever visited or called me while I was 'in' and they haven't now that I'm 'out,' either. She's moved on, and he apparently doesn't want anyone to know about me. Why do you ask?"

He ignored TW's question and changed subjects. "I heard that you recently came into a large sum of money."

TW replied, "More like a little bit of property. That doesn't necessarily mean money, especially in the

Bahamas. Converting real estate over there into cash can be tough. At least until the next American with a crazy dream of owning a bit of paradise and who has a boatload of money to lose comes along. Meanwhile I'll keep having to depend on my two marina managers that are robbing me blind. At least until I finish my probation, get this off, and get a new passport." He put his foot with the ankle GPS attached up on Dodson's desk.

"Get your damn foot off my desk, Wilton!" Dodson had finally spoken after silently deferring this whole time to Raymond.

TW smiled, and slowly returned his foot to the floor. "I know that it must be infuriating, me coming out of prison totally broke, and now ending up with enough assets to make a fresh, new start. With an income stream that you can't touch because I obtained it legally, long after my conviction. Like I've been telling you for fifteen years, Raymond, there's no other money."

"That's *Detective* Raymond to you, convict. And don't count on it being beyond my reach. See, Billy Thompson had dual citizenship, and that means he was still subject to US law. And we can't figure out where the funds to buy those places originated, nor why he would name you his largest beneficiary. But then it all started making sense when I got a call from Freeport Police. They're looking at your son for the murder."

TW was suddenly shaken. "That's insane! Timmy didn't even know Billy!"

Raymond saw that he had struck a nerve and loved drilling in on it. "And how would you know that? You said yourself that you haven't been in contact with him for fifteen years, how could you know who he might or might not be acquainted with? And why *did* Thompson name you his biggest beneficiary?"

TW leaned back, composing himself. "As his lawyer will tell you, he had no family. I guess the two closest people to him were me and Casey Shaw. We both

167

fished with him quite a bit. And I'll tell you where his money came from. It was my Northwood Hills subdivision and a dozen others just like it. He screwed me on every construction job and land deal. Of course, I didn't find that out until the IRS gave me a financial forensic colonoscopy over it.

And, while his overcharging me wasn't illegal, it should have been. If he was screwing all his other customers like he was me, *that's* where he got his money. Kind of ironic, don't you think? My own money coming back to me. Maybe in the end he felt guilty." TW smiled at Raymond, who knew it was all bull crap, but he couldn't prove it.

"Oh, and I'd love to see you try to seize my legally gotten properties over in a sovereign nation. Nothing like a good international incident for the headlines. As it is, I might already have a lawsuit against you, at least I'm assuming it was you, Raymond, that told my managers over there that I was prohibited from any international travel until after my parole period is up. That just opened the door for them to rip me off even worse. For all I know, they're leasing out Billy's house now and keeping the rent themselves. All because of you!" TW didn't have a clue about whether it was illegal or not, but he wanted to get Raymond to back off. Since he hadn't even corrected him about that detective part again, he figured it might just be working. That thought was reinforced when Raymond got up and left the room without saying another word.

*****

Ronnie ran his outboard over to Glenn Cetta's Lynnhaven Marina to look into it as a possible new base of operations for this season. After his dust up with Max went so badly, he didn't want to stay at Mallard Cove any longer than necessary. He hadn't really been sure if the hookup had been legit, so he figured it was worth

168

taking a poke at it. Originally his plan had been to discredit Max, who he saw as having been diverting attention away from him. And the MAFF board would surely have known about a record like that tuna in their own backyard caught by Max's crew. But if Ron could have discredited the catch and the crew, he would have been seen as someone who was upholding the highest standards and defending the integrity of the angling community. That should have gotten him even more attention, but instead, he was now having to do damage control. His new plan was to move his boats and keep a lower profile until this whole thing blows over. Then he could fish the Mallard Cove tournament, hopefully still meeting and impressing the MAFF representative. He wanted to see if he couldn't get an introduction to their board through him or her at some point during the tournament cocktail parties. Though that might be doubtful now if they heard about Ronnie's confrontation with Max. But it had been his only shot, and he had to take it.

After clearing Fisherman Inlet bridge, he set a course for Lynnhaven inlet across the mouth of the Chesapeake. Once past the Lessner bridge that spanned Lynnhaven inlet, he bore left into Long Creek and toward the Great Neck Road bridges. Just beyond those spans was his destination. As he pulled up, Ronnie was impressed with what he saw of the facility, although for some reason it looked pretty empty for the start of the season. He tied up to a floating dock in front of the office where two men stood outside talking. One was in what passed for marina a work uniform, so it chapped Ronnie's butt that the guy hadn't even quit talking long enough to help him tie up.

*****

All the way over to his Lynnhaven property Glenn Cetta had been thinking of angles to marketing the marina. Not to rent slips, but to sell the whole thing. For a couple of years, he had been trying to buy the huge piece of undeveloped waterfront parcel next door, but the owner kept jerking him around. The two of them clearly were as incompatible as oil and water. Then this marina had come on the market, and he quickly snatched it up, intending to eventually merge it into the property next door. He had paid dearly for the place, knowing that when he could add it into the adjoining piece, it would be worth every penny of what he paid and more.

Then, the worst possible thing happened. The M&S partners group had snatched the vacant property out from under him, just as they had done with Mallard Cove last year. Then he heard through a friend at city hall that they had a plan for a huge marina complex with condos, restaurants, and shopping. It also included more than ten times the number of slips that Cetta had next door. His friend told him that they already had enough votes on the planning board and city commission to get it passed.

This wouldn't be announced publicly and come up for that vote for a few more weeks, so Cetta knew he had to move fast if he was going to be able to unload his marina and still come out with his skin. Slip rent rates are dependent on supply and demand and he had misjudged after he bought the place, raising rents too far and too fast. He had lost a lot of business because of it, though he knew he'd pick it back up over time. At least he thought he would, until he heard about what M&S was doing. God, how he really hated that Murphy guy and his girlfriend. Once they build a larger marina next door with all those other amenities that his renters wouldn't have access to, he knew he could kiss even the original slip rent rates goodbye. So, he had come to Lynnhaven to tell his dockmaster, Brian, that he was free to negotiate lower rates as he saw fit if he locked people into long term leases. Better to get slightly lower

170

rent from a full marina than higher rates from one that was half empty. He needed to be able to show good cash flow to potential buyers.

*****

Ronnie walked up the ramp from the floating dock and addressed the guy with the uniform, not caring that he was already talking to Cetta. "Hey, are you the dockmaster? I need to talk to someone about renting some slips. I've got a hundred and sixty–footer, a seventy–five–footer and this outboard."

Cetta smiled. This would be perfect. The center console the guy came in on was a nice high end one, and if that was any indication then the other boats stood a chance of being head turners. This was exactly what he needed. He put on his best salesman's smile.

"Hi there I'm Glenn Cetta, the owner. This is Brian, our dockmaster." He motioned toward the guy in the uniform then stuck out his hand, which Sanders shook.

Ronnie puffed out his chest. He and Cetta were the same height, so he wanted to assert himself rather than let him think they were equals. "Ron Sanders. I noticed that you have the tee at the end of the center dock open, Cetta, and I think *Toolpusher* would look good right there." He said it in a way that implied that surely Cetta should know of his mothership.

Cetta gave him his best but totally fake impressed look. "*Toolpusher!* Yes, I think she'd look great out there, Ron. Of course, that is our most premier slip. But with as many boats as you have, I think we can work out a great deal for you. Why don't we go sit down in the office, have some coffee and talk it over." Of course, Cetta had never heard of *Toolpusher* before, but he had known dumb, egocentric guys like Ron Sanders his whole life. He had made a lot of money off of them because he knew exactly which buttons to push. This was going to be fun.

*****

On the ride back to Mallard Cove, Ronnie was grinning widely. He and Cetta had gotten along great, like a couple of old friends. Cetta had let it slip to him that he owned a string of marinas in the northern part of the Chesapeake, and he had his eye on a couple more up closer to where he lived. But first, he had to sell this one in Lynnhaven. Ronnie had cautiously asked him what his asking price was and was shocked that it was so high. But after he heard how much he wanted for his three slips, it seemed reasonable.

Ronnie hadn't actually ever owned a business himself; Caroline's income from her family business had always paid the bills, and before that he always worked for someone else, drawing a set salary. But the marina business looked so simple, and this would dovetail nicely into what he wanted to do. He would name the place *Sanders Lynnhaven Marina,* and *Toolpusher* would be out front and center, the focal point that would help draw other boats in. Then the first thing he'd do is announce his own high dollar white marlin tournament with a bounty for the biggest one brought in to the dock. The MAFF group wouldn't want that to happen, so they'd no doubt come to him with a proposal to make it a no-kill, all-release, tournament. And that's when they would find out the price for that was a board seat.

Chapter 19

Barry called Kari after Ronnie had returned, telling him he was taking his boats out of Mallard Cove immediately. Kari was having lunch at the *Cove* with Lindsay and Murph, so she passed the news along.

"Good riddance. Sorry to lose the income, but not the headache." Murph looked relieved.

Lindsay said, "After what that guy tried to pull, I don't want him anywhere near here. Good riddance is right."

*****

Ronnie stood at the railing on the deck in front of the bridge of *Toolpusher*, his huge smile back in place. All three boats were motoring along in a line across the mouth of the Chesapeake. The more he thought about it, the more he liked the idea of the name *Sanders Lynnhaven Marina*. He couldn't wait to get the deal finalized, and the tournament announced. He decided to call Marguerite and tell her about the location change, and about his acquisition. He liked the sound of that, *his acquisition*. Maybe there would be more of these in the future.

He had called his money manager to alert him to the amount of the funds he was going to need to close the all–cash deal. The guy then had the nerve to suggest that Ronnie slow down and take another look at the property, the numbers, and get a real estate expert involved. He obviously didn't have the natural instinct for spotting a good deal like Ronnie knew that he did. And Ronnie had been fortunate enough to catch this deal before it got listed with a broker, which would have only added to the price. His money manager might be good at picking stocks on the Dow and NASDAQ, but the guy had never bought a private company, so what did he know anyhow? Ronnie had been telling people that he was an investment genius for so long now that he had convinced himself that he really was.

"Hey, Marguerite, slight change of plans. We're moving the boats over to Virginia Beach, to my new marina."

"Well, that's fine, so long as there's good shopping nearby. Wait, did you say *your* marina, dear?"

"I made a deal for it this morning."

"Ron, what do you know about running a marina?"

"I didn't say I was going to *run* it, just that I'm going to *own* it. There's a dockmaster that will stay on, and he'll run it." Ron was irritated that she would even question his ability to operate a business, but it seemed lately that she was questioning more and more of what he did, and it was getting tiring.

Marguerite sensed that he was getting cross and wanted to quickly get off the subject. "Well, that's good dear. I'll be up there tomorrow, so please have our captain send a crewman to pick me up from our plane. Oh, and I have some great news. Timmy and his girlfriend will be joining us for a while; they have been fishing some tournaments in his boat on the way up. He has some business deal with some people up at that tournament you are in and I told him that you would simply love for him to fish it with you."

Ronnie rolled his eyes at the thought. Timmy Wilton was, in his opinion, an overaged juvenile delinquent in an adult's body. He and his actions had been at the center of many of the disagreements that had arisen lately between Ronnie and Marguerite. The old saying about not just marrying the woman but her family too had begun haunting him. Nevertheless, he answered with, "Great. Looking forward to it." No sense starting off with an argument before she even arrived.

*****

"Hey, bunkie, I need you to swap out some jewelry for me again."

Charlie Bates knew what the phrase meant, since he had done it for his friend before. "For how long this time? You know I'm sticking my neck out just being anywhere near you."

"I know that Charlie. I wouldn't ask if it weren't important. Maybe a week or a little more. Trust me, I'll make it worth your time."

Charlie knew he was good for it, but electronic deception such as this could get him charged with conspiracy, too.

"Alright, meet me in the back room of Savoia restaurant in an hour."

*****

Sam listened to Timmy's side of his conversation with his mom as they were idling out from Eagle Island, headed for Hatteras. So far for her, the trip had been a bust. They hadn't even placed in the top ten of any tournaments, and Timmy had kept her from siding up to any of the guys she had seen or met at them. His mood had soured continually as their streak of bad fishing luck continued. It wasn't her fault that he wasn't a big fisherman. She had had to do most of the work, rigging the baits and handling the rods. Timmy's end was to find the fish, and the only time they had any luck was when they followed someone else.

So, Sam had resigned herself to putting up with Timmy until they could recover his money and she could get the ten grand he promised her. But she began to worry more and more that he might not be content to let her take off after that. In fact, she wasn't that certain now she'd ever even see the cash. She looked over at him as he ended the call. There was a slight smile on his face.

"Good news?" She asked.

"Yeah. What my mom meant about seeing us soon when we left Palm Beach was because we're gonna stay for a while on her boyfriend's yacht up in Virginia. It was gonna be at a marina that's owned by the buttheads that took my money, but now her boyfriend bought a marina real near there. I'm gonna fish that big tournament with him on his sportfish and with his crew, so we'll have a real good shot at winning it and the prize money. Plus, I'll be able to keep outta sight until we can move on them to get my money back. This'll work out good for us."

She nodded almost unconsciously at him as she sorted through all this new information. Marguerite had mentioned her boyfriend was loaded, but a yacht, a sportfisherman, and a marina? One thing about guys with money was they usually hung out with other guys with money. She might be about to hit a target-rich environment where Timmy would be comfortable enough around his family to let his guard down. She might just get her shot at getting out after all.

*****

Rather than feeling like he was running away, instead Ronnie felt like a conquering hero, riding up Long Creek on *Toolpusher*. He smiled from his vantage point on the deck rail in front of the bridge. A few smaller boats were forced to move aside in the narrow channel leading under the bridges while she passed through. He watched as his crew pulled *Toolpusher* up to her new slip at the end of the dock tee of what would soon be his marina. This time Ronnie saw that Brian hustled out to catch *Toolpusher*'s lines, as well as those of *Gusher* and *Roughneck* as they both took their places in the slips adjacent to their mothership. Now the place looked much more full, and he saw that *Toolpusher* was already drawing a lot of looks from passing boats. Mostly because of her size, but several were because of

176

how ungainly and awkward she looked, though he never suspected that part of it.

Cetta walked down the dock and spotted Ronnie at the rail. He called up to him, "Wow, she certainly is big, Ron. Fills out the tee nicely." In reality, he thought she looked like an ugly research vessel, but he really wanted to close this deal and wasn't about to insult the man.

"Come on aboard, Glenn, I'll give you the nickel tour."

Fifteen minutes later the two sat in the large salon, each having a beer. It was "classic" Ron at his puffed–out chest best, holding court.

"Yes, this marina will fit perfectly into my portfolio, Glenn. How soon before we can close on the deal?"

Cetta had to fight the urge to roll his eyes upon hearing Ronnie brag about his portfolio. "I'm ready on this end. I've already spoken with my attorney; we'll just need yours to get in touch with him then we can pick a date."

"Uh, I haven't had a chance to look for one up here yet." Sanders looked concerned, like this might be a big hurdle.

"No problem, Ron, my guy has a big firm, so you can use one of his associates. It'll be faster that way, handling everything 'in house,' and that way they'll already be up to speed, being familiar with the property details. You'll like these guys, they're sharp and their fees are reasonable." What Cetta didn't add was that he had been doing business with the founding partner of that firm for years, and he was a good friend as well as a client. He'd make sure that they picked a young associate to represent Ronnie; one that wouldn't want to rock the boat. Ronnie hadn't done any due diligence, so he hadn't yet discovered what was going to happen next door. Cetta wanted to get this deal closed before that had a chance of happening. "We'll get it closed ASAP."

"Great! I'm going to go ahead and order the new sign. I want it up as soon as we close."

Marguerite's arrival the next day hadn't been the happy experience Ronnie had hoped for. For starters, it had stuck in his craw yesterday about her telling him to have "our captain" send a crewmember to pick her up at "our plane". Last time he checked, the boats and the airplane were still only in his name; he wasn't a damn travel agent, and the airport was only five minutes away by cab or Uber. But what was really irking him was the fact she just announced that Timmy and one of his sluts were coming to stay aboard. No request, discussion, or conversation over the subject, just an announcement that he was supposed to accept without question.

The final straw was the matter of the Black Amex Card she had talked him out of during a weak moment last month. It was only supposed to be used "for emergencies" she told him. When they first started dating, or rather, sneaking around, Marguerite had seemed to have plenty of money of her own. But his accountant had called him early this morning to confirm that the almost seventy thousand dollars' worth of charges from restaurants and shops on Worth Avenue over the past month were actually legitimate. Ronnie had hit the ceiling. If she would run up this high of a bill as his fiancée, how bad was it going to get after they were married? It wasn't that he couldn't afford it, he certainly could, but it wasn't what he had agreed to. He knew he had to put a stop to this before it got worse.

Ronnie's anger over the Amex bill had given him the courage he had lacked before to bring out the prenuptial agreement that he ordered drawn up several months ago. He had kept a copy in his onboard office desk, waiting for the right time to discuss it with her. It had turned out that this hadn't been it. Marguerite's anger over the document even exceeded his over the

178

credit card bill. Of course, it hadn't helped that he had tossed it on the table like an ultimatum. Her response had been to storm out and find the most expensive jewelry shop around, putting another fifteen thousand on the Amex card. Unfortunately for her, after this morning's phone conversation, Ronnie's accountant had set an alert limit on the card notifying him by text any time more than two thousand dollars got charged to it in a day. He called Ronnie right away.

Marguerite's text tone sounded, and she saw it was from Ronnie. "Stop, or I'll have it cut off." It upset and embarrassed her enough to prompt this reply, "I can cut you off, too." Instantly she regretted it after pushing the "Send" button. He didn't realize it, but at this point, she needed Ronnie more than he needed her. The money that she had taken from TW's account was almost gone. It had been used to prop up the expensive lifestyle facade she needed to project until she could finally "land" Ronnie at the altar. Unfortunately for her, he was more content to just stay engaged. He had been immune to her repeated suggestions about setting a wedding date, saying it was just too close to his wife's death. But once she had talked him out of the credit card, this had taken off some of the financial pressure. She figured that he wouldn't notice or wouldn't care if she used it in what she thought of as a limited way. But she had misjudged her position, and now he had brought a prenup into the picture. She hadn't even stopped to read the terms, because the best scenario for her of course, was not to have one at all. That ship seemed to have sailed, at least for now. But she was going to figure out a way to get this turned around and shred that document before she got him to marry her.

Back at the marina, Ronnie wanted to get away from everything, everyone, and even from *Toolpusher* before Marguerite returned. He went over to *Gusher* and told the crew to get ready to cast off, they were going for a ride. That caught both crewmen off guard as their boss never went out just for joyrides on *Gusher*. It further surprised them when he took the wheel right after they left the dock. They sat with him in silence up on the flying bridge, a little anxious about the weird change in the way he had been acting lately. From trying to scuttle Mimi's tuna record to impulsively buying a marina and moving the boats, now he was joy riding at the helm. Not that there was much they could do about it but keep an eye on him.

After they cleared the Lessner bridge, Ronnie shoved the throttles to the pegs as *Gusher* crept up to full speed, throwing a huge wake from the heavy boat on the nearly calm surface of the Chesapeake Bay. Ronnie was thankful that the bay was so smooth, allowing him to work out his frustrations without becoming nauseous and needing to return to the dock.

He had almost forgotten how much fun running his own boat on a calm day could be. He hadn't done it much since they sold the little Bertram. Max had run their boats after that since Ronnie wasn't really skillful enough to be able to dock anything much larger, at least in any kind of wind or current.

That damned Max. Just the thought of him and what happened the other day was infuriating. He started turning *Gusher*'s wheel back and forth creating a serpentine course, trying to concentrate on the feel of the boat in order to get his mind off both Max and Marguerite.

Up ahead Ronnie saw a midsized sportfisherman trolling, probably trying to pick up some early season bluefish. As he drew in closer he saw the hull was painted yellow, and the design looked familiar. He realized it was the *Golden Dolphin*, the boat that belonged to that smartass Bill Cooper from Mallard Cove who had nicknamed him Sandbags. Ronnie had even overheard some of his new "friends" starting to use that to refer to him when they thought he was out of earshot. He smiled grimly as he thought, *paybacks are such a bitch.*

"Boys, if I were you, I'd hang on," Ronnie told his crew, raising their anxiety level even higher. The boss just went from acting weird to a "full-on-crazy" alert. They knew he liked getting in close to other boats when they were trolling, but this was way different and much more dangerous at this higher speed.

Onboard the *Golden Dolphin*, Baloney was concentrating on watching his baits and the fishfinder's screen up on the flybridge. He didn't see the big sportfish rapidly approaching off his port beam until it was almost upon them. His reaction time was slow, and he wasn't able to get her turned far enough to starboard before the other boat was almost on them. He yelled down to B2 and his charter clients, telling them all to hang on.

Ronnie turned at the last minute, so close that he narrowly avoiding hitting Baloney's outriggers with his own. Right before he turned, he slowed Gusher until it was making its largest possible wake, over five feet high. The first part of his wake hit the *Golden Dolphin* broadside, rocking her hard to starboard before she rolled violently back as she "fell" into the trough before the second and most violent part of *Gusher's* wake hit her.

Baloney's lit cigar fell out of his mouth as he yelled obscenities at the top of his lungs at the lunatic that almost hit them. Then he recognized both the boat as well as the person at the helm, which only made him even angrier. He picked up the mic from his VHF radio and screamed, "Sandbags, you sonofabitch, are you crazy? You could have killed us!"

On the flying bridge of *Gusher*, Ronnie laughed as he picked up and keyed the mic, "Well, *Mister Chairman,* you don't own the whole bay you know."

"Yeah well, you try a stunt like that again around me and I'll own your ass, you idiot!" Baloney was even more livid now after Ronnie's snotty reply. Suddenly a scream erupted from the cockpit. Looking down, Baloney saw B2 frantically pulling his shirttail out of his shorts. Apparently, Baloney's fallen cigar, in a million to one shot, had gone over the edge of flybridge deck and down inside the neck of B2's shirt. He watched as Bobby pulled the hot cigar out from inside his shirttail, burning his fingers in the process and tossing it away from him. Baloney was horrified as he watched one of the good cigars Max had given him clear the gunwale and land in the Chesapeake. He was now even more determined to get even with Sandbags.

Back aboard *Gusher*, Ronnie's mood had lightened considerably. *Nothing like a little payback to lift the ol' spirits*, he thought as he smiled wide. His crew even relaxed a bit after he turned and headed north, literally leaving the *Golden Dolphin* in their wake. He set a course for Cape Charles, an hour and a half away. They'd grab lunch and he might even have a few martinis before letting the crew run the boat on the way back. He'd then have to deal with Marguerite back at the dock. Not something that he was looking forward to.

Chapter 20

Kari and I were sitting across from Murph and Lindsay, all of us listening to Baloney rail.

"That sonofabitch almost took off my outrigger!" Even though it was hours later, Baloney was still hot over his run-in with Ronnie. And this wasn't his opening statement to all of us in the Beer–Thirty–Bunch, he had already repeated it three times, in between various other rants about Ronnie. He wasn't showing signs of cooling down anytime soon, even with long draws from the second Bahamian Kalik beer that I had given him.

Spuds had just walked in and was lucky enough to have only heard the story once. But he had news that was going to add fuel to the Beer–Thirty fire. "That ain't all. I just heard from Brian over at Cetta's Lynnhaven place where Sandbags moved to, he just bought it."

"What, did he run up on one of the tunnel islands like Hard Rock?" Baloney looked hopeful as Hard Rock scowled at him.

Spuds shook his head, "Nah, I mean he's buying that marina. The one that's right in front of what you're building over there, Kari, the one where Shaker used to live. Deal closes tomorrow."

This was news to everyone in the room, including me, Kari, Murph, and Lindsay. It was just dawning on the three of them that they were now going to be Ronnie's neighbors with their new Lynnhaven project, and they weren't happy about it.

"Just when I thought we had gotten rid of that guy. But how the heck can he be closing on that place so fast? It would take weeks to get the loan approvals, documents, surveying, and title insurance all done and ready for a closing." Kari was bewildered.

"Brian overheard them, it's an all-cash deal. He said that Cetta's really taking this guy to the cleaners and ramrodding the closing." Spuds smiled, happy about this part. Everyone in the room was eager to see

183

Ronnie "get his," me included, because I hated how he had stressed out Kari. Now it looked like he might be doing it again. I saw she was biting her lower lip, deep in thought. I knew to leave her alone when this happened. Then slowly a thin smile formed on her lips. I gave her a quizzical look and she said, "Tell you later." Lindsay had seen the same thing I had and knew whatever it was wouldn't be good for our old pal Ronnie.

Marguerite had beaten Ronnie back to the marina by several hours and was lying in wait for him to talk over the prenup when he returned in the late afternoon. What she hadn't counted on was that he hadn't stopped with just two martinis at lunch and had continued drinking to the point where the crew had to help him up *Toolpusher's* gangway. At his direction, and over Marguerite's objections, a crewmember mixed another drink for Ronnie.

Eventually, he had passed out on the salon couch without ever being coherent enough to have a conversation about anything, much less the prenup. She was mad as well as a little concerned; she had always been able to exert some control over Ronnie, and that hadn't been the case at any point today. If things didn't go back to being that way this could all end up as a disaster. She decided to leave him on the couch overnight because if he was going to puke, it was better that it happened here than in the bed down in their stateroom. At least here he couldn't barf on her, and it would be up to the crew to clean up the mess.

*****

"I need a couple of guys for some muscle, bunkie. Ones that can keep their mouths shut afterward."

Charlie Bates grimaced, knowing that even their burner phones stood a chance of being compromised. "Okay, I got it. When and where?"

"Surfside Motel in Virginia Beach next Friday. Tell 'em to ask at the desk for Dr. Skyler."

"Done. But you really owe me for this."

"I told you that I'd take care of you after the score. I've always had your back, haven't I?"

Charlie started to say something when he realized the phone was already dead. He drew in a deep breath before making the next two calls. If for some reason these guys didn't get paid up in Virginia, he knew that afterward they'd be coming to collect from him.

*****

The next morning Ronnie woke up on the couch and found that someone had put a blanket over him at some point during the night. His head was splitting, and he reeked of the alcohol that had been almost oozing out of every pore in his body. Suddenly he remembered that he had to be downtown mid-morning for the marina closing. Marguerite was still asleep in his king–sized bed with her sleep mask on as he quietly walked through the stateroom heading for the shower. Soon the steam from the ultra–hot water was doing almost as much good as the four aspirin he had taken beforehand. He managed to get dressed and out of there without waking Marguerite. That would have been a complication that he really didn't want to have to deal with right now.

One of the best things about having a mothership is that there is a chef on the crew, and he hoped that his had anticipated Ronnie's condition and prepared some high carbohydrate breakfast items. A few minutes later Ronnie found this had been the case, and by the time he left for his meeting he was feeling almost halfway human.

Following the closing, he was then feeling well enough to insist on taking Cetta and both their attorneys out for a celebratory lunch. Toasting the deal gave him an excuse for some "hair of the dog" which brought him back to about ninety percent functionality, which was about as good as it was going to get without another full night's sleep.

It was after two when he got back to his marina, and he was happy to see the sign company guys finishing up the switch to *Sanders Lynnhaven Marina*. He walked over to their truck and noticed several other signs strapped down in their rack. They said: *Future Home of Lynnhaven Cove – Marina, Restaurants, Shops, & Condominiums* and underneath in smaller letters was *Another M & S Partners Project*. It took a couple of seconds for it to penetrate Ronnie's fog before he realized this was the same bunch that owned Mallard Cove.

"Hey! Where are these signs going?" He asked the sign installers as loudly as his head would allow.

One of the workers motioned to the broad open expanse beyond what was now Ronnie's parking lot. "Over there. They're gonna dig out a big marina with condos, restaurants, an' stuff. Gonna be huge."

Ronnie turned, cursing up a storm. His head was spinning, he had been thinking of approaching that property's owner at some point down the road himself, with the idea of expanding his own operation. Then at the closing, he found out that one whole section of his new marina's docks were installed on submerged land that belonged to that neighboring parcel, and it was only leased. This was something that Cetta hadn't volunteered before Ronnie read about it at the closing table. But since the property was vacant, he had just assumed he would be able to renew the lease which was due to end next spring. He figured the owners would want to continue that income stream to at least help cover the property taxes and they might even be ready to sell. It was in the name of some LLC company, so he hadn't made the connection to the Mallard Cove group.

This new revelation wasn't good; in fact, it was a potential disaster.

Ronnie walked up the gangway and into the salon. Marguerite was waiting there for him.

"Ron dear, Timmy just called. He's about five minutes away. I told our captain to have some of the crew standing by to help them tie up and bring their bags aboard."

She acted like nothing had happened, but Ronnie knew that was her style to ignore or deflect any conflict when there would be others around. He also noted the "our captain." Again, her overreach irritated him. He walked over to the bar and started making himself a drink.

"Dear, don't you think you should wait at least until our guests arrive and get settled then make drinks for everyone?"

Ronnie wasn't in the mood to be handled, especially after all he had learned in the past few hours. This should have been one of the best, most exciting days for him in recent years, but instead, it was becoming a nightmare. He ignored Marguerite and poured a healthy slug of Pilar rum over ice and squeezed a lime wedge over it. He figured he'd need it before Timmy and his "skank du jour" arrived. That's when he realized Marguerite was still talking.

"Don't you think, Ron dear?"

He took a huge sip of the ultra–smooth rum before answering. "Truthfully, I wasn't listening. It has been a rough afternoon that followed a rough morning, and I'd just like to sit quietly and rest a few minutes."

"Well dear, the morning was all self–inflicted, and whatever happened this afternoon I'm sure will work itself out. So, do we own the marina now?"

"Yes, *we* do." Ronnie noted that she didn't even flinch at the sarcastic way he said "we." It was either that deflection thing again, that or she really believed what was his was hers now, too. For a brief second he

187

considered saying, *"We will after you sign that prenup"*, but he didn't want to be in the middle of a fight when her kid showed up. Not that he really cared what Timmy thought, but he at least didn't want to start off the visit by being in a confrontation with his mother. That is, not if Ronnie was going to survive through the tournament with Timmy on *Gusher* and still be able to enjoy any part of it.

Marguerite looked out the salon window and exclaimed, "They're here!" But instead of going outside to meet them she walked over beside Ronnie's chair and struck what he knew to be her "hostess greeting pose."

Two minutes later Timmy walked through the door, going straight over to embrace his mother and as usual, ignoring Ronnie. But the girl that followed him through the door wasn't at all what Ronnie had expected. Yes, she had long blond hair and a great body like most of Timmy's previous concubines. But this one had stunning green eyes and was dressed in a long sleeve fishing shirt with Columbia shorts and deck shoes instead of a butt floss thong with a pair of band aids and some string. This girl looked like she had stepped right out of a yachting magazine. She smiled at him and came straight over to introduce herself as he stood up.

"Hi, Mr. Sanders, I'm Samantha Bronson, but please call me Sam. Thank you so much for letting me, er, *us* stay with you." Her handshake was strong, but it was her eyes that totally gripped him, almost pulling him into them.

Shaking off that feeling he said, "Then please call me Ron, Sam. And it's my pleasure to have you stay aboard." Too late he realized that he also should have said *"our pleasure,"* but fortunately Timmy and Marguerite were already too engrossed in their own conversation to have noticed. "You must be ready for a cocktail after that long run up the coast today. What can I get for you? We have just about anything you might want."

She noticed the glass on the table beside the chair he had been sitting in. "I'll have whatever you are having."

"I'm having a Pilar rum with lime. But seriously, I can make you whatever you want."

She smiled, "A Pilar with lime sounds great." She followed him over to the bar.

On noticing this, Marguerite called to Ronnie, "Thank you for bartending, dear. I'll have a vodka martini, and Timmy will have..."

Acknowledging Ron for the first time today as if he had just walked into the room, Timmy said, "S'up, Ron. I'll take a glass of Patron over ice. Somethin' Sam there has got me into lately."

Ron nodded, clearly only tolerating Timmy, as usual. He turned back to Sam. "If you'd rather have one of those, I can make two."

She shook her head. "I'd much rather have what you have." She smiled in a way that almost seemed to make her eyes look more alluring, as if that was even possible.

Ronnie wondered to himself if it was his imagination, or could she possibly be flirting with him? Or, did he just wish that she was flirting with him? But the way that she had said she wanted what he had...

"Ron dear! Our drinks?" Marguerite had an annoyed tone to her voice, not as if she had caught him flirting with someone else, but more like he was a slow-moving waiter.

He mixed and then brought their two drinks over to where she and Timmy were sitting and talking on the couch. Sam followed, bringing his drink along with hers. Marguerite raised her glass, "To having my son home again!"

They all raised their glasses and took a sip, then Marguerite looked over and said, "Samantha dear, why

189

don't you go with Ron on a tour of our boat, since you've never been aboard before. And in the meantime, I'll get caught up with Timmy. You two run along."

There was that "*our boat*" thing again, but this time Ronnie hardly noticed. He was happy to take Sam on a long tour and wasn't in any hurry to get back and listen to those two yack all through the cocktail hour. And Marguerite's reference to Timmy being "home" was another point of irritation for him. In no way did he want his yacht, nor his house in Palm Beach, becoming "home" for him. Timmy was to be a visitor, hopefully a very infrequent one, and that was the extent of that.

Ronnie and Sam went forward through the dining area into the huge galley where the chef was busy prepping for tonight's dinner. Sam struck up a casual conversation with him, asking questions designed to pick up cooking pointers. This was something that surprised Ronnie after being so used to Marguerite's standoffishness with the members of the crew. They then wound their way through each of the upper decks, finally ending up on the uppermost one, the open sundeck. Ronnie took Sam's glass and headed to the outdoor bar to refresh both of their drinks. He had quickly found that she was a great person to talk to; really bright and engaging. Yet for some reason, he didn't feel the need to have to embellish his stories nor to inflate his feeling of self–worth, despite his growing sense that she was flirting with him ever so slightly.

She took the refill he offered her and asked, "So, Ron, how big is it?"

He almost choked on his drink as he stared at her with a surprised expression. She laughed lightly then added, "Your *yacht*. I was wondering how long it is. Unless that's too forward a question."

"No, no, not at all. *Toolpusher* is a hundred and sixty feet." He was kicking himself for not having known what she meant and letting his imagination run wild. He motioned toward a built–in couch where they sat down, an arm's length apart. Wait, had she just asked if something was *forward*? Wasn't that more something you might say on a date?

She smiled and tilted her head slightly. "So, what's the meaning behind *Toolpusher*? It sounds like it could be a porn star's yacht." She laughed again lightly, already knowing the answer, but watched his eyes carefully for a reaction to see just how comfortable he was with her.

Ronnie was taken aback, but only slightly. This had become quite an interesting conversation. He finally chuckled himself then said, "A toolpusher is an oil rig boss. My late wife's family was in oil, and I inherited the business when she died." He surprised himself with the honesty of his own answer, and the fact that he hadn't felt the need to exaggerate or brag. There was really something about this girl, or rather this young woman. It was hard for him not to think of her as a girl since she looked like she was only slightly over half his age. But despite having met her less than an hour ago, she already had made him feel totally at ease, even with her frank and funny comments. Being at ease was something he almost never felt with anyone of any age anymore, not even Marguerite. And lately, *especially* with Marguerite.

She smiled, her green eyes twinkling. Looking out across the waterway and at the homes on the other shore she said, "You know, Ron, I don't think I could ever get tired of this view."

That statement caught him off guard. Not because he thought she was suggesting something, but because he hadn't really focused on the view himself before. He had been more interested in the marina, not in its surroundings. But Sam was right; it really was a nice view and a calming one at that. Lately, he had been so uptight he hadn't even noticed it. Now that he had, he was glad she was part of it.

191

"You know, Sam, not to bring up a bad subject but you don't seem to be like any of the other women that Timmy has had with him before. If you don't mind my being forward." Two can play at this game, he thought. If they were indeed playing a game.

Inwardly, Sam smiled to herself. This was going even better than she could have hoped. In less than an hour she had already determined that Ron had no intention of ever following through on his engagement to Marguerite. Not that he had told her in so many words, and in fact he might not yet be aware of it himself, but he soon would be. With the way that both Marguerite and Timmy treated Ron, he was starved for attention or adoration, and she planned on stealthily giving him plenty of that. She had quickly found exactly who she was looking for to help her get away from Timmy and back on her feet at least, if not even farther.

"Thanks, I think?"

Ronnie quickly replied, "I meant that in a good way. You're a great conversationalist, and really very smart. Not to sound overly judgmental but you don't seem like someone who would normally be attracted to him."

This was tricky, she thought. Best to tell the truth, but not the whole truth. Getting caught in a lie now could mess the whole thing up. And she knew that Ronnie was the best option she had seen in quite a long time. Screw Timmy; it was all a question of timing now. She made a pensive face, as if trying to decide whether or not to confide in him. Finally, she looked him straight in the eyes.

"I'm really not, Ron. I was dumped down in Costa Rica by my old boyfriend who took off with another girl. I was left with no money, and no family or friends back in the states to help me get back here. I met Timmy, and he was nice enough to help me out down there, bring me back to the US with him, and then give me a job fishing tournaments with him all the way up to here.

Virginia is as far as I'm going with him. After he pays me, I've got to figure out where I'm headed next, and what I'm going to do."

Ronnie was trying to assimilate everything she had told him as fast as possible. "The way that Marguerite was talking, I just assumed that you two were a couple."

"Well, that's complicated. I think he wanted her to believe that. But the long–term answer is 'no', we're not. At least we won't be. Long term, that is. But I couldn't have gotten out of down there if it hadn't been for him, and I am indebted to him for that. Though between you and me, I'm starting to worry if he'll actually make good on paying me what he said he would for the tournament work. I think he was counting on winning some prize money, and that hasn't happened, though that wasn't my fault. And I'm also worried that he might not want to let me go, either."

Ronnie looked shocked. "You mean try to keep you against your will?"

Sam gave him a rueful smile. "Just how well *do* you know your future stepson, Ron? He can be pretty rough when he wants to be." She grimaced and looked down at the deck.

Ron felt the heat rising in his neck at the thought of that lummox Timmy abusing Sam. Future stepson? He'd never really thought of him in those terms, more just as Marguerite's kid, but the reality was now hitting him like ice water in the face.

Sam looked back up at him, "Anyway, I really appreciate talking with you, Ron, but *please* keep everything I've said to yourself. I really shouldn't have told you; I don't want to make him angry at me again, or even you. Fortunately, I found that he and his mom can talk for hours when they get together, and it's like no one else in the room exists. I guess it comes from her raising him by herself for so long, and the two of them only having only had each other through some pretty

193

tough times. But I guess you've seen how they are when they're together.

This is only the first break that I've had in weeks, Ron. It's so nice talking with you. On the way up here, I couldn't even be seen talking with another guy or Timmy would get violent, either with them or with me, and sometimes both. I guess that he figures you're 'safe', so he doesn't have to worry. I really appreciate your just letting me unload on you."

Wow, Ronnie thought, thanks to Sam he had been shown a whole different side to his own situation that he hadn't even realized existed. He met her gaze and said, "Don't worry, that's all between us, and it won't go any farther."

Bingo, Sam thought, between *us*. He didn't say, *I won't say a word*; instead, now the seed had been planted that there was an *us*. Confidantes, each trapped in a bad situation, and she could sense that Ron was just now starting to realize how bad his really was. Sort of a comrades in arms kind of thing. Sam knew well that commiseration was a very powerful tool, and it should help her get where she wanted to be.

Chapter 21

It was the usual afternoon lineup at the Beer–Thirty–Bunch. Most of the talk centered on how good the fishing had been lately, though some was about how popular the beach bar had already become since its opening. The hotel wouldn't be ready to open for another week, but their summer reservations were filling up fast, especially the weekends. Chris Wagner had told me that the parasail reservations were already stacking up for this coming weekend, so it looked like I had made the right choice by getting into that business. Once the hotel opens, it should really be nuts.

Kari looked at her phone then went outside to answer a call. A minute later she returned, smiling as she hung up, looking at me. "Remember that thing yesterday I said I'd tell you about later? I had the sign guys that we use put some up on the Lynnhaven property, including one at the end of Ronnie's parking lot saying that our marina project was coming soon. They just called to tell me they finished, and that Ronnie went insane over it. I guess he didn't realize who owned the property until then."

Baloney chimed in, "I hope he had a stroke over it. Crazy sumbitch. Is he still registered for the tournament?"

I replied, "He is, and they can't bar him from fishing in it without raising a lot of flags about selectively choosing anglers in an open and high dollar tournament, especially an inaugural one. So, we're stuck with him in it."

"I hope it's rough as hell and he throws up his toenails." Baloney grumbled. He wanted revenge, and I can't say I blamed him after his run–in out on the bay. I hoped for rough weather, too.

*****

"So, Ron, we're gonna split all the tourney winnings 'tween you 'n me, right?" Timmy had continued drinking straight tequila through dinner and had gone way past the finish line for being snockered. The four of them had moved back into the salon where Timmy was now wedged into a high back chair. The high arms were the only thing keeping him from falling over.

"Well, Timmy, my crew gets half of any winnings, and then the anglers all split the other half. In addition to my friend Jay, I'd like you to fish it with us as well, Sam. If you want." Ron looked over at her questioningly.

"Screw the crew, ain't they on sal..er...salary? Whadda they need more 'n that for? An' I don' know this Jay guy. But Sam'll fish, won'cha?" Timmy gave her the most drunken stern look he could muster. As drunk as he was, he still figured out that he could take her portion of any winnings away from her, so he wanted her there for that reason alone.

"Well, Timmy, my boat, my rules, we'll divide any winnings as I say, and I'll invite whoever I want to invite. So, if you want to stay on the angler list, then you need to get used to that." Somehow, having Sam there had given Ron the courage to take Timmy head-on instead of deflecting.

Marguerite wasn't about to let it drop. She had polished off the better part of a bottle of wine during dinner after having had three martinis beforehand, so she was about on the same level of impairment as Timmy. "But Timmy is part of the family dear, not an employee, so he should get more of the split since he was the first one on the guest list."

"He wasn't on any list of mine, you were the one who invited him, *dear*. And again, my boat, my rules." While he hadn't imbibed as much as either of those two, the rum had still kicked in enough for him to be more aggressive than usual with Marguerite. He realized right

196

then that he was through with getting teamed up on again by those two like he had been in the past. Plus, there was the Sam factor. He didn't mind showing her that he had the "stones" to stand up to both of them.

"Well! Pardon me if I go turn in on *your* boat then," Marguerite said in a frosty tone. "And Sam dear, you should help Timmy down to bed now, too. Apparently we aren't wanted around here this evening." She stood up, swaying and trying to keep her balance before slowly and unsteadily making her way toward the stairs that led to the staterooms below. She still had her wineglass in hand, but it was leaning at a really bad angle.

Sam gave Ron a somewhat apologetic and rueful look as she helped pull Timmy up out of the chair. She steadied him as they followed Marguerite down the stairs.

Ron looked at his glass, which was now down to a third full. As he slowly sipped the remaining amber liquid over the next ten minutes he thought about what had happened. Not just since dinner, but throughout the whole day. How was it that by Sam coming to visit with Timmy, Ron had started to see his situation in a whole new way? Had he already realized he was in a bad spot, and somehow by just talking to her it had helped him admit that to himself? Maybe because she admitted to him that she too was in an almost captive situation. Captive situation? Was that where he was finding himself now with Marguerite?

"Hey, I hope you really don't mind some company." Sam had come back up the stairs. She had startled Ron at first, he had been so deep in thought.

"No, not at all. But I thought that you had turned in."

Sam shook her head. "Timmy did; passed out cold. But I figured that you had turned in, too."

"No, just sitting here thinking. And I was actually tossing around the idea of going up to the sundeck and making another drink up there. You got me thinking about that view from this afternoon; I want to see it at night. Care to join me?"

"Sure. Lead the way."

Up on the sundeck, Ronnie handed Sam a fresh drink. She had taken the same seat as this afternoon and was looking across the river at the lights reflecting off the water's surface. "I don't think I could get tired of this night view either, Ron."

He was thinking the same thing as he studied the backlit outline of her breasts as they were defined by those same lights. "Beautiful."

She glanced over and realized that it wasn't just the lights he was looking at. "I was talking about the lights." She said it in a teasing rather than accusatory way.

"Those are, too." Oh crap, had he really said that?

"Ron, you're engaged, and we've both had more than our share of rum."

He looked down at his glass, then up at her again. "Am I? That was something I was contemplating down in the salon. You saw the way I was getting ganged up on. Is that the way you would treat your fiancé if you really loved him, Sam? If you really wanted to get married because you loved him? Somehow I don't think so."

After hesitating a few seconds, she said, "No, I wouldn't. I felt bad for you when they did that. But you handled it well."

"Yeah, so well that we're both up here instead of downstairs asleep."

After a shorter pause she replied, "Well, I'm not complaining. I like the company up here better. Much more comfortable."

"Right now, I happen to agree on both counts. Probably even more so tomorrow. Things have been...deteriorating between Marguerite and me.

198

Though she might not want to admit it. Hell, I didn't, either. But you saw it for what it really is tonight."

"If I get too personal tonight Ron, I'll just blame it on the rum tomorrow, but here goes. So, why are you still engaged to her? If it's not good, why make each other miserable by staying together?" She had chosen her words very carefully, planting the idea that he was miserable so he would start thinking that. Or finally realizing it.

Ron sighed. What was it about Sam, who he barely knew, that could make him talk about things that before he had only dared to think to himself. "We were fooling around when I was married; even though my wife and Marguerite were friends. Then my wife was diagnosed with an aggressive form of cancer, and she was gone in less than a year. Marguerite stood by me then. I guess I asked her to marry me so that in some way it made me feel less cheap and guilty about the affair. Does that make any sense? It seemed to at the time, like I only cheated with someone who was worth marrying. I had never cheated on her before.

I know, I'm rambling. I'm telling you things that I've never told anyone before, and I've known you all of what, six hours? I'm sorry. There's just something about you that makes me want to get this all out."

Sam put a hand on his arm. "I've been told I'm a good listener."

"You are at that, but there's something else, and I'm not sure I know what it is."

"You know that every secret has its time, Ron. It's not good to take them to the grave."

"Hey, I'm may be about twice as old as you, but I'm not ready to croak any time soon."

She could just make out his worried smile in the low light. "I've known people younger than me that were much older than either of us, Ron. The thing about age is that it's really a state of mind, not a number of laps around the sun. If you don't mind, I'm going to give you

199

a bit of advice that a friend once told me; 'Life is not a dress rehearsal, and it's too damned short to dance with the wrong partner.' I'm with the wrong one now, you saw that right away, but this is about to change."

Ron sighed heavily. "You already know that I am, too. I've just got to do what you are going to."

Sam was silent for a minute then said, "You know why he wants me to fish with you in the tournament, right? He figures that if we win anything, he'll take my share away from me."

"I'm not going to let that happen."

"Timmy might have something to say about that, Ron."

"Timmy hasn't met my friend Jay yet, Sam. He's the other guy who is going to fish it with us. He's got six inches and fifty pounds on Timmy, and I guarantee he lifts more weight than him, too. Between the two of us, we'll make sure you get to keep any money that you win, and that Timmy pays you what he owes you. You said that you were afraid he wouldn't let you go, and that you had nowhere to go. You can keep staying aboard after he leaves, at least until you can get your plans together. That is, if you want. At least it gives you some options."

She hadn't seen this coming, not this quickly. Sam was the one that usually worked this fast, but he was very impulsive. She reached over and hugged Ron, kissing him on the cheek. "Thank you. I didn't know what to do, Ron."

He hugged her back and said, "You can quit worrying about it now, and try to enjoy the tournament. In fact, if it's not too rough tomorrow, do you want to go out and practice? I had already planned on going."

She broke the embrace and put both hands on his shoulders, looking directly at him. "I don't care if it is rough, yes, I'd love to go fishing with you." She saw the concern on his face. "Unless you're having second thoughts."

"Uh, well, there's something else I haven't told you. I get seasick at times when it's rough."

"You're kidding! All this ocean hardware and you get 'mal de mer?' Do you do anything for it?"

Ron said, "I have some pills, but they make me kind of foggy."

"Ron, do you drink beer when you fish?"

"Uh, sure."

"Good. Then I want you to do this for me, I want you to down a beer before you get on the boat in the morning. And I don't mean sip, I mean *chug* it. The combination of the alcohol and the carbonation will ward off any seasickness, but it only works if you do it before getting on the boat. And you need to keep having a few more during the day, consider it like having a booster shot, but with flavor." She grinned.

"I've never tried that, Sam."

"You will tomorrow. And Ron, is that hot tub heater on?"

"It stays on. Feel free to use it any time you want. There are towels over under the bar."

"I think I want to now. How about joining me?"

"I don't have a suit up here."

"I wasn't going to bother with a suit." She took his hand and led him over toward the tub.

Chapter 22

The next morning Marguerite woke with a crushing headache and saw that Ron's side of the bed had been slept in but was now empty. She showered and dressed then went up for brunch, still not seeing Ron anywhere. There was a note on the table: *Went fishing, took Sam along for practice. Didn't think that you or Timmy would be up to it, so I didn't wake either of you. Back tonight. RS*

If she thought she was going to get her leverage back on Ron this morning, that belief had just evaporated. She hadn't seen Sam as a threat when she arrived yesterday, but today the alarm bells were ringing. Ron could be so easily led when the right buttons were pushed, and now she had to make sure that they weren't. She looked up from the note to see her son approaching, looking like warmed-over death.

"You need to get Sam and get out of here. She's gone off fishing with Ron today, just the two of them. I need to get things patched up with him, and I don't need her providing any distractions while I do."

"Afraid you're losing your touch, mom? Don't worry, she's not gonna distract him, she'll do what I tell her. And I'm not goin' anywhere until after I take care of some business. That can't happen until the tournament; the guys I need to meet up with will all be here then. You'll do fine getting things back on track."

Marguerite was starting to really get angry. First, she was losing her grip on Ron, now her son as well? "I don't care, I just want you to get her away from him, Timmy. Now."

When he first got up, he had thought his headache couldn't get any worse. His mother had just proven that to be wrong. "Take it easy, mom. They just went fishing, it's no big deal. He's probably scared to face you like always. And I need her to help me with this thing I gotta do, so I'll fix it. Hey, you still have his Amex card, right? You always feel better after some shopping. Lemme get some carbs and a beer in me, then how about we spend the day together outta here? I'll let you buy me a new gold bracelet or somethin'. It'll be fun." Timmy was willing to do anything to get her to calm down, even if it meant tagging along while she shopped. Especially if there was something made of gold for him involved in the deal. He wasn't worried about Sam going out fishing with Ron, his mom was freaking out over nothing.

"I don't know, he was so different last night. She was the only thing that had changed around here."

Timmy rolled his eyes, "You two got into it almost the same time they met. It ain't her, I'm telling you. You guys were already starting to get into it back in Palm Beach, too, way before Sam. So, let's get some breakfast and get out of here. You'll feel better, and I know I will."

Ron had peeked into Timmy's room, but quickly realized that Sam wasn't there. It was still an hour before dawn when he walked over to *Gusher* where the cockpit was well lit, and the engines were idling. He saw that the crew had everything all set and ready to go. Sam was sitting on the aft facing cockpit bench.

"Hold it, Ron! Remember what I told you last night." She walked over to the gunwale and handed him a can of beer.

"You were serious about that? It really works? I have my pills onboard that I can take."

Sam nodded. "Yes, I was serious. An old boyfriend was a mate on a boat where the owner's teenaged grandkids kept getting sick whenever they went out. So, he tried this. The owner was mad at first when he found out about him giving the kids beer, but then he realized it worked and the kids enjoyed going out with him. Eventually, they overcame being prone to seasickness altogether, but they never told their grandfather so they

203

could still have beer on his boat. So, bottoms up, what do you have to lose?"

He gave her a skeptical look, but then upended the can. When it was empty he stepped onto the boat and said, "I feel like a frat boy."

"And I forgot to wear my toga," Sam laughed. "Hey, your chef left some breakfast sandwiches and lunch inside."

"Normally I don't eat before or during a boat ride. I do better on an empty stomach." Ronnie was still skeptical.

"It's okay, trust me, that beer trick works, with food or without. I'm going to have a sandwich; they looked great."

They went inside the cabin where the crew had just finished eating and were headed out to get them underway. Ronnie poured coffee for both himself and Sam. They sat across from each other in the galley nook just as they felt the boat start to idle out of the slip. Sam noticed that Ronnie kept looking down at the table instead of her, and he wasn't saying anything.

"Feeling awkward now, Ron? I told you last night that I'd blame anything I said or did then on the rum. But truthfully it was more than just that, it was about finding a friend; an ally who had my back, as well as finding a way out of a bad situation. Unless you're having second thoughts about helping me. I couldn't blame you if you did; Timmy can be pretty tough when he wants to be. Just tell me so that I can figure out a new plan. I won't hold it against you, I just need to know up front

He looked up, "It was easier to talk about this last night after a few rums. After just one beer isn't the same but, no, Sam, I'm not having second thoughts. I meant what I said; I'll make sure that you get and keep whatever money is yours, he's not going to hold it back or take it from you. Also, as I said, you're welcome to continue to stay on *Toolpusher* after they leave." He

204

paused a minute, "You were right you know. About life being too short to stick with the wrong partner. I just didn't want to admit to myself that I've been miserable for quite a while."

Sam thought, *Bingo!* Not only did Ron use the word *miserable,* but he had again made the invitation to stay on *Toolpusher* an open-ended one. This situation was getting more and more promising. "Hey, Ron, we all kid ourselves about things from time to time. Relationships are probably the number one thing that I've lied to myself about. But Timmy, too. I saw him as a way back to the states, telling myself that he'd let me go after he paid me what he had promised, and that I could walk away any time I wanted. I really do know better than that."

"Walking away. That's what I've decided to do, Sam, as soon as this tournament is over. Marguerite is headed back down south then, and that's when I'm going to break everything off, just as she leaves. I'm tired of being miserable and played. I kind of bought this marina on a whim, but I like being here now. I think I'll look around for other opportunities, maybe add some more real estate, open a new chapter in my life. There's a fishing foundation here that I want to become part of. And it might be time for some new experiences."

Sam gave him a wry smile, "Like ours last night? We've covered most everything that we said together, but just not what we *did,* Ron."

"That was something that probably never would have happened if both of us hadn't been treated the way we were. And I'd be lying if I said that I didn't feel a bit guilty about it, to both her as well as you. Still not nearly as guilty as I did back when I cheated *with* Marguerite. Which tells me all I need to know, Sam. Why, are you regretting it now?"

She caught the part about how it *probably* wouldn't have happened. "The only reason I'd regret any part of it is if it made you uncomfortable, or if now being

205

around me makes you uncomfortable, Ron. You don't need to feel guilty to me, if you'll recall it was my idea. And *I'd* be lying if I said that I didn't need that last night; being with someone because I *wanted* to be, instead of because I didn't have a choice."

Ron's brow furrowed as he thought of Timmy forcing himself on Sam, and again he felt the heat and anger rising within him. "You always have a choice! Why not leave him now?"

"For the same reason that you aren't breaking it off with Marguerite right now, because it's complicated. And because it'll be easier if they both leave when they are scheduled to, after he finishes his business with some guys in the tournament. That's when he said that our 'arrangement' was through, so I'll just be making him keep to his word. Meanwhile, at least we both have someone to commiserate with. We still do, right? Or, did last night screw that up?" She gave him a worried look.

"Yes. I mean no! Yes, we can get through this together, and no, that didn't mess things up. At least not for me. It's all good from my standpoint."

Sam winked, "Well, from my standpoint, it was great."

After two and a half hours of running, they spotted several large sportfishing rigs out at Norfolk Canyon, sixty miles offshore. The seas were running about six feet high. The size of these waves would normally have been enough to have had Ronnie already losing whatever was in his stomach, but Sam had made him drink two more beers on the way out. Whether her explanation about how this worked was correct, or maybe it was psychosomatic, but in any case, Ronnie felt fine. It also helped that the fishing was red hot and they caught several tuna and mahi in the morning. That afternoon the white marlin "bite" turned on, as pack after pack of them came through. The cockpit became a madhouse with singles, doubles, and even a triple hookup. The mate ended up grabbing the third rod on that one as well as wiring and releasing both of their fish. The three of them fought all the fish standing up, without the advantage of the fighting chair.

Ron could easily see that Sam had almost the same amount of skill as his late wife, and that she was really enjoying herself, which made for a great combination. They had been fishing all day with twenty and thirty–pound–class rods when Ron looked at the mate and said, "Break out the twelve–pound rods, I think Sam is ready for a good workout."

Sam said, "I've never fished twelve–pound test offshore before, Ron."

"Just don't horse them, Sam, use that same finesse that you have with the twenties, but just more of it. You've got this."

She managed to catch and release a half dozen more on the twelve–pound rods with the help of the captain backing down on them fast and hard, and with Ronnie coaching her. Despite his long track record of seasickness, he had still been watching Caroline enough over the years to know some decent light tackle tips. They started to back on the next fish when Sam called out, "I want to fight this one dead–boat." Meaning that she would have to do all the work herself. By "dead boat" rules, the captain could only use the engines to keep the transom turned toward the fish, he couldn't back down on it at all. Catching a white marlin dead–boat on light tackle was something that only the absolute best anglers could accomplish; an extreme challenge for a billfish angler.

The mate looked over at Ronnie who was nodding and grinning. Sam was really gaining confidence in the light tackle fast. As luck would have it, this one ended up being the largest billfish of the day and took almost an hour to land. After releasing this fish Sam was exhausted, the spent muscles in her pulling arm still quivering slightly but her face was totally glowing with excitement. She wrapped Ron up in a hug, squeezing him tightly.

"Thank you, Ron, this was fantastic!"

"So was watching you work that fish. Plus being out here without getting sick, Sam, so thank *you* for teaching me that trick. I can't believe it was so simple. Are you ready to catch another one?"

"I think that after that last one if I tried to catch one more marlin on twelve–pound, my arms would fall off."

"Think you could manage to hold a Pilar and lime?" He raised an eyebrow.

"If that's another challenge, it's one I think I'm up to."

They went into the salon where Ron built their drinks in tall glasses. Then he joined Sam on the built-in curved sofa as the captain brought *Gusher* up to cruising speed for the ride home.

"This day was totally amazing. I can see why people get hooked on light tackle and don't want to fish with anything else. I think I want to try billfishing with a fly rod at some point." Sam's green eyes were still lit with excitement.

Ron nodded. "Light tackle and fly fishing separates the real anglers from the rest. And you, my friend, are incredible. With you in the tournament, we've got a real shot at it. So, how good is Timmy?"

"You're so much better. And I'm just talking about last night." She winked at him and took a long sip of her drink while leaning back into the sofa.

"Hah. Well, thanks. But I'm serious, I meant at angling. I haven't fished with him before."

She said, "You're better at that part, too. He tries to crank fish in too fast. Like with everything and everyone else, he thinks he can overpower anything."

"Well, we've got several days before the tournament; I'd like to get in a few more practice sessions so that you and I are both at the top of our game before then."

Sam smiled seductively, "Fishing or...?"

"I was talking about fishing."

Sam frowned, "Still feeling guilty then." It felt like more of a question than a statement.

Just then Ron's phone chimed, and at first, he didn't know whether he should be irritated or relieved at the interruption. It was a message from his accountant; another almost eight grand charged on Marguerite's Amex card today. He scowled as he looked up from the phone.

"Maybe not feeling as guilty as I was before, Sam."

Ronnie then downed the half drink that was left in his glass. Sam took it as another challenge and locked eyes with him before doing the same thing. He then got up and refilled both their glasses, sitting closer to her when he returned. Glancing down at his phone again, she could see his jaw tighten. Sam didn't know what that message had been, but she figured whatever it was it had been good for her. She was thankful that *Gusher* had satellite internet. She ran a hand up his arm and rested it on his shoulder.

"We're still a little over two hours out, right?" Sam asked.

"Give or take, yes."

"It's just that this has been the best day ever. And two hours would give us enough time for that other kind of practice session, maybe let me make it up to you for the fishing. I mean, if you want to. Like you said this morning, you always have a choice, Ron."

"You don't have to make anything up to me for fishing, Sam, you don't owe me anything, especially not that. You've already done a lot for me today."

She drew back away from him, looking rejected and embarrassed. "Sorry, Ron. I didn't mean to push, I just felt connected to you after everything we've said. I don't want you thinking this is something that I do all the time with just anyone, especially because of Timmy, or that I'm..." She looked down again.

He grabbed her shoulders and pulled her to him in a hug, as she rested her head on his shoulder. "Of course, I don't. Trust me, I get it. But you don't need to feel obligated to me about anything."

She leaned back and looked up at his face. "I don't feel *obligated* as much as it's more like a connection with you. A lot of it is because it's now my choice for the first time in a long time."

She told him the story of Jimmy/Reggie and the bar in Costa Rica, leaving out only the part about leaving him tied up when they left. She knew that at some point the story would probably come out, and better that he hear it from her now than from Timmy at the wrong time. At first, Ronnie was shocked, but a part of his heart went out to her as he realized the desperation that she had felt at the hopeless situation she had found herself in while down there. He was disgusted and angry over how Timmy had first rescued her but then taken advantage and forced her into this 'arrangement' with him.

"Where do you want to go, Sam? I can have my plane take you wherever you want. I'll give you the money Timmy promised you, and I'll get it back from him."

"I don't want to go anywhere else, Ron. I want to stay here and fish the tournament with you and learn to catch billfish on a fly rod. And I want to win that tournament while fishing it with you. You said it yourself, we have a good chance if we fish it together. Ron, I want something good to happen in my life again, it would be the first time in a long time that it has.

Do you realize that you are the only guy I've met in months that hasn't just wanted sex? The only guy that *I've* asked to go to bed with me because it was *my* idea? The only guy I've felt like I wanted to for me? This is the first time in months that I've felt truly safe, and

210

it's because of you, a guy that I didn't even know twenty–four hours ago. I feel like I can really trust you.

Like I said this morning, I needed you last night. I needed a closeness that was on my own terms. Maybe in part to prove to myself that I was still able to get back to having things on my own terms. I really needed to feel that way again. Make that I still need to feel it." Again, she looked down, but it wasn't an act. She realized that most if not all of what she had just said was true. For too long her life had been totally out of her control. Maybe there was a chance at some kind of stability and normalcy after Timmy leaves, whether it was either with or around Ron, or maybe just in this area. But she desperately wanted to find out, and she didn't want to leave.

Ronnie got up, went over and pulled out a drawer in the galley. He took several pills out of a bottle and put them in a plastic bag. He handed Sam the bag and said, "These are the prescription seasick pills I was talking about. It's a kind of sedative that really makes me so relaxed I feel like a zombie, so I hate taking them. They aren't supposed to be mixed with any alcohol. I made the mistake of doing that once and it knocked me right out for almost twelve hours. Another side effect of mixing this with alcohol is that it puts things out of commission for almost twenty–four hours, if you catch my drift. So, if you just happen to bartend for Timmy, you won't have to worry about him getting frisky either tonight or even tomorrow. Just one pill in his tequila should do it."

Sam stood up and kissed Ronnie, again pulling him into a hug. "Thank you, Ron. I don't know what to say."

"How about, 'Bottoms up, Timmy!'" They both laughed.

Sam said, "Grab your glass, and show me where your stateroom is. I'm not in the mood to take no for an answer."

He looked down at the phone again then back up at her. Marguerite had made a choice, now so could he. "Not in the mood to give you a 'no' answer, either."

An hour and a half later, Gusher's captain got a call over the intercom to head for a little waterfront restaurant and bar just inside the Lynnhaven inlet. Ronnie also said to slow down a bit, he wasn't in a hurry to get there. The fact that the call had come from the master stateroom intercom wasn't lost on the captain as he slowed to just above trolling speed.

Chapter 23

"You keep grinning like that when we get back to the marina, and it won't take a genius to figure out that there was more than just fishing going on today." Sam looked worried.

They were sitting across from each other in the waterfront restaurant, after having had a couple more drinks and splitting an appetizer. Ronnie answered, "I've had more than my share of drinks, and I had a ball today, so I can't help it if I'm grinning. Watching you fish with light tackle for your very first time while being able to relax and enjoy myself out in rough seas without getting seasick was great. This was one of the best days I've had on a boat in a long time."

Sam looked slyly to the left and right then said in a low voice, "So, it was all about fishing and not getting sick... Nothing else?"

"Hmm, let me think, there might have been something else."

Sam feigned being annoyed and kicked Ronnie playfully under the table as he burst out laughing.

"Sam, I haven't laughed like this in years. What the hell is it about you? It's like you're like some kind of catalyst. I haven't felt this good since I don't remember when; like huge weight has been lifted off of me. I've realized, or at least finally admitted to myself, that I haven't been happy for quite a while. I was the one who felt obligated, and for all the wrong reasons. Now I've got a plan to do something about it. Don't get me wrong, I'm not looking forward to doing what needs to be done in order to get there, but at least I know that it's just around the corner. If it wasn't for Timmy still going to be here during the tournament because of that business deal he has going, I'd go ahead and do it now. But I think you're right, he can't complain too much if you just make him stick to his own timeline; we'll just make sure he does what he said he would. Then you don't have to worry about him being around here anymore."

Ronnie looked down at his phone then back up at her. "You have no idea how great it will be to not be hounded about setting a date to get married when I don't want to be married again, especially to someone who I've realized that I really don't love. And to no longer get questioned about every single decision I make. Plus, no more messages from my accountant telling me that she just spent another eight grand on my Amex card today. She's supposed to have her own money, but all of a sudden she's out spending mine."

Sam looked down to her left, and Ronnie caught it.

"What? You know something I don't?"

She looked up at him, "I guess telling you won't matter since you two are breaking up. Before we came up here I spent some time with her down in Palm Beach and she did a ton of shopping. A lot of it was for me, so that 'Timmy's girlfriend' would look nice. All the new clothes she gave me I thought she bought, but I guess it was with your money. I'm sorry, I didn't know, Ron. But it's starting to make sense. She was complaining to Timmy about running out of money while she was still taking me shopping on Worth Avenue and out to expensive lunches, racking up thousands of dollars in the process. Everything went on what I thought was her own Amex card. It didn't make sense to me how someone that qualified for a black Amex card could keep it and yet still be out of money. Then she told Timmy that she was listing her condo for sale and moving into your house when you came back down for the season, and that you two would be married not long after that."

This was all news to Ronnie, except the part about her wanting to get married soon. He knew that something was wrong but figured she might have had a temporary financial setback of some kind. Now it was sounding more like she was broke and looking for an

214

ATM instead of a husband. Well, that wasn't going to be him. He had kept insisting that they keep separate places after Caroline died. At first, it was for appearances. Then, he had said it was because he still needed space to adjust. Now he was coming to realize that at least subconsciously he knew that something wasn't right, and he didn't want her moving in because he might never get her out.

Ronnie sighed deeply, suddenly very tired. "Thanks for telling me all that, it explains a lot. Don't worry about the clothes, I'm glad you have them. But we had better get going, it's already dark out."

Sam really had hated breaking the mood by telling him about what happened down in Palm Beach, but she didn't want him knowing that she figured it out and held it back from him. Not if she was going to have any future around here. It was funny, Timmy had said that Ronnie was a pompous ass and all full of himself, but he hadn't acted that way around her. Now he was suddenly very down, so at least she didn't have to worry about him giving anything away about their "afternoon" activities by looking so happy.

Back at *Toolpusher,* their extended cocktail hour had taken its toll on Timmy and Marguerite. They had started with Bloody Marys' at lunch and kept rolling from there. Marguerite was primed for a fight when Ronnie and Sam walked in.

"Where the hell have you two been? It's after eight o'clock! And why didn't you call?"

Ron replied coolly, "Fishing, Marguerite. This isn't Palm Beach where you fish only a mile or so offshore. Here we have to run over sixty miles each way; it's like going over to the Bahamas and back in the same day. And I wasn't aware that I had to check in with the den mother." There was no way that Ronnie was going to let her get the upper hand. "I didn't call because I really wanted a chance to cool down before talking to you about your credit card purchases today."

"What? Oh, well, there's nothing to do up here so I had to find some way to entertain myself."

"Eight grand is a hell of a lot of entertainment. And I'm guessing that new gold anchor chain around his wrist is a big part of it." Ronnie motioned toward Timmy. "Practicing for this tournament is what I'm going to be doing, but shopping with my card is not something you're going to do while I'm out. Am I making myself clear?"

"It's clear that you don't give a damn about me being back here and bored while you're off having fun!" She was steaming.

"Hey, you don' get tuh talk to my mom like that." Timmy got up very unsteadily.

"Hey, I'll talk any damn way I want on my boat. You don't like it, feel free to leave, bucko."

Marguerite glared at Ronnie, then headed out to the back deck. Timmy looked at Sam and said harshly, "Make me 'n my mom drinks and bring 'em out to us." Then he headed outside as well.

After Timmy pulled the door closed Ronnie said, "That's not a bad idea, Sam. Another drink for each of them, if you don't mind. *Special* drinks. And please tell Timmy that I said Gusher leaves at five a.m., so if he wants to practice he needs to be on it." He winked at her and got an evil looking grin in return.

"Two specials, coming up."

He added, "Hopefully tomorrow will be another hot bite day, and we can get you on some marlin with a fly rod. I'm going to hit the hay; I'll see you onboard in the morning."

The next morning Sam was waiting at the gunwale with Ronnie's beer.

"That worked like a charm last night, he barely made it onto the bed before he was out. He was snoring as I left this morning."

"Same thing with Marguerite, she never said a word."

Sam smiled at Ronnie, "Best night of sleep I've had in a month."

Sam proved to be just as adept with a fly rod as she had with the other light tackle, landing several marlin in the morning. Salt water fly fishing is tricky; the fish have to be attracted to the boat using hookless "teaser" baits. Once the fish is after the teaser, it has to be yanked away and the fly rod's lure presented simultaneously. Even for an experienced fly–fishing angler it can be a daunting task. Then once the fish is on, fighting it can be a really lengthy process. The rod is extremely flexible, and the leader is light. The challenge is totally addictive. It makes fishing with twelve–pound test look like using steel cable. But Sam handled it like she had been doing it for years. Ronnie knew that she had a heck of a fishing career ahead of her if she chose to go that route.

They had to head back to shore early, as Ronnie's friend Jay was due to arrive early that evening. Sam didn't suggest a repeat performance of yesterday's "practice" on the way back, and Ronnie didn't bring it up, they just talked. In a way he was relieved, and in another, disappointed. But he had a lot on his mind this week, and he wasn't going to worry about that today. Even though Jay would be fishing with them from now through the tournament, and they wouldn't have any privacy to be able to talk much about their situations until after then. Nor to do anything else in private. Sam knew that, too.

*****

217

Captain Jeff Scott brought Casey Shaw's fifty-five-foot custom Jarrett Bay Carolina sportfisherman down from his other Atlantic side marina, the Bluffs. Similar to Murph and Lindsay's Merritt, *Predator* had the lines of a seagoing gazelle, and ran like one too. Slightly faster and equally as stunning as *Irish Luck,* they were now tied up next to each other for the duration of the tournament.

"Saw Casey's boat pullin' in today. Place'll be a madhouse real soon," Baloney commented at the afternoon get-together.

We were two days away from the tournament's captain's meeting and the kickoff cocktail party. I was already a bit nervous because I had to speak at it as a representative of MAFF, even though Casey, Murph, and Max would also be on the stage behind me.

I replied, "The marina is totally booked, and so is the hotel. I suspect that it'll be tough to get a meal or a drink at the *Cove* or the *Steak & Fin* for the next few days." The *Steak & Fin* had just opened. So far, all the reviews were very positive It was being called the best steakhouse on southern ESVA and being compared to *Bayside's Rooftops Restaurant.* I was really proud of what Kari and her team had accomplished.

"Mimi has been running flat out for days, the *Beach Bar* has already been three deep for drinks at the bar on the weekends, and they're almost fighting over tables when one opens up. She's got a list of job applications half an inch thick for servers. Her crew is cleaning up on tips," Max said. I couldn't tell if he was happy for her or complaining because he hadn't seen her. Maybe a combination of both.

I commented, "She's going to need a bigger crew during the tournament. They're coming to put up that huge tent by the beach in the morning, and it'll have the stage and four bars. I hope that's going to be enough. And don't feel bad, Max, Kari hasn't slowed down half a

218

knot in the last week either." I was apparently already a "marina widower" and we weren't even married yet.

"I saw your buddy offshore, Big," Baloney said.

"Who would that be, Baloney?"

"That sumbitch Sandbags. Though he was mindin' his manners. Had some new guy in the 'pit that looked like a fullback, and a young blonde on a fly rod. She caught a few whites that I saw, and she really seemed to know what she was doin'. I put the glasses on 'em, and she looked real easy on the eyes."

Max had no clue who the girl could be, but he was willing to bet the 'fullback' was Ronnie's pal Jay. A fair angler and a decent person who was very well off. Max never could figure out why he hung around with Ronnie. "Probably practicing. You sure the woman wasn't middle-aged with strawberry blonde hair?"

"Trust me Big, this one's young, blonde, and a looker. If she's one of his anglers, she could be trouble. You shoulda seen her work that fly rod, she knows her stuff. Who knows, they might even end up bein' a boat to watch."

Chapter 24

Things had been tense but quiet on the Marguerite front since Jay arrived. He was one of her favorites of Ron's friends back in Palm Beach, so she was on her best behavior around him. She even went as far as to go offshore with them once, though she complained about the long ride. However, she all but totally ignored Sam now, especially since Sam, Ronnie, and Jay all seemed to enjoy chatting together so much while they were out fishing.

And Timmy now seemed to be having a really tough time lately waking up to make the boat and declared he'd rather sleep in, that he really didn't need the practice anyway. Sam whispered to Ronnie that this wasn't the only thing Timmy was out of practice on, then smiled and stealthily winked.

The tournament was a two–day affair, set on Thursday, and Friday. Ronnie was still planning to be able to talk to someone from MAFF in private after the captain's meeting. So, on Wednesday after lunch, they moved all three boats over in front of Mallard Cove and took a break from fishing. They anchored *Toolpusher* two hundred yards off the beach; *Roughneck* and *Gusher* were tied alongside her with huge fenders separating them from her hull. The repositioning was mostly for convenience; Ronnie wanted his office close by for his highly anticipated meeting. But it also let him show off to all the other tournament anglers by having his private navy sitting out on display where it couldn't be missed.

But Ronnie appeared to be mellowing somewhat, not even getting that upset when Baloney passed by in the *Golden Dolphin* only twenty yards away, throwing a purposely big wake and violently rocking both *Roughneck* and *Gusher*. Ronnie knew it was in payback for that stunt he had pulled in the bay. He watched

220

from the exterior companionway rail and could hear Baloney laugh and curse him even over the sound of the *Dolphin*'s engines as she ran past.

"What a jerk!" Sam had appeared at his side.

"I waked him out much worse when he was out with a charter, so that was just payback. I deserved it."

Sam looked surprised, "You know that guy?"

"Kind of."

"Why did you do it?"

"I was frustrated over some things and took it out on him. None of it was his fault, but he just happened to be there at the wrong time. Didn't have anyone around to talk to at the time like I do now." He looked at Sam and smiled until he saw Marguerite emerging from the salon and making a beeline for them.

"There you are, Ron dear. So, *this* was where you were going to base our boats all summer? I'm glad that we bought our own marina, this looks so tacky and touristy. But I think I'll still go over to that little beach bar for a cocktail and see if I know any of the other boat owners. How about joining me?" Except when she was in front of Jay, Marguerite had taken to ignoring Sam as if she was invisible. Not that Sam cared.

"You go ahead without me; I need to respond to an email." Ron didn't want to start drinking before the meeting that he was scheduling. Not that he drank all that much during a tournament anyway. Though his "beer therapy" each morning was now going to be an exception to that rule.

"Alright, in that case, I'll take Jay along with me. Remember dear, the captain's meeting starts at five. Ta ta." She poked her head into the salon, then Jay came out and followed her aft where a crewmember was waiting to take them over to the marina in *Roughneck*.

"Sorry she's acting like that, Sam." Ron sounded sad.

"It's okay, I don't care Ron. I get it, she sees me as a threat. I'd probably act the same way if I were in her shoes."

"Somehow, I doubt that." He shook his head slightly.

"You're right. I'd be a hell of a lot bitchier." She smiled at Ron, who couldn't help but smile back at her and chuckle.

We were having an impromptu MAFF meeting with Murph, Lindsay, Max, Rikki, Dawn, and Casey aboard *On Coastal Time*; we were only missing Kari, who was too busy with tournament preparations to attend. I was looking at an email on my smartphone. "He says he wants to meet on *Toolpusher* tonight. His outboard will pick up our representative at the fuel dock at seven." Ronnie had contacted MAFF via our new email address that was now listed on the foundation's website. We were still keeping the identity of the board members confidential.

Casey asked, "Do we really think he's serious about making that a 'kill' tournament?"

Max spoke up, "Absolutely. This is all about him, not about preserving a species. He'd do it just for spite, trust me on that. Wanting to be on this board is purely to spite the other foundation that booted him; he's not that interested in what we're about."

"The guy is a total jerk. There's no way that we would want him on the board, or in any way connected with MAFF. So, what do we do, just ignore him and his tournament?" Lindsay asked.

"I have an idea. A board seat is one type of leverage, but it might not be the only thing he wants. In fact, we have something else that he might *need*." Casey had the attention of all of us now as he laid out his plan. We all liked it. Casey continued, "Okay, we've now got some leverage to take with us. So, who do we send?"

"Not me. We're not on good terms." Max was out.

Lindsay said, "He wants me dead after that whole 'Chairman Baloney' gag, so I'm out."

I jumped in, "I'm out too, since he has issues with Kari and me. Plus, whoever goes should be a marina partner as well as on the MAFF board."

"It should be more than just one person; we need a solid looking front," Murph said.

"I agree. How about you and me, Murph?" Casey asked.

As I said earlier, Casey and Murph go way back, and they work well together; a huge plus.

"Done. Even though I have issues with him, too. Those might actually be a good distraction." Everyone could see that Murph was looking forward to this.

Max looked at me and nodded. We had picked the best team.

"Ron dear, aren't you coming over? I've spotted the Lainharts and the Edwards. I didn't even know that they both come up to Virginia for the summer. I can't wait to show them our new marina." Marguerite was slurring her words slightly like she had been at the bar for too long. Because she had.

Ronnie had no intention of leaving the boat; he sent his crew to attend the meeting, they could give him a recap on the way out in the morning. And the person from MAFF was due in ten minutes, so Ronnie wasn't going anywhere.

He sighed, "I have a meeting in a few minutes. Just give them all my regards, and I'll see them at the awards party. Now I've got to go."

"But they haven't seen..."

Ronnie hung up. He wasn't interested in being social, he wanted to nail down that board seat and get some sleep before tomorrow. He looked across the water in the growing dusk from his spot at the companionway rail. The lights from the tent and the beach bar were starting to reflect across the water. His thoughts were interrupted when the salon door opened, and a very loud Timmy stepped through it. Apparently he had already mixed a few drinks on his own, and unfortunately hadn't had any "specials".

"You just stay here. I don' want you talking to strange guys at that bar. Get some sleep, we gotta tournament ta win tomorra. I'll be back in a while." Timmy intended to do some reconnaissance after dark, to make sure that all of his targets were here and then he'd figure out a plan about how to get his money back. Ronnie watched him stumble a bit as he went down the gangway headed for the outboard. The crewman running the boat would bring back the MAFF guy on the return trip. It was almost showtime.

Ronnie looked out toward the bar again. The reflection of the bar and tent lights was now even prettier as the last rays of sun disappeared to the west. It saddened him to realize that for the first time since he had first started dating Caroline that he really no longer had anyone to share things like this with. He hated the idea of being alone, almost as much as he hated the realization that he had come within a hair of marrying someone who wasn't worth sharing this view with. He didn't realize that Sam was next to him until he felt her arm around his waist, and he jumped. She withdrew her arm and stepped back.

"Sorry, Ron. I didn't mean to..."

He reached over and pulled her back toward him. "You didn't. I was just startled. It actually felt really nice."

She replaced her arm as she looked out over the water. "Wow, that's so beautiful. You know how I love water views, even at night."

"I'm learning that about you. And I'm glad you do because I like them too. I was just taking it all in before my meeting person shows up."

"Meeting person? You don't know who it is?"

He sighed, "Long story. I'll tell you later."

"I'll hold you to it. The part about being around later to hear it." Sam looked at him, trying to get a fix on where she stood. Things might start to get really bad really fast between Timmy and her, so she was trying to feel out her alliance with Ronnie, if that was what it was. He seemed to have become a different person after he decided to break things off with Marguerite.

"I already told you that you can stay here. I meant it; I'm not tossing you out with Timmy."

At that moment, Timmy was still on *Roughneck*, which was approaching the fuel dock. He recognized Murph and Casey before they spotted him, and he ducked behind the console. Quietly he told the crewman that was at the helm, "I'm ain't here, you're the only one on the boat, you got that?"

The confused crewman said he did and watched as Timmy opened the side console hatch that led into the small cramped head with the porta potty. He closed the hatch behind him.

Murph and Casey climbed the gangway steps on *Toolpusher* and followed another crewman through the salon and over to Ronnie's office door. The look on Ronnie's face as Murph followed Casey through the opened the door and sat down was priceless.

"*You* are part of MAFF?" Ronnie was staring slack-jawed at Murph. He hadn't even considered that Murph could be involved with a three billion–dollar organization.

"Both me and my business partner here, Casey Shaw. Casey, this is Ronnie Sanders."

"That's Ron." Ronnie hadn't bothered to get up nor extend his hand.

Murph looked at Casey and said with a smile, "Chairman Baloney calls him sandbags."

"Did you come here just to insult me?"

"No, but I figured that as long as we were here..." Murph would have kept going if Casey hadn't reached across and put a hand on his arm.

Casey looked over at Ronnie. "No, Ron, we came because you contacted our organization about your planned tournament and wanting to become more involved with MAFF. Since you've apparently studied us and know about our goals, you also know that your proposed tournament rules and MAFF are at odds."

"I do. And I have a solution. I'm willing to change my tournament to 'release only' in exchange for a seat on the MAFF board of directors." He sat back, looking very pleased with himself, thinking that he had them backed into a corner.

Casey glanced over at Murph, who shrugged. "Everybody agreed, Case."

Ron couldn't believe that it would be this easy. He at least expected them to put up a fight. If he hadn't been so excited about the prospect, he might have been a little disappointed that there hadn't been more of a challenge involved.

Ronnie interlaced his fingers as he smiled triumphantly. "So, when is our next board meeting?"

"Board meeting?" Murph feigned being confused. "Oh, you think that we all agreed to add you to our board. I guess I gave you the wrong impression. See, everyone on the board agreed to keep you off of it. We don't respond well to ultimatums, and with you willing to do the one thing that we're trying to stop just so you can satisfy your own ego, well, there's no way that you'd ever fit in at MAFF. Hey, Case, you want to give him the other thing that we all agreed on?"

Casey passed a letter across the desk as Murph continued. "That's from Kari Albury, I think you know her from the marina. But she's also a partner and the managing member of the LLC that owns our Lynnhaven property. It's to put you on notice that we are declining to extend or renew your lease of our underwater property that's occupied by your marina's south dock. The current agreement expires next April, and by the terms of the lease, that dock has to be physically removed before that date. Otherwise, we'll remove it and charge you our cost plus a twenty percent management fee, as the lease allows. Hey, thanks for the boat ride, and we'll see you offshore tomorrow."

The two of them started to get up but Ronnie said, "Hold on now, let's not be hasty."

"Hasty? Hasty? You summon us like a couple of dogs, and then try to extort a seat in an organization that you don't even care about, and we're hasty?" Murph was selling Ronnie his best pissed off look. Then again, it wasn't hard, the guy had irritated him from day one, but this was really just part of the negotiations.

"I'm sorry about that, I should have been a bit more genteel in my invitation. But we're all reasonable here, and I'm sure that we can come to an agreement that will satisfy everyone. I'd like a seat on your board, and an extension on my lease. And what would you like?"

"I'd like the money these two assholes stole from me." Timmy was standing in the office doorway, waving a semi-automatic pistol back and forth between Murph and Casey.

Chapter 25

Max, Kari, Dawn, Lindsay, Rikki, and I were sitting on the upper deck of *OCT*, winding down after the captain's meeting/kickoff party. Everything had gone off with only one hitch, and we were all just waiting for Casey and Murph to get back before giving them the bad news. Small craft warnings had been posted for the mid-Atlantic tomorrow, as a tropical system was rushing past just offshore before it was to turn and go farther out to sea. Wind gusts of up to forty knots had now been forecast for out at the canyons, so the tournament committee had declared Thursday a "lay day". Meaning that the first day of fishing was now going to be Friday, with the final day on Saturday. The news had been followed by an immediate declaration of a "Rum Front" at the *Cove Beach Bar*, and it was currently slammed.

Linds had the lights turned off up on the party deck so that we could see Ronnie's boat better from there. *Toolpusher* was off our stern and thirty degrees to the right out well beyond the breakwater. We should also be able to spot the outboard bringing the guys back. So far, there was no sign of them.

The darkness made all of us up on the deck all but invisible from the dock, though the low post lamps behind every other slip softly illuminated everyone walking down it. That's how I was able to first spot TW. I reached across to grab Lindsay's arm in the chair next to me, and hissed "shhh". She looked at me, then over at the dock. I felt her arm stiffen when she saw him. We silently watched as he passed by, headed for the *Beach Bar*. Then I said to the other three, "That's TW. If he's here, chances are that Timmy's not far away. We have to warn the guys."

Dawn and Linds both grabbed their phones and called Murph and Casey. They looked up, shaking their heads. Linds said, "No answer, went straight to voicemail."

Max didn't know what was going on, nor who TW or Timmy were, not yet having made the connection. "Could they have turned their phones off because they were in that meeting?"

Dawn said, "No way. Case told me he'd have his with him because they didn't know for sure how Ronnie would react, and we might have to pick them up. Since they won't answer, something is really wrong."

"Who are Timmy and TW?" Max asked.

Rikki filled him, including their last name. Max looked around at all of us as he said, "Uh, guys, Timmy Wilton is Ronnie's fiancée's son. There's a huge chance that he's on *Toolpusher*. They might have just walked into some kind of a trap."

Marguerite had walked down the beach to the water's edge with her cocktail, admiring the view of *Toolpusher*. She loved the way her lights were now shimmering on the water. The surface had been stirred up by a sudden, very warm breeze, and now the reflections on the ripples looked like a million shining diamonds. And she loved diamonds.

"Hello, Margie."

Her blood froze. Only one person had ever called her that. She turned and stared into the face of someone she hadn't seen in a decade and a half. And she hoped never to have seen again.

TW sneered as he jammed a revolver into her stomach. "Miss me, babe? I sure missed you. Fifteen years without a single visit, not even a postcard, and you wouldn't answer my calls from prison. Fifteen years of never getting to see or talk to my son or to watch him grow up. Then I get out, figuring I had millions waiting on me and him. But no, it was all gone. I found out that it wasn't just you that stole it, but that he helped you take and spend it. I only wanted to reconnect with him,

229

but he just wanted more money. My money. You had turned him totally against me. All that time, waiting and hoping to see my son while you were poisoning his mind and spending my money.

You know, you and Timmy now owe me that money, and I'm going to collect it. By the way, where is that boy of ours? I know he's also got a half million of Billy's cash, which is also mine."

Marguerite glanced down at the pistol then back up at TW, the adrenaline now counteracting the alcohol as she started to panic. "He was supposed to meet me here, Tim, but he never showed up. He must still be on the boat."

"What boat is that, Margie?"

"My fiancé's boat, *Toolpusher.*" She pointed out to it.

"Wow, you've been a busy girl while I've been gone. A man with a rig like that should sure be able to pay what you two owe me. A fiancé, eh? Then we'll just call it a dowry. Let's go pay our son and your fiancé a little visit. How can we get out there?"

Marguerite held up her phone. "I just call the captain and he sends a boat."

"Do it, Margie, have him pick us up right here on the beach. And no tricks. I'd hate to have to clean my gun tonight."

Max's news totally stunned us about the connection between Timmy and Ronnie. As we were all digesting the news Dawn said, "Hey look! The outboard is coming back this way, but I can't see how many are aboard, it's too dark."

"They picked the guys up at the fuel dock, they should be headed back there to drop them back off so let's go," Lindsay urged.

First, though, Kari, Dawn, and I raced to our boats to pick up our pistols. Lindsay got hers from OCT, and Rikki's security business meant she always carried a concealed pistol. The six of us took off around the marina basin, hurrying to the fuel dock on the very far side. We walked fast but didn't run, not wanting to draw attention to ourselves in order to keep TW or Timmy from spotting us. We didn't know if one or both of them might be waiting at the fuel dock as well. Still, we made it over there in four minutes only to find it was deserted. And there wasn't yet any sign of the outboard. Several minutes passed, and we became concerned because it had had plenty of time to reach us. Max went over to Deb's Emerald to grab a pistol and see if he could get a better view from the flybridge.

My phone rang, Max was calling. "They're almost back to Toolpusher. If they picked up anyone, it must have been from the beach. Come on over, I'll dig out some more binoculars."

The five of us met up with him on the flybridge and by that time the outboard had already tied up to the mothership. Max handed Lindsay and me his two spare binoculars, keeping a set for himself. We had a clear view across the basin, over the top of *Why Knot*'s low profile. I could see four people walking along *Toolpusher*'s exterior companionway. They passed under several overhead lights, and even at this angle I was able to identify TW. He was right behind a woman I didn't recognize, and in front of two men that were also strangers to me.

Max narrated, "That's Marguerite James at the front, Timmy's mother and Ronnie's fiancée. Wait, that's a gun! The guy behind her has a pistol stuck in her back, I saw it for a split second."

I replied, "That's TW, Timmy's dad."

Marguerite opened the door to the salon and all four disappeared inside. This time Lindsay and I both saw the pistol as well.

Sam had gone up to the sundeck to be out of sight while Ronnie conducted his meeting. This was her

231

favorite place on *Toolpusher*, the highest point, and from it she had a great view of the shore and most of the marina as well as the approaching center console. She watched as two men boarded *Toolpusher*, no doubt here for Ronnie's meeting, though she remembered he had only expected one. A couple of minutes later something strange happened, as Timmy climbed out of the head in the center console then also came aboard. Since he hadn't had his "special" cocktail, she was content to stay up here out of sight, out of mind.

She watched when a little while later the outboard again took off at idle, headed for the shore. Only this time it aimed for the beach instead of the marina, which she thought was strange. After it returned she saw Marguerite climbing aboard in front of three men. As they passed under a light at the opening to the companionway she realized that they were all strangers, though the first one bore a striking resemblance to Timmy. And he had a pistol stuck in Marguerite's back.

Her mind raced as she tried to think about what to do. It was obviously a robbery. If it had been a kidnapping, they wouldn't have brought Marguerite back here, they would have taken her somewhere else and contacted Ronnie. Since Sam was unarmed, she wasn't about to go below and get caught or worse. She could dive off into the water and swim for the beach but again she might be seen or heard and at least one of them had a gun. She would be a sitting duck every time she came up for air.

Timmy had made certain that she didn't have access to a cell phone. There was a VHF radio up here, but she knew that any call for help she made with it would be picked up by the radio on the bridge, which was always kept on. Chances were good that it could be overheard by one of the robbers. In the end, she decided that her best play was to stay put and hope that the men just robbed Marguerite of her jewelry and cash and left. Though she couldn't help but worry that they might hurt Ronnie. It was strange, she hadn't worried about anyone else for a long time. While he had started off as just a mark, he really had become more of a friend, which was something that she hadn't had in what seemed like forever.

Ronnie could have put the moves on her that last day that they fished with just the two of them, and she wouldn't really have minded. But he hadn't. And she hadn't made another pass either, as kind of a friendship test by her even though she hadn't known why at the time. And now in recalling it all, she realized that it had been her that had been the instigator in both of their trysts. Then he had laughed a lot at that cute restaurant after the last time. Laughed along with her, like a friend would do.

Sorry Ron, she thought, *I'm not much help as a friend right now.*

Seeing the pistol stuck in Marguerite's back and the two guys that were obviously with TW had changed everything. What it was now, we hadn't quite figured out yet.

Rikki looked at Max. "Okay, we have to assume that Casey and Murph are still aboard. You know that boat, and you know Ronnie. Where do you think they might be?"

I could see Max thinking about it a second before he said, "It's likely that he would have taken them into his office. He would have wanted to project power so he'd go where he could be the central focus, sitting behind his desk and in front of his power wall with all his photos of him with famous people. The office is just off the forward part of the salon; it has no windows and only one door for access. I doubt that he would have wanted to hold a meeting in the salon, it's too informal and too spacious. No, they would definitely have been in his office."

I asked, "Could those walls be blocking their cell phones?"

Max shook his head, "No, Ronnie's and mine always worked in there. If they kept them on, they would work anywhere on that rig. They had to have been taken away or turned off. TW was still here onshore when we called, so it had to have been someone else. My money is on Timmy. He must be working with his dad. So, we have to assume that there's at least four of them."

"This doesn't make sense. All this for sixty grand? TW is taking a hell of a risk, especially since he has that ankle GPS tracker thing the Feds put on him that he showed us, Mar. And he has now violated his probation when he had less than a year left. He is willing to go back to prison now when all he had to do was wait a few more months before coming after us? That's crazy." Lindsay was bewildered, and frankly, so was I.

Max had an epiphany. "Maybe it wasn't about that sixty thousand. What if it is about kidnapping Ronnie? If TW knew that he was going to be here fishing the tournament he could have been planning this for months."

I didn't buy it. "But we think Timmy grabbed Case and Murph before TW ever got onboard. Why do that if you are only after Ronnie? Why not wait until after they're safely off the boat? Now Ronnie knows that Timmy is part of it."

Rikki's voice was cold, "Unless it didn't matter that Ronnie knew because he was never meant to come out of this alive."

I realized that if they were going to kill Ronnie, they would have to kill Casey and Murph as well. We had to get aboard *Toolpusher* before that happened.

Chapter 26

"Well, look who's here, if it isn't my spendthrift son." TW pointed his pistol at Timmy's head while shoving Marguerite over to one of his men who were both also armed with pistols. Timmy started to swing his gun toward his father. "Ah, ah, ah, just put that pistol down there, junior. I'd hate to have paid fifty grand to keep you safe only to end up shooting you myself."

Timmy glared at his father as he bent down and placed the pistol on the deck.

TW addressed his guys, "Look at this, guys, I kept him safe, yet he stole piles of money from me and now he's the one who looks mad and all 'put out'. That's gratitude for you. And speaking of stealing, my old partner stole three million of my hard-earned dollars from me, then gave it to these guys for 'safekeeping'. I had a heck of a time getting that out of him. Admitting it almost killed him. Oh, wait, it *did* kill him."

Murph said, "What guys?"

"Are you going to try that same thing Billy did, Murph? 'Cause it didn't work out so well for him. You really should learn from the last mistake he ever made. Just tell me where you and Casey stashed my three million, and I'll leave you alone."

"TW, we don't know anything about three million dollars." Casey looked confused.

Murph said, "He didn't give us any money, TW. Timmy took the fifty grand in cash from his house, and another hundred from his bank. I've got the fifty, and Billy got his hundred back. He had it when we let him off in West End. We don't know anything about any three million. But I'll give you the fifty grand to let us go."

TW sounded sad. "Murph, what happened to you? Back then you were so straight and honest, now you've turned into a pathetic liar and thief. You really disappoint me."

"He's telling you the truth, TW, there is no three million," Casey stated flatly.

"Dad, I'm tellin' ya, there wasn't any three million when I got there, only the fifty K. I turned the place upside down. I'd a found it if he had it."

"You know Timmy, don't ever call me 'Dad' again. You forfeited that right when you stole from me while I was rotting away in jail. And did you find the ledger that was in the desk drawer false bottom? The one that showed the three million?" When Timmy barely shook his head, TW continued, "I didn't think so. Billy knew that you would be coming back, which is why he sent the cash back to the states with them. So, he had done a great job of hiding it, you just never discovered where it was."

"TW, you know I've never lied to you. That's why you trusted me with your boat. And I'm not lying to you now. There is no three million."

"You know Murph, that is true. You've never lied to me that I know of. So, maybe you just didn't know about the cash, and Casey's got it. What about that, Casey? You were closer to Billy, he even left you his airplane. If he was going to trust anyone with that much cash it probably would have been you." TW cocked the hammer on his semi-automatic pistol and pointed it straight at Murph. "You've got five seconds to tell me where that money is or Murph dies. Three seconds. Last chance..."

"Wait! It's on my boat at *Chesapeake Bayside's* marina. Sorry Murph, I wasn't supposed to tell you." He looked over at Murph who realized that Casey was lying, just stalling for time.

"You son of a bitch! You were going to keep all that money for yourself? You never said a word, even after Billy died!" Murph was trying to help sell the idea.

It didn't take much, since TW really believed that the money existed.

"Ah, so sad when money divides friends like it finally did with Billy and me. But oh well." TW turned his attention to Ronnie who had kept silent through the whole ordeal. "You must be Margie's fiancé. Congratulations old man, or I guess I really should say, my condolences to you. A word to the wise: if you don't already know, you need to watch your wallet with this one or she'll steal you blind. Speaking of which, she owes me nine million bucks. Since she's your problem now, so are all her debts. Especially this one to me. How much cash do you carry on this rig?"

Ronnie involuntarily glanced at the original A.D. Maddox tarpon painting on the bulkhead to his left, and TW smiled.

"An onboard safe behind a painting. Not very original, but still pretty smart."

"Look, TW or whatever your name is, I'm not her fiancé any longer, I was just about to break up with her."

"You were *what?*" Marguerite yelled from the salon.

TW laughed, "Ouch! I bet that smarts, Margie. But it's too little, too late pal. You still owe me at least what's in that safe. And even if it's twenty million, you're getting off light. Trust me, she'd milk you 'till you were dry and sore."

"You son of a bitch! When were you planning on telling me this?" Marguerite was more concerned with her relationship status than her present predicament.

"Margie, shut the hell up. See what I mean fella? You're welcome. And speaking of welcome, you're quite a great boss. You're about to give your crew the night off. They declared a 'lay day' tomorrow because of some weather coming in so the timing is perfect. You'll want that sportfish and outboard in where they're protected in the marina. Tell your crew that the captain and we

237

are going to take this rig around to the lee side while they all go ashore to party. In fact, get your captain in here. My pal Al is gonna keep an eye on him, so he doesn't do anything he'll end up regretting."

The six of them were devising a plan to rescue their friends, but things were quickly changing. "Look, there's a bunch of people loading onto both boats." Kari was keeping vigil on the binoculars.

Dawn asked, "Are any of them Casey or Murph?"

"Not that I saw, though it's kind of dark. They're cranking up and casting off."

Both boats headed for the marina this time and tied up at the vacant fuel dock. Kari and Lindsay went over to the fuel dock to look for the guys and find out what was going on. They returned a few minutes later.

"Ronnie gave the crew time off because of the lay day. He and the captain are going to move *Toolpusher* to the lee side of the Shore ("shore") for the storm. There's no sign of the guys," Kari reported.

I was watching *Toolpusher* through the binoculars. "Gang, she's moving."

Rikki spoke up, "I can have a team here in assault boats in just under an hour."

"She's really starting to move out, we don't have an hour to wait. Hey, didn't her crew say that the captain was taking her to the lee side? That would be the east side of the peninsula. She's headed south, toward the mouth of the Chesapeake. No place to get out of the weather there." It made no sense to me.

Max said, "He could have been lying, and they're headed into the bay through the Chesapeake Channel. She's too high to clear the Fisherman Inlet bridge. And forget about approaching her from the water. She was built for going past some dangerous waters inhabited by modern day pirates. There are all kinds of detection equipment for waterborne attacks including cameras on all the lower decks. They would see us coming a mile away."

I looked at him as an idea hit me. "Literally a mile?"

"Well, her surface radar goes out fifteen miles. But the stuff I'm talking about can pick up approaching small craft at five hundred yards. It has a computer that assesses threats and sets off warnings about unfamiliar vessels."

I asked, "What about a vessel that's running parallel out a couple hundred yards?"

He said, "It wouldn't set off any alarms unless it turned in toward her. What do you have in mind?"

I told them my plan and looked at Max. He nodded. "This could work. Let's get rolling."

"I still say I should be one of the ones going. Murph's my partner." Lindsay was ticked off at having to stay aboard *High Flier*.

I shook my head. "Rikki has the most experience in these things, followed by me, and Max knows the layout better than any of us. You, Dawn, and Kari just need to stand by and be ready in case we need the cavalry. Besides, you didn't ever want to go parasailing, remember? Just keep your eyes peeled for glow sticks on the water in case things go south, but don't worry, we've got this."

Toolpusher had indeed gone through the Chesapeake Channel, over the northernmost tunnels of the CBBT. Then she set a northerly course up the Chesapeake. The wind had already picked up and was coming over her port bow; perfect conditions for what we had planned. Fortunately, I had been able to reach Chris Wagner, and he met us at the dock five minutes later. I really like Chris, not just because he was a great parasail boat captain but because he just accepted what we told him that we had in mind and didn't ask any questions. While he didn't yet know Casey, he liked

Murph and wanted to help. And tonight, his skills would be tested at a level he hadn't ever dreamed of.

Even though *High Flier* had a thousand feet of line on the reel, with the drag and lift of the parasail the three of us should max out at about six hundred feet of altitude with the line angling up at just over a fifty-degree angle. At this height, we shouldn't be spotted from *Toolpusher*. If they would be looking for threats from anywhere, it should be at surface level. Max said that none of the threat detection was aimed skyward.

With this wind angling just right, Chris will be positioned just forward and well to the side of Toolpusher's bow when he starts to slow down, basically doing a 'dip drop', letting the parasail lose altitude. But instead of the surface of the water, our target was the sundeck forty feet above it. We were counting on being able to use the wind to push us sideways and over our target. Chris and I had worked out a system of directional signals that I could use to guide him with my LED penlight instead of a phone. We didn't want to take a chance of our voices being heard from above by anyone out on deck. The open part of the sundeck was only about thirty feet wide by sixty feet long. This would be a daunting task for us to hit in broad daylight, but on a cloudy and dark night, it was going to be a real challenge. And once we hit the deck we only had seconds to simultaneously unclip our harnesses from the triple bar, so we won't get carried back up or even over the side.

We are keeping our fingers crossed that there won't be any sentries on the sundeck, so then we'll be able to move stealthily down the interior stairs to the bridge and take control of the helm. Then we'll split up and take both the port and starboard interior companionways back to the salon. Hopefully, Casey and Murph will be there, and we can overpower whoever is watching over them. We had made a lot of what we hoped were logical assumptions, but there were still a

240

lot of parts to this plan that all had to come together at the right times. Winging it could become a real bitch.

All three of us had glow sticks pinned to our clothes. If things went bad we were to go over the side and activate the sticks once we were clear of *Toolpusher*, and *High Flier* would pick us up. In theory. It looks good on paper. Yes, I'm trying to be funny, because I'm trying to relieve the tension. My tension. The truth is I'm scared. Not just for me, but for all my pals. It's my plan, so that makes it and them my responsibility. I just hoped that I wasn't getting them all killed.

Chapter 27

High Flier was now a half-mile behind *Toolpusher* and closing. All three of us donned our harnesses over our dark clothing and shared what hopefully would not be final hugs and fist bumps with our friends. Lindsay took the wheel while Chris hooked us to the triple bar as he deployed the parasail, filling it with wind. One last check of our gear and weapons, and then we were airborne. In addition to our sidearms, we each carried a taser. And we weren't leaving our pals unarmed in the towboat, either. More pistols, shotguns and a pair of Ruger mini-14's in .223 caliber. I know, it sounds like between all our boats, we keep an arsenal. We do. Stuff tends to happen along the waterfront, and you can never be too careful, or too well-armed. Hopefully, nothing bigger than a taser would get any use tonight.

It was eerie, ascending into a dark sky behind a blacked–out boat that wasn't even burning its running lights. The lights from *Toolpusher* as well as from ESVA, now a few miles away, were the only reference points that kept us from getting vertigo in the black void above. Again, as we rose we couldn't talk for fear that our voices would carry, and then we might lose our element of surprise. We were each left to our own private thoughts in silence.

As the line played out, *Toolpusher* kept getting smaller and smaller, even as we were blown farther over toward her. We felt the line come completely tight as we reached the end. I directed Chris using our signals, and a minute later we felt ourselves starting to descend. The lights on *Toolpusher*'s radar and communications mast just aft of the sundeck were a great reference point for me. It was also a huge obstacle; we had to land far enough forward so that the parasail didn't end up tangled in it or we would be totally screwed.

But if we had marked an "x" on the deck for the perfect spot to land, it would have been right under my feet when we touched down. When we get back, Chris is going to get a big bonus; nobody else could have pulled that off. Two seconds later we were all unhitched, and I tapped out three dashes with my penlight. Off in the distance and out of sight, Chris hit the throttle, and the parasail, which had now become slightly visible from the mast lights, disappeared back into the dark sky. Now focusing my attention to the sundeck, I sensed motion about ten feet from me by the forward rail. My penlight revealed a terrified looking young blond woman. On a hunch, I said quietly, "Hey, fly fisherman, we're the good guys."

"How... how did you know about that?"

Rikki was closer, so she almost whispered, "Because we are the good guys. Who are you?"

"I'm Sam, I'm a guest of Ron's."

Rikki was in her element. "Okay, Sam, keep your voice down but is anyone else up here?"

"No, I'm hiding out. Nobody has even come up looking around, they must not know I'm here. They're all on the lower decks."

"Okay, there's Timmy, and Ron and who else?"

"How did you know about Tim...never mind. There are three other guys and at least one has a gun. Oh, and Marguerite plus the captain. All the other crew left."

I went over and handed her my glow stick. "We're going to take the boat back, but you need to stay up here. If any of those three comes up, I want you to dive overboard and get away from this boat. We have our own boat following behind us that will pick you up, you just need to snap this glow stick and get their attention with it, got that?"

"Yes. Thank you. Be careful, I know that one definitely has a pistol, but I don't know about the others."

TW and his guys had moved Casey, Murph, Timmy and Marguerite over to a pair of couches in the salon while his other helper watched over them with his pistol in hand.

TW forced Ronnie to open the office safe where he had just shy of a million in cash as well as a bag with several hundred gold coins and a small pile of watches and gold jewelry. Then he forced him back out of the office and over to the couches. One look at Marguerite and Ronnie decided to sit over with Murph and Casey.

"You know, that's not nine million, but it's a good start." TW smiled evilly as he took a seat across from them. "The three million you've been hiding will run the total up nicely."

Casey wanted to get his mind off the non-existent cash. "TW, how can you be out of Palm Beach County and not have the Feds already tracking you?"

TW smiled and pulled up his pants leg, revealing that his leg was wrapped in some kind of black fabric and secured with Velcro. "That's a Faraday bag that I re–engineered. It blocks all incoming and outgoing radio signals."

"But that would just shut off the signal and alert them that you were missing."

"It would if I didn't have a cloned transmitter running around West Palm right now. It pays to have an old cellmate who went up for electronic related theft." TW grinned.

Casey's heart sank. There was no way that TW was planning on letting them live since they could now prove how he had beaten the electronic tracking system. He had the perfect alibi; the Feds would figure that he had been in Florida all this time. If he and Murph wanted to live, they had to find a way to overpower these three. Four if you counted Timmy. And they had to do it before they got to *Bayside* and he couldn't produce the three million in cash.

Rikki led the trio down the enclosed stairs to the bridge. Reaching the last few steps she saw that the bridge was bathed in muted red light since they were running at night. She raised her hand silently, stopping the advance of the others. In front and to her left a man in a captain's uniform was at the wheel, and another man in plainclothes was just to his right, peering through the windshield. In his right hand was a pistol.

Rikki judged the distance from her to the man at roughly twelve feet. The Taser's range was fifteen. She extended the gun, taking careful aim between the man's shoulder blades and pulled the trigger. Two metal darts embedded themselves in the man's back as over a million volts passed between them, supplied by the thin wires that ran back to the gun. The man made an almost gurgling sound, lost control of his legs and fell backward, hitting his head hard on the corner of the footrest on the helm's chair. Rikki rushed forward to check him, only to find that he wasn't breathing. His neck had snapped when his head hit the footrest.

I came up behind her and picked up the man's weapon, shoving it into my waistband. The captain's eyes were wide, and he started to speak but Max quickly covered his mouth with his hand from behind him. He turned and looked at Max then obviously recognized him. Max put his finger across his own lips, and the captain nodded that he understood.

Rikki motioned that I should go down the port companionway and beckoned to Max to follow her down the starboard. Both passageways emptied out into a deserted galley, then picked up again across the room, leading toward the salon about twenty feet away. Max had said it was a large room the full width of the boat, with doors leading out on either side and two more leading aft. I crept forward slowly then flattened myself against the bulkhead, now inching forward until I could just see around the edge of the bulkhead corner at the end.

Casey and Murph were facing over toward my direction, while TW and his guy had their backs to me. I saw Casey glance to his right for a second, so I knew that he must have seen Rikki and Max. I took the pistol we had taken off of the guy on the bridge and faked an underhanded toss then held up three fingers. He nodded faintly. I made two false swings and then released it on the third one. It sailed perfectly through the air, headed straight for his now outstretched hand.

Unfortunately, Timmy had also seen me, and he jumped up, intercepting the gun in midair. He then fired in my direction, missing me as I ducked back while all hell broke loose. Ronnie made a break for the side door as TW and his accomplice started firing at Rikki and Max. Someone rushed past from behind me as I drew down on Timmy, taking him out with a perfect pair of center mass shots. Meanwhile, Murph and Casey had dived over the back of their couch just as Rikki took out TW's guy from her spot at the companionway entrance. TW took a wild shot at her then fired in Ronnie's direction just as he went out the salon door. TW then half dove, half fell through the opposite salon door as Max fired at him twice. Max followed him through the door a few seconds later, intent on finishing the job.

Marguerite was now wailing as she was sprawled across Timmy's chest, hugging his lifeless body. Casey rushed over and grabbed the pistol that had been meant for him, then looked down, confirming that my two shots had indeed done their job.

"Oh no, nooo, someone help me!" It was Ronnie, who had fallen backward and partially through the door, after being pushed down by Sam. She had taken TW's bullet that had been meant for Ronnie. A growing wet red spot had appeared on the upper right side of her chest. Ronnie was sitting on the deck, his arms wrapped around her from behind, telling her that everything was going to be okay. He looked up at me. "Over there, in those side cabinets are medical supplies. We've got to stop the bleeding."

Rikki sprang into action, quickly opening the cabinets and finding that they carried a wide array of medical supplies onboard since they were set up for long-range travel. She grabbed a couple of packs of Quick Clot to help stop the blood loss. She went over and ripped open Sam's shirt, applying one of the patches to the wound. Sam was still barely conscious, but going into shock, and in a lot of pain.

Ronnie looked down in Sam's face asking, "Why did you do that, Sam?" She had jumped between him and TW while shoving him down.

Sam gritted her teeth through the pain then said simply, "Because we're friends." Then she passed out.

Now following just out of sight in *Toolpusher's* wake, it had seemed like an eternity of silence for the crew on *High Flier*. Then they saw the muzzle flashes coming from the salon windows and heard the gunshots. A side door opened, and seconds later they saw a large splash alongside, but no light from a glow stick. "Screw it, we're going in," said Chris as he pegged the throttle, heading for the boat launching deck on the stern.

I called Kari's phone, "Kari, we need *High Flier*. We're all okay, but a passenger was hit, and we need to get her off and to a hospital...Right, got it." I went over to the intercom and punched the bridge button. "Captain, full stop! We have a boat coming alongside."

Max came back into the salon after making a thorough search outside. "I found a blood trail and a smudge on the railing. TW was hit, and then he must've gone over the side."

Rikki was still attending to Sam. "We need to get her aboard *High Flier* and to shore."

Ronnie said, "We have a rescue backboard on the boat deck."

Max retrieved the backboard and they gently strapped Sam to it. He and Ronnie carried Sam down to the landing deck where *High Flier* was waiting. They set the board on the parasail launch deck. Ronnie rode on the deck beside her as Chris headed out for the Coast Guard station at Cape Charles. *Toolpusher's* captain had radioed the station about the hijacking and we could see several blue lights now headed in our direction.

The next several hours would have been even crazier than they ended up being if it hadn't been for Rikki. She had made a few phone calls to some of her government clients and called in a few markers. The Coast Guard interrogated us about our involvement, but the interviews were short, there was only a perfunctory crime scene investigation. The incident investigation's outcome and narrative had obviously been predetermined. The official ruling was that this had all been in self–defense of an armed hijacking, and no charges would be filed against any of us. We never brought up the Bahamian connection. According to the Coast Guard media relations department, the details of what happened could not yet be released to the press due to "security concerns and the ongoing investigation." The investigation that was really already closed.

Yes, we had broken and bruised more than a few laws in the process of getting our friends back. But other than Sam getting shot, it was the bad guys that had all paid the price in the end, and I wasn't going to lose any sleep over their loss, especially that of Timmy. TW was still missing and hopefully crab food on the bay bottom by now.

We helped Ronnie's captain return *Toolpusher* to Lynnhaven then Chris ran us all back to Mallard Cove in *High Flier*. I owed him more of an explanation as well as that bonus which he didn't yet know about, but it would all have to wait until later. We wanted to get to the hospital to find out how that woman named Sam was doing.

We found Ronnie and Max sitting together in the surgical waiting room, quietly talking together. When Ronnie looked up, he looked like he had aged ten years.

Ronnie addressed us all, "Thank you for coming to our rescue. I know that it was mostly for Casey and Murph's benefit, but you saved the rest of us, and I'm grateful. Now I just pray that Sam is going to be okay."

We all took seats in the otherwise empty room where he told us the story of what she had been through in Costa Rica and subsequently with Timmy. It made me glad I hadn't missed that son of a bitch. Then he told us how she had helped him get over his seasickness, and how she was such an outstanding natural angler.

"I hate to admit it, I did think there was a good chance of her being just another gold digger, but she was, or rather is, so great to talk with. And face it, it wasn't my youthful good looks that must've attracted her to me." He had a sad, grim smile. "But I don't know anyone else who would have jumped between me and a bullet, and she said that she did it because we're friends, and I have no doubt about that now. I probably wouldn't be alive except for her, and I want the chance to make it up to her. I just hope that I get it."

This was not the Ronnie Sanders that we had all grown to dislike so vehemently. This Ronnie was humble and contrite, after apparently having gotten a glimpse of what truly was important in life. We all absorbed her story in silence. She had been bullied, abused, and led for so long by so many, but in the end, she had taken control of her own life and used it to help save someone else. Hopefully, this wouldn't be the end of that life.

Her surgeon came in fifteen minutes later. "It's a good thing she got here when she did, even another few

249

minutes could have been fatal due to her blood loss. The bullet shattered a rib, then it and the bone fragments damaged the top of her lung. We removed the damaged part and had to do a lot of vascular repair. The next twenty–four hours or so will be critical for her, but if she gets through that time period and doesn't develop any subsequent infection, she has a very good chance of making a full recovery."

Ronnie actually had a tear running down one side of his face, and a huge smile was slowly forming. He had learned a lot about himself from Sam, most of it in the past few hours.

Chapter 28

"Where did you sleep last night, Ron?" Sam asked Ronnie after she found him sitting on a couch in the newly redecorated salon. It was the morning after her release from the hospital, a week and a half after the shooting. She sat down next to him.

"I took one of the guest staterooms."

"I could have taken that one, or you were welcome to sleep with me." This time there were no bedroom eyes involved, just a look of concern.

"That bed is the most comfortable one here. And you needed a good night's rest, all by yourself."

"Oh, like you didn't? Sleeping in a chair in my hospital room every night for over a week. That couldn't have been comfortable."

He shrugged. "It was necessary. I wanted to be there in case you needed anything."

She looked out the side windows of the salon across the water and at the homes on the other shore. "What I needed was this view. This is the best medicine ever. I kept thinking about it when I would wake up at night in the hospital."

"Well, you've got it back, and nobody is going to take it away from you, either." He pulled an envelope from his pocket and handed it to her. Inside was ten thousand dollars in cash.

"What is this?" She was confused.

"Well, ten grand is what Timmy owed you."

"You don't have to pay me that."

"It isn't even a down payment on what I owe you." He smiled. "And about your view, I'm taking care of that in a few minutes."

At first, Sam gave him a questioning look but then said, "I can't accept this."

"It's not a carnal bribe or anything, Sam."

"I didn't think it was, Ron. But it's not your responsibility."

"That hole in your shoulder could very easily have been in my heart or my brain if it hadn't been for what you did. Nobody else would have done that for me. Face it, Sam, we're the only real friends each other has."

"I was after you for your money, Ron."

"Maybe at first, but not when you pushed me through that door, Sam."

"What about Marguerite?"

"You knew from day one we were toast, before I was ever willing to admit it to myself. She went back to Florida to bury Timmy and to try to keep a lid on this story. She's scared that the Feds could seize everything she has and charge her with conspiracy if the full story gets out about where that money came from. I suspect that she'll sell her condo like she planned and then move away. At least she will if she has an ounce of sense. The Feds arrested TW's old cellmate after a second identical signal was picked up in Richmond. He's alive, or at least he was. They found his ankle bracelet and some bloody bandages in a motel there. They think he's headed out of Virginia." He looked out the dockside window. "And here comes the second part about fixing your view." His grin got wider now.

Sam looked confused as there was a knock on the door and Ronnie got up to answer it. Kari, Casey, Murph and Lindsay all walked in and Ronnie shook hands with each. Kari sat next to Sam as the others took spots on the other couch. Ronnie sat on Sam's other side. Ronnie and Sam had gotten to know each of them better over the last week when they came to relieve him each day so that he could run back to the marina to shower and change.

Kari asked, "How's the shoulder?"

"It's sore. But I'm supposed to start taking my arm out of the sling some starting next week."

Kari looked at Ronnie. "Did you tell her?"

He shook his head, "I figured I'd wait until you were all here."

"Tell me what?" Sam asked suspiciously.

Kari handed an envelope to Ronnie and one to Sam who opened it and pulled out a stock certificate. She looked really confused now. "Shares to a Limited Liability Corporation made out in my name? What is this and where did it come from?"

Ronnie explained, "It turns out that by adding this marina property to the project next door, it allows them to add a lot more square footage to what they want to build because they can totally change the site plan. Remember I said that I bought it on a whim? I found out it wasn't worth as much as I paid for it by itself. And I thought running a marina would be easy. It's more complicated than you might think.

In talking with Kari, she convinced me that my best deal for the long term was to throw in with them. They'll handle all the management, I'll just be an investor, with my three slips reserved and at a discount of course. And they've even agreed to hire Brian as the dockmaster for the whole project. So, he'll stay on here in the meantime, then he'll get a promotion and a few assistants when the new marina opens."

Ronnie could see that she wasn't grasping the whole concept. "I swapped this property for shares in theirs. No more headaches, and in two years when the project is complete, my investment should be worth double what I paid for it. Your certificate is for half of those shares. The view comes with it. Permanently."

Sam leaned back into the sofa, looking at everyone and finally at Ronnie. Quietly she said, "I can't accept this, Ron. A month ago, I'd have taken it in a heartbeat, but now I don't feel right about it."

"Which is exactly what I hoped you'd say. But it's my turn not to take no for an answer. Again, if you hadn't shoved me down, this would have been a moot point. But you did. And because of that, I've been doing a lot of thinking about why I was doing certain things, and I didn't like the answers I was coming up with.

I bought this marina to feed my own ego. I'd been doing a lot of that, too. Had they gone ahead and built their project without this property, it wouldn't have been worth as much, and in two years this property wouldn't have been worth even half of what I paid for it either. I'd have been competing against them and would have had to lower my rates. Instead, now these slips will have all the same amenities as the ones next door.

So, my half of those shares will not only recoup my original investment in two years but will also throw off a decent return. When you look at it that way, your shares will have cost me nothing. And they'll be throwing off a decent amount of income for you as well."

Sam still looked dubious, but said she'd think about it. Then Murph handed her another envelope which was stuffed with cash.

Casey spoke up. "You now know the story of how this all started when Murph was kidnapped. Well, remember that we agreed with TW not to hurt Timmy when we caught up with him in exchange for the fifty thousand dollars that he offered us. I didn't want it, Marlin wouldn't take it, and we gave it to Murph who, as you can see, didn't spend it. Since it was TW that shot you, we figured he should at least pay for your medical bills."

"Thanks. Since it came from him, I'll take it. I haven't gotten the hospital bill yet, so hopefully this will cover it. But I still don't feel right about the marina stock."

Kari said, "I know it's between you and Ron, but just think it over. We'd love to have you as a partner."

The group stayed and chatted another five minutes then headed back to Mallard Cove, letting Ronnie and Sam have a chance to talk things over.

"You know, Ron, today is the first day in years that I am really free. Before I always had an obligation of one kind or another to someone else. In one way it's

254

really exciting and in another it's kind of scary. I don't know what to do next, I've always had somebody that was pushing me in one direction or another, and I was dependent on them."

"Sounds like a good time to start making your own choices, Sam."

"I don't know what to do."

"I'm your friend, so I'm not going to tell you. If you ask me for advice, I'll give it to you, but it's time for you to start spreading your wings and setting your own direction. Is there something that you've always wanted to do?"

"I've figured out that I really like to fish."

He nodded. "You're good at it. And I'm not pushing you, but the income from that stock would fund a lot of fishing time."

"What about you, Ron, what do you want to do?"

"I don't know, Sam. It's funny, we're a lot alike. I actually went after my wife originally because of her family's money. Then somewhere along the line I really fell in love with her. And I loved watching her fish. Then I was stupid, hooking up with her friend, and getting serious after she was gone. I guess I didn't want to be alone, and I didn't care what I had to put up with from Marguerite. Along the way, I just got older but now I'd like to think I'm getting wiser. This is the first time in two and a half decades that I've been alone. Probably since before you were born."

"Not quite, I look younger than I really am."

Ronnie chuckled at that. Then he said, "I've realized that I was trying to live a life that others thought was cool, and in that way, I was always living it for someone else. Like wanting to be involved with MAFF, that was just to prove something to somebody else. It was for all the wrong reasons. I've finally decided to do what I want, and live life on my terms doing what I think is cool, starting right now."

"Mind if I tag along and watch?"

Ronnie replied, "You said yourself, this is the first time in a long time that you're free. Don't blow the chance to get out there and enjoy yourself."

"Ron, the best time that I've had in forever was learning about light tackle and fly fishing for billfish with you. So, I've figured out that *is* how I enjoy myself, and it wouldn't be the same without you. You said you're my friend and you would give me advice if I asked. So now I'm asking, is this something that we can do together?"

"Maybe. With certain conditions. You're happy about not having any obligation to anyone right now, so I'd stick to that if I were you."

"Okay. What else?"

"Take the stock. You never want to find yourself again in a situation like you did in Costa Rica, and that could guarantee you won't."

She was quiet for a few minutes, mulling it over. "Okay. Thank you for that."

"I'm happy to do it. To really be free you need a safety net that guarantees you can walk down the dock anytime that you like."

She asked, "Anything else?"

"Just one thing, and it's a deal breaker."

"What?" She asked worriedly.

"Never, and I mean never call me 'Ron dear'. My god, you have no idea how much I hated that."

She laughed and put her good arm across his shoulders. "Done deal."

Epilogue

It turned out the tropical storm that caused the delay in the tournament was only a precursor of things to come during this early storm season. A week after Sam was released from the hospital a huge storm built in the lower Caribbean, packing some of the highest winds ever recorded in a tropical cyclone. It peaked right before it hit the Abacos, causing massive destruction and flooding. Then its forward motion slowed as it came across the flats, pushing the water up from the shallows over Grand Bahama like a giant invisible bulldozer.

Right after the shootout, TW had cautiously made his way from Virginia down to Stuart, Florida. He had shoved enough of Ronnie's cash from the safe into his pockets before all the shooting began to pay for the trip down and a "no questions asked" boat trip from Stuart to Bootle Bay. He was dropped off under cover of darkness, and once inside what was now his house he pulled the drapes on all the windows then used only minimal light inside. Fortunately, no squatters had taken up residence, and Billy had left over a month's worth of canned and dried foods, so he wouldn't have to go out for provisions for a while.

The bullet hole in his side hadn't healed and instead started to fester, leaking a green pus that soaked into the bandage that the antibiotic cream hadn't been able to cure. He brought enough replacement bandages to last a week, but then he knew he would have to make a pharmacy run. Fortunately, Billy's truck was still parked in the driveway, and his keys were on the table next to the door.

Nothing was missing from inside the house, possibly due to native superstitions regarding murdered souls looking for vengeance. That could be why there weren't squatters as well. But when he tried the television, TW found there was no signal. Looking out into the yard past a slightly drawn curtain he saw that the pole which had held the satellite dish was now vacant. Apparently, superstitions and murdered souls only reached so far.

After a few days there TW knew he was really getting sick and had a rising fever. He was sweating profusely, even though the air conditioner seemed to be running fine. He had lost track of time and mostly slept. He suddenly woke to the sound of sheets of rain assaulting the windows. Then he noticed his infection was getting worse and now had a putrid odor. When he went to change the bandage, he found that he had already used the last one, he just couldn't remember when.

The rain sounded like it was getting louder. No, that was wind. Now the house was shaking. It felt like it was lifting up. Damn, the rain was so loud he couldn't hear himself think. No lights, the storm must have knocked out the power, and he hoped it would come back on soon; it was already getting hot in the house. He looked out the window only to find that the yard had disappeared, it was now all water. And it was raining so hard he couldn't see past the railing on the back deck. Wait, waves were now coming across the deck and slamming into the door, but that wasn't possible, the deck was six feet above the seawall. He looked out the side window into the driveway, or where it should be, but it was gone, replaced by water. Billy's truck was gone, too. What was happening? What was real?

This time he was sure of it, the house lurched, he hadn't imagined it. But he didn't know if it was caused by the rising water or the wind which was screaming. He had sudden pressure on his ears as an upstairs window exploded inward. The house moved again, twisting as some of the pilings were pushed off of their foundations. The metal straps that fastened the wood posts to the concrete had succumbed to decades of

258

exposure to the salty environment. But all TW knew was that the ceiling was falling in spots, and the floor looked warped.

Suddenly the wall by the canal collapsed inward, and all of the other ribs of the A-Frame construction were then pushed down like dominoes. TW was trapped under tons of debris, one leg crushed, and an arm pinned. The water was rising rapidly now, and it was up to his chin. A minute later a wave broke over his head, and he had to struggle for air.

Then everything went silent. The storm was still raging, but it was like someone had pushed the "Mute" button on the television. Then he heard the voice. He knew exactly who it belonged to. Billy.

"I've been waiting for you, TW. At least it wasn't a long wait." The maniacal laugh that followed was the last thing that TW ever heard on this earth as the water level rose above his head.

Author Notes

Thanks for reading **Coastal Paybacks**! If you read this one before reading the first two books in this series, Coastal Conspiracy and Coastal Cousins, don't worry. While it's better if they are read in sequence, each can still be read as a "stand alone" book with a minimum of "spoilers". I used the phrase "that's a story for another day" to refer to things that were covered more in depth in those other volumes.

Max's story about the kids' fishing day is a true one. In 1990, I was a founding board member of the **Palm Beach County Fishing Foundation**, the charitable arm of the **West Palm Beach Fishing Club**. That first year, we took 500 at risk and disabled kids out on a single day in boats that were chartered and borrowed from Jupiter down through Boynton Beach, Florida. For many of those kids it was their first ever time being out on a boat. To date, this amazing organization has had over ***13,000 kids*** come through the program. To find out more about it, go to http://www.westpalmbeachfishingclub.org/foundation.php
And the story about the young woman who answered the phone when Max called, telling him how that day had given her life a new direction? It was based on a true story that actually happened to me and remains one of the best feelings I've ever had in my life.

Bootle Bay exists. The owner of a boat I worked on as a kid had a place back in there. The boat was a 53' Hatteras, so my description of how tight it was getting the 60' *Irish Luck* back into those canals is dead-on accurate. Tight fit.

The beer story is based on something which might have actually happened in another country over 40 years ago. Maybe. After all, this book *is* a work of fiction. But if it did happen, it wasn't within the jurisdiction of US laws. Anyway, I'm happy to report that if it really happened, then all those then teenaged grandkids grew up and became happy, healthy, and upright citizens who now no longer need a beer prior to boarding to ward off mal-de-mer. Though I've been told they have been spotted having a "booster beer" from time to time. Maybe.

Hey, if you liked **Coastal Paybacks**, I'd really appreciate it if you wouldn't mind leaving a review on Amazon or Goodreads.com. Just a line or two would be great! If for some reason you didn't like it, please drop me an email instead. You can reach me at contact@donrichbooks.com Actually, please feel free to send me an email even if you liked it, I'd love to hear from you!

I also have a **Reader's Group** where I share pictures and stories that inspire the books. Members also get advance notice of any upcoming releases at discounted rates Like **Coastal Tuna**, the next book of this series that will be coming out in early 2020. You can sign up for the Reader's Group on my website, http://www.donrichbooks.com

Printed in Great Britain
by Amazon